The

ANTIQUE STORE
DETECTIVE

and the

May Day

Murder

BOOKS BY CLARE CHASE

CLARE CHASE

The
ANTIQUE STORE DETECTIVE
and the
May Day Murder

bookouture

Published by Bookouture in 2025

An imprint of Storyfire Ltd.
Carmelite House
50 Victoria Embankment
London EC4Y 0DZ

www.bookouture.com

Storyfire Ltd's authorised representative in the EEA is Hachette Ireland
8 Castlecourt Centre
Castleknock Road
Castleknock
Dublin 15 D15 YF6A
Ireland

ISBN: 978-1-83525-289-5
eBook ISBN: 978-1-83525-288-8

For Charlie, George and Ros, with much love

1

THE FIRST SIGNS OF TROUBLE

It was four fifteen in the morning on 1 May. Bella Winter had been treading carefully over the tussocks and tree roots, getting a small amount of solace from the sight of her replica Edwardian boots. Now, she looked at her colleague John Jenks through three-quarter-closed eyes. The moon was setting but the approaching dawn meant John's lantern was no longer essential.

He met her gaze warily. 'You didn't *have* to come.'

'Oh yes I did. You made me. I can't believe I left my bed before dawn on a day when there's no sale to attend.' Bella had visited two antiques fairs the previous week, travelling outside Shropshire to reach them. Both had involved horrendously early starts. The trips had been worthwhile, though; she'd found several treasures to add to the stock in her shop, Vintage Winter. The benefits of the current escapade were less certain.

'I seem to remember you saying, "That does it, I'm coming!"', John said.

Bella felt the dew infiltrate her boots. *The icing on the cake.* 'You told me I'd be the only person in Hope Eaton not to come to the Sacred Spring if I stayed in bed. I call that forcing my hand.'

She and countless townsfolk were walking along an ancient route through the wood. Known as the Sacred Way, it was a narrow, steeply banked path crowded on either side with hawthorns, hollies and plum trees.

John's sister-in-law Carys was next to Bella. Her face conveyed stoicism, which was relatable, but she'd pushed Bella to attend too. Bella was still wondering why.

The Sacred Way was the route the ancients had used to reach the spring on Kite Hill. These days it ended at the gate of Springside Cottage, but there was a right of way through the grounds.

Bella peered ahead, past John's mum, Jeannie. Normally, the pub landlady would be leading the procession. Today, the headteacher of Hope Eaton High School had overtaken her. It clearly rankled. Every so often Jeannie raised her head in the man's direction and tutted.

'What do you think of him?' Bella nodded in the head-teacher's direction, addressing Carys, who taught at the town's primary school and was in the loop.

'Adrian Fitzpatrick?' She tucked her long, jet-black hair behind her ears and shrugged. 'A stuffed shirt who excels at PR. Well off. Family money. All heated gilets, horses, jeeps and sherry parties.' Bella had noted his tweed jacket. 'Good at getting people to do his bidding. The memorial to his brother after he died in a car crash is a case in point. Everyone said how touching it was that he'd arranged it, but it was his secretary who did all the work and it was a right pain to organise, I gather. William – the brother – wrote poetry about the spring, so they wanted to site the memorial here, but the council took ages to agree.

'Adrian's just been appointed head of a government scheme involving schools across Shropshire, which is irritating. On the upside, the kids call him Fitzcatsick.' She smiled.

Jeannie glanced over her shoulder at Carys's words. 'I've

had to adopt a firm line with him. He's been trying to take over the organisation of every town function. People don't like it.'

Bella imagined Jeannie liked it least of all, since that was *her* role. It had been that way since Bella had visited Hope Eaton as a child, when her late father had lived in the town. The townsfolk were used to Jeannie and vice versa. She waded into every situation, clucking over them like an uncompromising mother hen. She might not always get it right, but she wasn't bothered about self-aggrandisement or appearances. That counted for a lot. Bella would back her to the hilt against the likes of Adrian Fitzpatrick.

Jeannie looked behind her again and raised her voice. 'We must keep up, everyone. We're racing the dawn, and it won't wait for us!'

The ever-growing light infected Bella with a sense of urgency despite herself. She quickened her pace. It was important to reach the spring before the sun crested the eastern hills on the other side of the valley. Apparently.

Up ahead, they saw Adrian Fitzpatrick greet a woman at the gate of Springside Cottage. She was made more visible by the glow of an outside light: she had strong bone structure, and a thick well-styled bob. As Bella got closer, she decided the woman was probably in her early fifties – a similar age to the headteacher. She wore a padded navy jacket, brown pleated skirt and a red scarf. No nonsense. Mary Roberts, presumably, cottage owner and high-school secretary.

'She's renowned for being strict,' Carys said, under her breath, 'but she's all right really. She used to babysit for us and she's a point of contact between the schools. I've always liked her.'

There was a 'For Sale' notice in Springside Cottage's grounds, though except on May Day, not many people would see it. The place was remote. The only vehicular access was a narrow track off a lane outside the town.

'She's moving out?' Bella asked Carys. She'd probably have heard about it on the grapevine. The Jenkses knew everyone in Hope Eaton. Bella was working towards the same goal, instinctively and for the sake of her business. She'd made good progress since she'd relocated from London ten months ago, building on her childhood contacts. It helped that her dad had been a well-liked community figure: the town's cop when it had still had one. He'd had time for the locals and minded about them.

Carys indicated the far end of Mary's large garden with a slender, outstretched hand. 'She's not leaving; she loves the spring too much to relocate. She's keeping a plot of land to build on. A much smaller place.'

'Ah, so she's downsizing.' Bella caught John's eye. 'Interesting.' She might have items to sell, in that case. John gave her a quelling look which she met head-on. 'You do realise we'd be a stockless shop if I didn't spot opportunities?'

He gave a half-smile and shook his head.

They were following Adrian Fitzpatrick and Mary Roberts through the cottage's grounds now, past drifts of tulips.

John pushed his glasses up his nose and peered at her expectantly.

She met his look. 'Yes, all right, the plants are lovely, but I dare say they'd look even more stunning when they're properly open in daylight.'

Moments later, they were through the garden and onto the hillside.

Bella had visited the spring long ago with her dad, but they'd come a different way, approaching from beyond the town over a stile, ploughing through vegetation. Nostalgia put a lump in her throat.

Suddenly, Adrian Fitzcatsick and Jeannie held up their hands at the exact same moment, and Bella realised they'd arrived. The pre-dawn light revealed water flowing from a rock in Kite Hill into a small pool. Around the waterspout, the stone was carved into an image of Sweet Agnes, the medieval mystic who'd lived in Hope Eaton. She popped up everywhere in the town. The water was trickling from a jug she held.

Bella turned to look behind her. The townsfolk were pouring onto the hillside. There were huge numbers, all following the same route. Their annual pilgrimage, echoing down the long years, hit Bella with a wave of emotion. It was special, and a little eerie too. She couldn't help feeling that anything done with such regularity and fervent dedication would leave a mark. If, one year, no one came, perhaps an onlooker would see ghostly shadows of the faithful approaching the spring.

At last, everyone had filed onto the hillside, spreading out, filling the space.

Down below, Bella glimpsed the River Kite, running through the valley. There was a hush, and as she raised her eyes, the first tiny sliver of sun came over the eastern hills.

It seemed as though everyone was holding their breath. Rays of light wove through the woods on the other side of the valley, dazzling, crisp and perfect. The break of day was breathtaking and Bella's eyes were pricking.

As she looked back at the near hillside, she saw the children of the town approaching the spring in a (mostly) orderly queue. They laid down offerings to Sweet Agnes in thanks for the spring and coming summer.

Bella had seen the after-effects when she'd come with her dad. Flowers of the season, gathered locally, woven into patterns. They'd been wilting in the sun, reminding her that nothing lasted. She'd thought of them when her father died twelve years earlier. He'd provided a quiet, calm refuge after her parents divorced. She'd spent most of her time in a crumbling London house with her mother, younger half-siblings and a sea of bohemian guests. Then suddenly her father was gone,

his flat sold and Bella was left with a horrible feeling of empti-
ness. It had felt like fate when that same flat came up for sale,
just when Bella decided to relocate.

She sighed and turned her mind back to current proceed-
ings. Most of those laying offerings were primary-school age.
Carys appeared to be hiding from one or two of them.

But now, a young man with shoulder-length blond hair
swaggered towards the spring. Late teens. Definitely too cool for
school.

Mary Roberts was standing close to the spring, her eyes on
the carving of Sweet Agnes, seemingly lost in thought. The
young man glanced over his shoulder, as though making sure he
had an audience, then walked towards Mary.

Bella's radar went off immediately. It was his stance and the
way he stared at the school secretary.

He didn't break his stride, but barged into her, knocking her
violently forwards. *Unbelievable.* It was so clearly deliberate.
Bella stepped towards them automatically, ready to intervene,
but Adrian Fitzpatrick got there first, in time to save Mary from
falling. He might be a stuffed shirt, but his reactions were quick.
He gripped her arm and steadied her, his fierce eyes on the
youth.

'So sorry.' The young man smiled at Mary with what looked
like the utmost pleasure. There was an uncomfortable pause
before he continued towards the spring.

What was he holding? Not flowers, that was for sure. When
he backed off, having put his offering amongst the others, Bella
saw it was a small wooden effigy, dressed in hand-sewn clothes:
a pleated brown skirt, a padded navy jacket and a red scarf.

Bella glanced at Mary Roberts. The effigy wore a crude
copy of the outfit she was wearing, as well as a bob made from
wool. It was shocking, all the more so given the pins sticking
into it.

2

GINNY GREENTEETH

There was a collective intake of breath. In the crowd, those close enough to see the effigy either looked shocked or intrigued, though a rugged-looking guy with grey stubble produced a satisfied smile. Bella was filled with the urge to wipe it off his face. What did he mean by reacting like that?

Mary Roberts's eyes were burning, as though anger and grim determination were doing battle inside her. She certainly didn't look cowed.

And nor did Adrian Fitzpatrick. The headteacher stepped forward and rolled up his sleeves. Bella was sure he'd love to punch the young man, but from what Carys had said he wouldn't do it. You didn't get to lead a government initiative by going around thumping people. Or not publicly, anyway.

'What? What!' The youth's infuriating smile sent Bella's heart rate surging. She'd love to give him what for.

'You know what, Noah!' Fitzpatrick gestured towards the effigy.

'That?' The teenager mimed exaggerated confusion. He looked very deliberately at the doll he'd made, then shifted his gaze to Mary Roberts and put a hand over his mouth. 'Oh! Oh, I see. You've got it wrong. The effigy's Ginny Greenteeth. You're meant to leave something to ward her off.'

Bella's dad had told her the legend. Ginny was a green-skinned, sharp-toothed hag who was said to lurk under the duckweed in ponds, ready to drag the unwary underwater and drown them. She was clearly a busy character, haunting wells, ponds and the like in several English counties. The thought had sent a thrill through Bella as a child. The current Hope Eaton children were edging back from the pond at the reminder.

It was abundantly clear that the effigy wasn't meant to be Ginny. She wasn't known for wearing a pleated brown skirt. Noah was smirking as though he knew no one would dare to state the obvious: that the doll was modelled on Mary.

'If you think you can—' Adrian was puce in the face.

Noah cut across him. 'I don't just think. I know. I can do what I like now.' He smiled lazily. 'I'm not at school any more.'

He looked infuriatingly relaxed as he slunk off into the crowd. It was Fitzpatrick who appeared to be fighting to keep his cool. It took him several seconds to wave the next child forward, who thankfully had a more conventional offering in hand.

Carys edged closer to Bella as the ceremony resumed. 'Noah Elsworth is an abominable worm,' she said, her voice low but forceful. 'Picking on Mary is the pits, especially now. I've been worried about her, as a matter of fact, and it's a bit of a puzzle. I was hoping you'd give me a second opinion if you came today.'

It explained why she'd been so persuasive. 'You think I'll be able to help?'

Carys raised an eyebrow. 'Don't come over all coy on me. You're good at getting to the bottom of things. I've seen the proof and I think you may have mentioned it yourself, once or twice.'

Hmm. It was possible. Growing up she'd done most of the childcare for her three half-siblings. Picking her way through their tall stories had been excellent training for her role in antiques, where reading dealers and customers was essential. Digging for the truth went with the territory too. She loved using subtle signs to unveil the history of the objects she bought and sold.

'Couple that with the way your dad trained you in his methods,' Carys went on, 'and who else would I turn to?'

Bella's father had once hoped she'd join the police like him – train to be a detective, perhaps. He hadn't pushed when he'd realised she had other ideas, but she'd always felt slightly guilty that she'd let him down. Not that she'd change anything. She loved her work.

All the same, she was intrigued about Mary and angry with Noah Elsworth. She edged a little further from the crowd. 'So tell me, why are you worried about Mary?'

Carys sighed. 'I've been wondering if she's spent too much time out here, all on her own. I'm beginning to think her mind is playing tricks on her. One time recently she let her guard down and told me she'd seen footprints on the garden path that didn't go away until she scrubbed them.'

It was a well-known Ginny Greenteeth myth. Anyone who'd spent time in Hope Eaton would know it.

'I think she's seen other things, too,' Carys went on. 'I saw her staring into the woods, and honestly, Bella, the look in her eyes was enough to make my skin crawl. But when I asked her about it, she changed the subject.'

'After what Noah just did, do you think he could be responsible? Maybe the effigy's part of a campaign.'

Carys nodded. 'It's possible. It would be a relief in some ways, but more frightening in others.'

Bella could see that. 'Adrian Fitzpatrick seems protective of Mary.'

'Superficially chivalrous. Though they're old friends, to be fair. She's worked for him for years.'

Bella's eyes were on the key players. 'Noah must really hate Mary to humiliate her in front of everyone like that. And the effigy feels like a threat.' Saying it was meant to be Ginny Greenteeth showed the legend was high in his mind. That could fit with him creating the footprints. She wondered how he'd have done it. With an oil mix maybe. Something that wouldn't evaporate. 'Why would he have it in for Mary?'

Carys frowned. 'I'm not sure. He's been in trouble – the police were involved. But I can't see how that would relate to her.'

Bella would have been determined to find out more even if Carys hadn't asked. She was jumping in at the deep end, but this was important. It was what her dad would have done, to help Mary and keep the peace that mattered so much to the community. 'I was going to ask to talk to Mary anyway, about her downsizing.' In the meantime, she could ask her godfather for the background on Noah's criminal activity. He was a retired member of CID and had been her dad's best friend, back in the day. He still sat on some committees, was unashamedly nosy and had no regard for the rules, which was handy. As for the cause of Noah's grudge against Mary, she'd ask around town. The third prong of her swiftly put-together plan would focus on getting Mary to open up about what she'd seen. She needed to work out if Noah had been tormenting her repeatedly, or if he'd picked up on her existing fear for today's one-off nastiness. If it was the former, it was a matter for the police; if the latter, then more research was required.

She and Carys were still talking about the drama when Jeannie joined them.

'I've said it before and I'll say it again,' she said, 'what Noah Elsworth needs is something legal yet exciting to occupy him. The trainee mechanic job his father got him is no good.' She shook her head. 'He'll get bored and be in trouble all over again, you mark my words. I'll have to see if I can arrange something.'

That was typical of Jeannie. Bella made sure she didn't catch her eye. She had a habit of allocating miscreant youths to family members to nurture. John could be next in line.

She wished now that she hadn't waxed lyrical about their work: the thrill of the chase at fairs, the excitement of knowing you were about to make a sale, the delight of foraging through a box of old junk at a house clearance. Jeannie might think her and John's profession fitted the bill.

But as luck would have it, Jeannie was distracted by a passing neighbour. As she turned away, Bella saw Noah pass the rugged-looking guy with grey stubble who'd grinned when he'd seen the effigy. She might not have noticed the subtle interaction between them if she hadn't been monitoring Noah. As it was, she spotted it: a raising of Noah's eyebrows, as though he was asking a question, then a tiny nod and a warning look in response from Mr Grey Stubble, as if to say yes, but not here.

Bella turned to Carys. 'Who's that man? I noticed him earlier.'

'The one with the mean look and the muscles? He's Mary's ex.'

How on earth had two such different people got together? 'He looked delighted when he saw the effigy, and he and Noah have just exchanged glances.'

'I can imagine them hitting it off,' Carys said. 'Birds of a feather and all that...'

The connection could prove interesting. Watching the dynamics made her think of her dad again. He'd been a neighbourhood officer, not CID like her godfather, but his work had still involved divining relationships and solving puzzles. He'd done his utmost to protect the townsfolk. Since moving to Hope Eaton, Bella had felt an extra connection with him, though they'd always been close. Two owners had come and gone between his death and Bella buying his old flat but the sense of him there was still strong.

A moment later, a woman of around Mary's age with short dark hair and a silk scarf walked over and took Noah to task. This would definitely have interested her father, because Noah was letting her. He looked grumpy but he didn't move away and his cocky laugh had gone. She must hold some sway with him.

Bella turned to Carys again and indicated the woman. 'Who's that?'

'Adrian Fitzpatrick's wife. Former nurse, now well-to-do woman about town and charity worker. Mary's best friend.'

It explained the scolding, but not why Noah was treating her differently to her husband.

John joined them. 'Enough excitement for you?'

She smiled. 'Is it always this eventful? I might turn up every year.'

'In my experience, you will anyway,' Carys said, 'disturbed sleep or not. If you've come once, it's hard to let it go.'

Bella could imagine but decided not to admit it.

'Come on,' Carys went on. 'I spy refreshments.'

John and Bella followed in her wake as she went to join the rest of the Jenks clan, who'd gathered on the hillside for coffee and scones, which were rich with fruit and spread generously with butter from a local farm. John poured the drinks, working very precisely, not spilling a drop.

'Your very good health,' Jeannie said, raising her cup with such gusto that she ruined John's efforts by slopping some over the side.

As they ate and drank, Bella continued to monitor Noah. It was deeply irritating to see some of the younger teens watching him with admiration. Hope Eaton could do without a gaggle of imitators. Noah's attitude needed sorting.

While chatting with John and his family, Bella made it her business to keep an eye on Noah, Adrian and Mary, and when the gathering of Jenkses broke up, she followed her quarry. It was how she came to hear the headteacher talking to the gossipy proprietor of Hope Eaton's grocers.

'... shocking, what Noah did,' the grocer was saying.

Adrian Fitzpatrick nodded. 'And it's the last thing Mary needs. I've been worried about her recently.'

Just like Carys. Bella pricked up her ears.

The grocer leaned forward eagerly. 'Really? Why?'

'She says she's seen some strange things out here. It's a lonely place. I wondered if it was playing on her imagination, but of course, she's determined to stay.'

The fact that Mary had confided in Adrian showed they were close, though Bella didn't think much of Adrian passing on his worries to the biggest gossip in town. She lost track of what they said next. Noah was her top priority and she had to move to keep tabs on him. When she saw Fitzpatrick again, he was off to one side, in earnest discussion with Mary. Bella edged closer, but she couldn't hear well enough to discover the topic. The one word she caught from Mary was 'Fitz'. A nickname from Adrian's family name, presumably. It seemed like an informal way for Mary to address her boss, though Carys had said they were old friends.

At last, the crowds began to disperse. Someone had removed the effigy from the spring and the carving of Sweet Agnes was surrounded by nothing but flowers again. It would take more than that to remove the stain of the memory though. Bella would need to work on that, just as her dad would have. The thought of Noah frightening Mary and getting away with it made her blood boil. Even if he hadn't been tormenting her long-term, he needed to know that a single hateful prank was unacceptable. She just needed to work out the best way to drive that message home.

As Bella and John retraced their steps through the garden of

Springside Cottage, Bella made a beeline for Mary. 'It's so lovely to walk through your grounds. They're beautiful.'

Mary's smile transformed her face. 'I love them too. I could never leave altogether.' She stared up at a pussy willow, then beamed and nodded at the branches, as though she saw something there.

Bella found herself looking too, then failing to stave off a shiver. At least Mary seemed happy now, not scared, but Bella had seen nothing.

After a moment, Mary's attention was back with her.

Bella fastened on to practicalities and told her about Vintage Winter. 'We buy and sell, if you're ever interested.' Out of the corner of her eye she saw John wince, but Mary looked thoughtful.

'I would like to sell some of my belongings,' she said at last. 'I'll never fit everything into my new place. Could you visit me tomorrow evening and have a look?'

Excitement pricked Bella. It was the first step to getting more information from her, and she'd get to see her bits and pieces too. She flicked John a small I-told-you-so smile and took out her diary. It was a thing of beauty with gilded pages, decorated with tiny hummingbirds. It made every entry feel important, which was just as it should be. You only got one life, after all.

They arranged for Bella to visit at eight the following evening. Very satisfactory.

A minute later, they neared Springside Cottage itself. Bella hadn't been able to see much of it on the way up the hill, but now she took in the house, squarely built in red brick and oak. Sixteenth century at a guess. It was a pretty place with its period casement windows and tiled roof. Someone would be very glad to buy it.

Bella was thoroughly looking forward to seeing inside and busy speculating when she heard Mary's sharp intake of breath.

On the doorstep of her cottage sat a pool of water and pondweed. Far too much to have come off someone's boots, even if anyone had been paddling in the pool.

Mary was silent now, and a shade paler than she had been. She pinched at the material of her padded jacket, twisting it in her hand.

'The curse of Ginny Greenteeth,' she said at last. 'If she leaves her mark your days are numbered. Only of course they're not. Someone's having a game with me. How very amusing of them.' It was a brave response, but her voice trembled.

Bella wasn't entertained either. It was a nasty, cruel thing to do, and she'd watched Noah throughout the event. It hadn't been he who'd left Ginny's mark. Whatever was going on, Mary had more than one enemy.

3

I MET A MAN WHO WASN'T THERE

Bella managed to meet her godfather Tony after work on May Day, in the grotty surroundings of his favourite pub, the Mitre in Shrewsbury. She'd explained what she wanted to know in advance, and Tony had said he'd put out feelers to get Noah's history and any gossip going. In the meantime, Bella had googled for information herself. She knew Noah had been had up for thieving, but nothing beat the inside track.

She tried to ignore the horrible swirly carpet as Tony rose from his usual corner table to give her a half hug. After that, she patted Tony's dog – a black Labrador called Captain – bought his master a pint of Hobsons Twisted Spire, along with a Coke for herself, and sat down.

Tony was grinning with a sort of dark relish. 'Interesting one, this. He's not well-liked down the nick, your Noah. On the face of it, he's a small-time thief. Arrested for stealing a quad bike from a farm outside Much Wenlock aged seventeen. But he had an awful lot of money on him when they brought him in. Wouldn't say where he got it and the police never worked it out.' He sniffed. 'Too much to do, too little time.'

'He was still at school when he was arrested?' Bella sipped

her Coke and rued the lack of ice and lemon. The Mitre took its no-frills approach to extremes.

Tony nodded. 'Got a community sentence. Volunteer work and a curfew.'

She couldn't imagine either sanction deterring someone like Noah. 'Do you know anything about his family?'

Tony referred to some notes. 'He's got a dad, sister and step-mum.' He gave Bella their details, which had to be against data protection law.

'And the curfew's over now?' Bella asked, stuffing the note into the pocket of her cigarette pants.

'Yup. Ended around a month ago. But here's the interesting thing – it was this woman you mentioned, Mary Roberts, who reported him.'

Bella sat back in her seat. 'Ah.' So that explained the vendetta.

'Her involvement was hushed up at the request of Noah's headteacher.'

'Adrian Fitzpatrick?'

Tony squinted at his notes again, all in smudged pencil. 'That's the one. Didn't want the press associating Noah's wrongdoing with his school and our lot didn't need Mary's evidence. They had a witness who saw him take the bike. They didn't know him from Adam, but they identified him all right once Mary called it in. By the sound of it, your Adrian Fitzpatrick was cross with Mary Roberts for going straight to the police rather than to Noah's parents.'

'He's a mover and shaker, apparently. He's been picked to run a government project, but it probably wasn't confirmed back then. I can imagine him shying away from bad publicity.' It fitted with what Carys had said about his character too.

'From what my colleagues say about Noah, I can see him wanting the last laugh.' Tony leaned back in his seat, laced his fingers and looked at Bella. 'What you told me about this morning's antics is in keeping. Question is, is that it, or will there be more? What do you think?'

Bella bent to make a fuss of Captain, who'd stirred and was after attention. 'Noah certainly enjoyed himself. I could see him giving a repeat performance, and today's might not have been the first.' She explained what Carys had said. 'But it's not just him we need to worry about.' She told him about the pondweed on Mary's doorstep.

'So there are at least two people at work. Any idea who the second one is?'

Bella mentioned Mary's ex, who'd seemed to give Noah a signal. 'But it might not be him. There were hundreds of people there and Noah was the only one I never lost track of.'

'You'll find out more when you visit Roberts,' Tony said, grinning for a moment over his pint. 'One thing you should know is that Noah's not the only person she's reported. She sounds like a bit of a one-woman moral guardian. Most of what she called in dates back a bit and she hasn't always had proof.'

Not good news. Her enemies could be countless. 'Did the police lose patience?' Bella probably would have.

Tony chuckled. 'They've got used to her. They say she seems compelled, as though it's down to her to straighten out wrongdoers.'

'So her motives are good?' Carys liked her, so it made sense.

He nodded. 'Seems so, even if her methods are a bit OTT. And she got the message in the end about when to make things official.' He smiled. 'It's a worry if someone's menacing her repeatedly, but I know you can take care of it. You're a chip off the old block.'

Bella said nothing. He appeared to share her dad's opinion that she'd have made a good detective. She was starting to realise he hadn't given up on the idea yet, even if she was just acting informally. She was determined to help Carys help Mary, and just as curious to understand the background, but she didn't tell him. It wasn't as though he needed encouragement.

As she approached Springside Cottage the following evening, Bella realised she was about to walk in on a row. She paused but the raised voices continued. *Oh joy.* Perhaps Mary had forgotten she was coming.

On the upside, the quarrel might be relevant to the duckweed on her doorstep. In her mind's eye she imagined Tony rubbing his hands and telling her to listen in.

Bella raised her eyes to heaven and waited behind a viburnum for the storm to pass. She peered through the leaves to see Mary and a woman in her forties emerge from Springside Cottage.

'How many times do I have to tell you, Mary?' The younger woman's voice was thick with upset and desperation. 'He's done nothing wrong! Haven't you done enough to my family? I think it's time you left well alone, don't you?' Her long blonde hair fell over her face and she turned away quickly.

Mary stood still, head held high. 'I was only trying to help.' Her voice was firm and calm. 'I can't ignore it.'

It sounded similar to the situation with Noah, and the way she'd reported other people to the police. Perhaps Mary really did see herself as the moral guardian of the town.

The younger woman groaned. 'I don't know what more I can say to you!' Her voice shook. She was afraid as well as furious. 'Give it up!'

Bella decided to show herself. If Mary knew she'd been overheard, she'd have to offer an explanation and if the blonde woman had left pondweed on Mary's doorstep then it was relevant.

'Hello.' She strode towards them as though she'd just come through the garden gate. 'Sorry to interrupt. Am I early?'

Mary stepped forward. 'Not at all.'

The other woman's jaw was tight. 'I was just leaving.' She dashed past Bella and the air crackled with tension.

'I'm sorry about that,' Mary said, looking after her.

Bella decided to take control of the conversation. 'It's difficult when you want to help someone but they won't let you.' Mary would be hard put to move on without elaborating.

'I expect I was patronising.' She ushered Bella inside the cottage. 'I chose Olivia's estate agents to market my house because I know business has been difficult recently. She disapproves of my wanting to hold on to some of the land. It's making the sale harder. I hear she'll lose staff if her cashflow doesn't improve. Though it's histrionics to say I'm out to ruin her family.' She fixed Bella with a firm gaze, her arms folded. 'As I said, I was only trying to help when I picked her firm.'

But that didn't explain the blonde woman's protestations. *He's done nothing wrong.* Who was 'he'? Bella would probably burn her boats with Mary if she asked outright. She'd look at the 'For Sale' sign as she left instead, remind herself of the estate agent. After that, she could find out more about Olivia. See if she had any reason to leave Ginny Greenteeth's calling card on Mary's step. Whoever was guilty needed reporting, even if they felt Mary was being difficult.

'What are your plans for the land you'll hang on to?'

'I was going to live in a caravan, but I've been persuaded to have a chalet built. I'll move into that eventually. I won't be pressured to leave altogether.'

'Of course not.' Though Bella would leap at the chance to move into town if it were her. It was magical but eerie here. And a long way from the shops, Jeannie's inn and John's brother's café.

'Let's get down to business,' Mary said. 'Can I get you a coffee? Or a glass of wine?'

After Bella had accepted coffee, she surveyed her surroundings as Mary disappeared into the kitchen. The front door led straight into a sitting room with wooden beams, a tiled floor and an inglenook fireplace. There were a couple of coats on hooks by the entrance. The rug in front of the dresser was glorious. Early twentieth century Persian at first glance. Unfortunately, it wasn't large. It would probably fit in Mary's new home. The same went for an intriguing statuette on the dresser. A representation of Sweet Agnes at the Sacred Spring, done in walnut. The work of an amateur. Saleable, but only to locals for a modest amount.

The dresser itself was something to behold. Leaf-carved columns and a central decorative panel. Seventeenth century. And big. Now, if Mary wanted to sell that...

Her host reappeared with coffees for them both. Bella was holding her breath, wondering which pieces Mary would offer her. She managed not to dance a jig when the dresser was mentioned, and produced a good offer. She played fair, then priced her goods to sell. Greed was ugly but also, as it happened, bad for business.

Most of the other items they discussed were also sizeable, including a country farmhouse table which was almost too big for her shop. She could feature it online instead, and Jeannie would let her store it in the old coach house at the inn. It was a handy arrangement, offered when Bella had hired John. The table would sell quickly, or she was no judge. They also discussed a seventeenth-century oak chest and a tallboy, but Bella's favourite item was tiny and Victorian. A carved owl inkwell.

'It's beautiful.'

'I suppose it is,' Mary said, 'but who writes with a fountain pen these days? It's just gathering dust.' Her words came out harshly.

So dust it, Bella wanted to say. Surely it must give her joy?

But as she looked up, she realised Mary's tone had come from suppressed emotion. Her eyes were damp.

Bella named a price. More than she should, but she felt for Mary. She must be running out of money. She wouldn't get rid of something so delightful and small otherwise. And she clearly had no desire to leave her lonely house.

At last, they finished. 'Have a think,' Bella said. 'There's no pressure. If you'd like to go ahead just give me a call and I'll make the arrangements.'

Mary nodded. 'Thank you.'

Bella wondered how she'd come to own this palatial house but not the funds to go with it. At least she'd still be on the spot, if the sale went through. Bella thought of her looking into the trees in that otherworldly way. Perhaps it was earth, leaf and stone that bound her there, not bricks and mortar.

Mary loaded their empty coffee cups onto her tray and swept through to the kitchen. Bella followed her, ready to offer help and slip Noah into conversation, but before she'd reached the other room, there was an almighty crash.

She leaped forward to check Mary was all right. The woman looked as white as the broken porcelain at her feet. What on earth had happened? It was as though she'd forgotten what she was carrying and tipped the tray sideways. Her gaze was on the woods beyond her garden and Bella felt the hairs on her head lift.

'What is it?'

Mary pointed, but Bella couldn't see anything.

'Where do you keep your dustpan and brush?'

'You're not to trouble.'

'I'd prefer to. Honestly.'

She let Bella help in the end, gesturing at a cupboard under the sink.

'What did you see?' Bella asked, as she got to work.

Mary sank onto a stool. 'It doesn't matter. I must have been mistaken.'

'I doubt it.' Playing the waiting game tended to work.

'A figure in the wood wearing a long, dark cloak,' she said at last. 'Its hood pulled over its face.'

Bella noticed her use of 'it', not 'their', but even without that it would have been creepy. The hooded figure was another feature of local folklore: a demon in human form who'd come for Sweet Agnes, desperate to drag her down to hell. Legend had it that her goodness had saved her. Anyone in Hope Eaton could have decided to reference the story. People learned about it on their parents' knees. Adrian Fitzpatrick's brother William, whom Carys had mentioned, had even written a poem about it. She'd looked him up.

'It's not the first time I've seen it.' Mary's voice was almost a whisper. 'It's visited me a few times over the last month.'

Bella reminded herself of her own theory: that the original hooded demon had been some powerful local who'd felt threatened by Sweet Agnes, and it was the townsfolk who'd saved her, because she was beloved. 'Have you told the police?'

But of course, they'd told her to stop coming forward unless she could make a good case against someone.

She shook her head. 'What would I say? They'd never believe me.' Her voice got lower again. 'I hear it chanting sometimes.'

Bella was still crouched down, sweeping up the last few shards of porcelain when Mary exclaimed again: 'There! Quick, look!'

She shot up so fast she spilled some of the debris and this time she thought she caught movement, though she didn't see anything in detail. It could have been an innocent passer-by or an animal even.

Mary had seemed to see something in the pussy willow the previous morning. She might be imagining a hooded figure now, but it would be dangerous to bank on it, and the pondweed had been real enough. 'You don't think it's Noah? I saw what happened at the spring. Has he bothered you before? Or since?'

Mary shook her head quickly. 'No. And anyway, wrong height.'

But in the woods, someone might stand on a log or in a dip. All the same, there were other candidates: Mary's ex and the blonde woman who'd visited, plus anyone she'd accused of wrongdoing. 'Is there someone else you think it might be?'

Mary closed her eyes for a moment. 'No.'

She *could* be speaking the truth. 'I think you should inform the police. Just to be on the safe side. You've got the evidence of your own eyes and you could tell them what Noah did at the spring too. Even if he's not the one hanging round in a cloak, I'm sure they'd investigate.' Bella would tell Tony as well.

A short while later, they said their goodbyes and Bella walked back towards the garden gate. She'd asked Mary if she should call someone to keep her company but she'd said it was fine.

But was it? Or was there someone out there who might be a danger to her? Carys was right to be worried; this needed resolving, and with her upbringing and contacts, Bella might be best placed to do it.

She kept her eyes peeled as she made her way home, crossing to the edge of the holt as quickly as possible, then joining Holt Lane. It was the long way round, but the tall trees felt threatening.

It was only as she reached home that she realised she'd forgotten to check Mary's estate agent's board. She looked up the sale online.

The Nest – an outfit on the high street, run by the blonde visitor, Olivia Elsworth. Realisation hit her. She must be a relation of Noah's. She looked at the note Tony had given her with details of his family members. Olivia was his stepmum. Her conclusions about the conversation she'd overheard shifted. It looked as though Noah was in trouble again and Olivia was pleading his case.

Mary could have told her she thought Noah was her long-term tormentor, but it seemed unlikely. She'd said the hooded figure was the wrong height, and Bella had a hunch she half believed in the demon.

No, she guessed Mary was onto something else. It would be a second offence, if she reported him, and he was no longer underage. The police would be harsher this time. He had more to lose, and that was a worry.

4

AN INTRUDER IN THE NIGHT

Mary Roberts was on Bella's mind after her visit. She called Tony when she got home and he said he'd flag her stalker with his former colleagues. All the same, she doubted much would be done unless Mary reported it herself. But perhaps she would, if she got in touch about Noah's latest wrongdoing, as discussed with his stepmum. She'd made it clear to Olivia Elsworth that she couldn't ignore it, whatever it was. It made Bella deeply curious. It had to be something beyond his bad behaviour at the spring, if Olivia was denying it.

The following day, Bella opened Vintage Winter for the Saturday trade and wondered if she'd hear back from Mary about the items she'd offered on. It would be a wrench to let them go though; Bella would be in denial if she was in Mary's shoes. Thoughts of the beautiful dresser flitted through her mind.

Of course, she might get other valuations too, though Bella was always surprised by the number of people who didn't.

As the day wore on, she trawled for gossip from her customers and the lunchtime crowd at John's brother's café, the Steps, then later that evening at the Blue Boar. She was at the inn for Jeannie's sixty-ninth birthday party. She met plenty of people who wished Noah would leave Hope Eaton.

She also managed to confirm that Mary had been forced into her house sale. Her family hadn't had much money. Her rag-and-bone-man dad had been a single parent after her mum died when she was small. Then the value of scrap metal went down and councils established recycling centres, so he was out of work. But her uncle on her mum's side had done better. Mary had inherited Springside Cottage from him. Although she owned it outright, her salary wasn't enough to keep it going. It was cavernous, old and chilly. She could release a lot of capital if she found the right buyer. Enough to build the chalet she'd mentioned and have some fun, perhaps.

Very late that night, Bella made her way home from Jeannie's jamboree. It had been a raucous affair, though Jeannie's husband Peter had been quiet as a mouse, as ever. Bella enjoyed the couple's double act. Peter let Jeannie get on with it, in her loud and forthright way, but he was there in the background, stoically running the business side of the inn, or in this evening's case, making sure there was enough to eat and drink. Bella had managed to dodge Jeannie's youngest son Matt and his current girlfriend by hanging back as they'd left. The last thing she wanted was to have to walk back to the seventeenth-century hall where both their apartments were located, making awkward chit-chat. Talk about third wheeling...

It was well after one in the morning, but Bella felt safe as she crossed the high street and cut through St Giles's Close, home to Vintage Winter and the town's church with its twelfth-century origins. It was a world away from the woods. She listened at the top of St Giles's Steps, her shortcut to where she lived, down by the river. It was a lonely route, but she could hear Matt and his love interest ahead of her. If she ran into difficulties she could yell, though that would be deeply embarrassing, obviously.

She passed between John and Matt's brother's café and the next building along, descending the tiled steps, taking care not to catch the lovebirds up. At least there was no direct line of sight: the steps curved gently to avoid making them too steep. As she reached the bottom and the junction with Boatman's Walk, she saw Matt and the model-like beauty turn the corner towards the river, the water glinting in the moonlight. All good. Bella followed slowly to ensure no interaction, then prepared to dash for home. Her feet were killing her. But as she passed Friar's Gate, a lane leading off Boatman's Walk, she caught an unusual sound from the rear garden of the house on the corner.

Adrian and Fiona Fitzpatrick's place, as she'd discovered during her research.

There'd been a clatter, as though someone had dropped something. A sizeable item, but not heavy.

The house was in darkness.

Bother. If something was going down at the Fitzpatricks', she wasn't especially keen on dealing with it. The shoes she was wearing were exquisite: 1940s peep-toes with high heels and an ankle strap. Not suitable for anything more energetic than sipping a cocktail. She'd known they'd be hellish when she put them on, but Jeannie's birthday called for something special. Besides, it was fun to cut a dash.

She sighed and approached the Fitzpatricks' side gate. She'd check out the situation through a knothole, just to show willing. After all, it might be Noah; he seemed to hate Adrian as well as Mary.

She held her breath as she watched a figure dressed in black dashing away from the back of the Fitzpatricks' house towards their boundary wall. They weren't hooded like Mary's spectre. This one looked more like a cat burglar in skinny trousers and a long-sleeved top. The security lights had come on, so Bella got a good view. The figure was slight and lithe, with a black beanie covering their hair. They carried something over their arm which swung wildly as they leaped onto a garden bench, using it to launch themselves over the back wall. As they scrabbled, almost dropping their cargo, Bella realised what it was. A paint pot, visible in the security lights. The figure's hat slipped, and some long hair escaped. Reddish-brown.

Bella was certain it was a woman. She couldn't chase her from where she was. The house backed onto the eastern edge of St Giles's Holt and there was a high brick wall blocking the way. Giving it up as a lost cause, she peered at the back of the house.

The graffiti the intruder had daubed was visible for a moment before the security lights timed out. The message was written in pale green paint. *Tasteful.*

Leave her alone!

A spur-of-the-moment job? Using a spray can would have been a lot quicker.

Bella thought about calling the police, but there'd be no one to catch by the time they arrived. They'd have to send someone from Shrewsbury. Not like in her dad's day.

Instead, she strode up Friar's Gate, made her way through the Fitzpatricks' front garden and knocked on their glossy front door. If they were in, they needed to know they'd been visited. They probably wouldn't thank her for waking them in the small hours, but leaving it until morning would be cavalier.

Bella wondered about the intruder's message. Who was it intended for, Fiona or Adrian? And if it was Adrian, was the 'her' Fiona or someone else? Bella thought of the headmaster's bunched fists as he'd rounded on Noah Elsworth on May Day morning. She guessed he had a short fuse.

No one came to the door, but as Bella stood back and craned her neck, she caught sight of a shadow at an upper window. Someone was home.

She waved to make sure they knew they'd been seen, then knocked again. It would be quite nice if they'd hurry up.

At last, she heard footsteps. The door opened a crack, with the chain on.

It was Fiona Fitzpatrick. She looked fed up and weary but Bella clearly hadn't woken her. She wasn't even in her night things. 'Yes?'

Bella explained who she was and why she was out so late. 'I'm afraid you've had an intruder. I heard a crash, so I peered through a hole in your back gate. They've graffitied your wall. If you call up to Adrian now, he might catch sight of them through a back window.'

Fiona opened her mouth, then closed it again. 'No. Thank you. It's not worth it. We'll report it to the police.'

What an odd response. Bella would have wanted to look, even if she had a good idea who'd done it. The chances of the police having the resources to investigate were next to none.

Fiona looked pale in the porch light. 'Did you see what the graffiti said?'

Bella didn't relish explaining when the words were so accusatory. Still, discussing it would give Fiona the opportunity to confide. '"Leave her alone!"'

Fiona put a hand to her face and Bella lowered her voice. 'Do you need help? I was worried in case the "her" referred to you.'

There was a long pause. At last, Fiona looked Bella in the eye. 'That's probably what the writer intended. That's the hell of being a headmaster. You're in the public eye, you make enemies, and the rumours go round. But you needn't worry, there's nothing in it, just some busybody who's completely wide of the mark. Adrian's never laid a finger on me, nor would he. So thank you for letting us know, but I'm fine. You should go and get some sleep.'

Bella wished her goodnight and the glossy red door closed in her face. So that was that. *Highly unsatisfactory.*

As she made her way towards the river and home, Bella considered Fiona's words. It felt as though she'd been protesting too much, with her story of her persecuted husband. But if Adrian *was* treating her badly, why hadn't the intruder knocked on the door to check she was all right, rather than daubing paint on their house, out of the public eye? Graffiti wasn't the most logical route if you wanted to save someone from an abusive partner. And besides, Fiona's statement that Adrian wasn't violent was the one bit of her speech which had sounded convincing.

Inside her flat, Bella sat down in the palatial hall. It was excessive for the size of the place, but Bella liked the luxury. Her childhood home had only been borderline habitable. All those buckets under drips...

At last, her shoes were off and she wriggled her toes. Pure heaven.

Why would Fiona Fitzpatrick protest too much? The answer came in her father's voice: *Because she's anxious and the truth is explosive. She's determined to keep it quiet, whether it refers to her or Adrian.*

There were other questions too. Why had Fiona been awake at that hour, and why had she not reacted to the crash that Bella had heard?

Bella went to wash, then slipped into her satin pyjamas. She could imagine Fiona not going to tackle the intruder if she was on her own. She'd let Bella think that Adrian was at home, but that seemed unlikely. She couldn't see him ignoring an intruder or hanging around upstairs while Fiona answered the door in the dead of night. He was the sort who pushed himself forward and whose blood was easily heated.

She was all but certain he hadn't been there at all, and that Fiona had been determined to hide the fact.

5

GINNY GREENTEETH'S CURSE

Vintage Winter opened late on Sundays, for which Bella was deeply grateful. She woke blearily at nine to the sound of frantic meowing.

Cuthbert. Honestly! How had Matt's cat got in again? She hadn't noticed him last night but he seemed to like Bella's place better than his own. It was probably more serene. Matt's love life was hectic and he came and went at odd hours – she still hadn't found out why. She stumbled through to the flat's hall and hefted Cuthbert up, to immediate contented purring.

'I thought you wanted to go out.' The tabby kneaded her with his paws, then butted her with his head. 'So fickle.' She opened the front door.

Perfect timing. Not.

The name of the model-like brunette came back to her now. Debra. And she was just leaving Matt's flat opposite. Bella would have preferred not to be seen unmade-up and in her night things. At least she'd put her kimono on. Velvet and satin, mustard yellow. A favourite. She tried not to imagine her bed head and the potential for streaked mascara. She hadn't been too careful about make-up removal the night before. She'd been thinking about Fiona.

Debra turned to her with an amused smile and held out her arms to Cuthbert.

Bella was delighted when the cat wriggled free and jumped into Matt's open doorway instead.

'Honestly, Cuthbert,' Matt appeared, 'you must stop bothering strange women in the middle of the night.' His twinkling eyes met hers.

Bella turned on her heel and retreated into the flat. Twenty minutes later she'd showered, dressed and entered the shared hallway in 1950s black vintage elegance, only there was no one to see her. She made for the Steps for coffee and something restorative to eat before she opened the shop.

Her walk was the reverse of the one she'd taken the night before, along the River Kite heading out of town, then up Boatman's Walk to reach St Giles's Steps. As she passed the leafy entrance to Friar's Gate, she paused by the Fitzpatricks' back gate. It was daylight now. Anyone walking up the lane might see her looking. She checked over her shoulder then put her eye to the knothole she'd used previously. She wanted to see the graffiti again. Think the whole incident through. Curiosity gnawed at her. But the daubed paint had gone.

That was weird. Had they really had time to report it, get the police in and clean the words off? Bella continued her journey as she thought. Maybe there'd been no one available, so they'd taken photos and emailed them. And of course Adrian (or possibly Fiona) wouldn't want the neighbours seeing the words.

Leave her alone!

What did it mean? And who was 'her', if not Fiona?

John and Matt's middle brother Leo distracted her from her thoughts as she entered the Steps café. 'Feeling delicate?' He looked unreasonably cheerful, his extravagant blond hair waving as he bounded over.

'I didn't overindulge. It was just the late night.'

He gave her a knowing look. 'Coffee as black as a raven's feather?'

'If you insist.'

'And an Eaton sausage sandwich?' He caught her expression. 'Ah. Or some nice plain sourdough toast perhaps?'

'It's as though you'd read my mind. Have you seen John this morning?' He didn't work on Sundays unless Bella had a sale to attend.

'Up horribly early, cycling up hill and down dale with Gareth.'

He and his partner were both bike enthusiasts. It took all sorts.

Bernadette, who was in charge of the Steps' new-and-used book section, bounced over to join them. 'What time do you open today, Bella?' She was breathlessly excited as usual, eyes wide and slightly poppy.

'Half eleven. If I can lever myself out of my seat again.'

Bernadette's smile widened. 'There's just time then.'

Bella felt faint misgivings. 'Time for what?'

'For you to go with Carys to see Mary Roberts.'

Carys appeared at that moment, the imprint of a creased pillow still on her cheek. Leo pressed a cup of coffee into his wife's hands.

Bella seemed to have missed part of the plot. 'Lovely.' Well, lovely-ish. It would be good to check in, though it was a shame it involved moving. 'But why?'

Bernadette bounced on the balls of her feet. 'Mary ordered some books and Carys has volunteered to take them over, but Mary wanted to see you too. I found an answerphone message from her when I got home from Jeannie's party.' She'd left a lot earlier than Bella. 'She mentioned wanting to sell some of her things and asked if I could vouch for you. It was before ten, so I called her back. I said she couldn't do better, of course, but there's a couple of extra pieces she'd like you to consider. Isn't that good news? She said she'd call you about it today, but you could go with Carys, as you're here.'

She finally paused for breath. As a seller of beautiful books, some of them antique, Bernadette understood Bella's fascination with her work and her delight in finding new clients. It went way beyond making a living. The feeling of connection and understanding people's hopes and desires was everything. Though there was a massive buzz when you struck a deal, of course. Nothing beat it.

Carys put her coffee on Bella's table, then flumped down into a seat opposite her. She didn't look like someone with a strong urge to run an errand.

'I could go on my own if you like.' Bella was keen now she understood the situation, and not just because of the business deal. Each time she saw Mary was another chance to persuade her to talk to the police.

'It's okay.' Carys looked at her blearily. 'I think the walk might do me good. Kill or cure.'

'All right then. It'll give us the chance to catch up too.' Bella hadn't managed to fill her in on her chat with Tony yet, or her visit to Mary on Friday night. They'd tried to talk at Jeannie's party but the music, dancing and games hadn't lent themselves to the plan.

Leo set down Bella's toast and coffee.

'Thank you. You're a lifesaver.'

He saluted.

The combination of the food and the news of Mary was a shot in the arm. 'I'll get on the right side of this coffee and toast, Carys, then lead the way.'

. . .

Trudging along the Sacred Way in daylight was a joy, especially as Bella had worn flats. All around her, the trees were a lush green and the birds sang in the undergrowth. She was even enjoying the smell of earth and leaf matter stirred up by their progress. The sunlight traced dappled patterns at her feet and once again she felt the power of the ancient route. Its antiquity made travelling it feel momentous.

Carys had her hands shoved in her pockets, her eyes half closed against the sun that reached them.

'Have an afternoon nap.'

She groaned. 'I can never sleep in the day. It means I'll still feel rubbish tomorrow morning and a Monday teaching the small-but-loud ones is always horrendous on too little sleep.'

She needed distracting. 'Shall I tell you my news about Mary's trouble?'

Carys nodded. 'Definitely.'

Bella relayed what her godfather had said. 'It's no excuse, but it explains Noah's grudge.'

'It certainly does.'

'Mary never told you she'd reported him?'

Carys shook her head. 'That said, I know she tends to get involved if she spots any wrongdoing. I remember Lucy telling us very solemnly one evening after Mary babysat that "Doing wrong only leads to misery." We eventually got it out of her that she was quoting Mary.' She gave a wry smile. 'It turned out that Lucy had eaten our secret supply of Hallowe'en sweets when Mary wasn't looking. She was right about the misery. The sweets came back up.'

'Ah.' After that, Bella told Carys what had happened when she'd visited Mary on Friday evening.

'So she's seen the hooded figure from "Sweet Agnes and the Demon" as well as Ginny Greenteeth's footprints.' Carys shook her head.

'I glimpsed movement, out in the woods. There was something there, but I can't say for certain that someone's dressing up. It's possible it was an innocent passer-by and her mind's playing tricks. I'm not entirely sure she's convinced the hooded figure's human. You know her better, what do you think?'

Carys frowned. 'She's an unusual mix. Tough and no-nonsense in some ways, but I've always thought of her as spiritual too. Before now it seemed like a happy thing. She hears voices in the trees, and it makes her smile. She doesn't try to cover it up.'

A chill crept up Bella's arms as she remembered Mary's focus on something invisible in the pussy willow. Of course, some people said Ginny Greenteeth could ascend into the canopy of trees and lurk there at night. And Mary had gone pale when she'd seen the water and weed on her step. Maybe she believed in her. But Carys was right, that was different. The look in her eye had been fond and emotional when she'd stared up at the tree.

'Has she talked to you about the voices?'

'No, I just got used to it. I've heard her reply to someone who isn't there. Just very quietly. Things like, "Ah yes, I remember that." And, "I believe you're right."' She gave a quick laugh. 'I thought she was talking to me at first, but when I went to answer I realised she wasn't looking at me at all. It never worried me until she started fretting over what she saw. As soon as things changed, I realised something needed to be done. I just wasn't sure if there were outside forces at work.'

Bella nodded. 'I wish I'd been quick enough to get a good look at the figure she saw.' Mary had been terrified, and Bella was kicking herself. Whatever the truth, she mustn't go on suffering like that. 'What's her taste in books like?' She nodded at the satchel Carys was carrying.

'Diverse. Bernadette says she bought the most beautiful

edition of *Grimm's Fairy Tales* from her recently, but she also reads about politics and sociology.'

Bella would have been interested in the fairy tales. She had a weak spot for distinctive illustrations and bindings. 'What have you got for her today?'

Carys gave her a sidelong look. 'Several volumes on witch-craft for a start, so you can see the way her mind's working.'

The poor woman. Bella imagined her poring over the books late at night, wondering what was beyond her curtains. 'She was impressively stoical about the effigy. Outwardly at least.' Bella was glad Noah hadn't seen her cower. 'If we can't convince her to go for help, is there anyone else she might listen to? I think she's scared no one will believe her.'

'I suppose there's Adrian.' Carys looked doubtful. 'But I suspect he thinks she's imagining things.'

Bella remembered hearing him say so on May Day morning.

'His wife Fiona's probably a better bet,' Carys went on. 'She's Mary's best friend.'

Bella thought of the graffiti again. *Leave her alone.* Mary probably wished whoever was plaguing her would do just that. 'It sounds like the worry over the hooded figure is relatively new. She's seen them over the last month, since Noah's curfew ended.'

Carys's expression hardened. 'I wouldn't put it past him, especially now we know it was Mary who reported him to the police. It's annoying that the pondweed on the step can't be him too.'

It muddied the waters, but it was another example of something that wasn't in Mary's imagination.

As they got nearer to Springside Cottage, Bella wondered about the extra possessions Mary had earmarked for Vintage Winter. If Friday's items were anything to go by, they'd be inter-esting. They didn't have to be flawless. Back in London at the antiques shop she'd managed, the owner had only zeroed in on perfect items, worth a small fortune. Bella had rebelled against that. She rarely stocked anything truly expensive. Vintage Winter was more Paris flea market than Christie's showroom, and that was the way she wanted it.

They reached the other side of St Giles's Holt and Bella opened the gate onto Mary's land. To the left were crowds of green alkanet, and a couple of bees, but they weren't the only creatures buzzing. To the right, flies were congregating.

Too many flies. And what was that horrible smell?

Bella leaned far enough forward to see, then sprang sharply back. *Ugh*. Maggoty meat of some kind. It undid all the good work of Leo's sourdough toast.

Carys lurched back too. 'Oh, weird! Who on earth could have put it there?'

An effigy, pondweed, a hooded figure and now rotting meat. Bella wondered what her dad would have made of it. One thing was certain, it was getting out of hand. Mary *must* call the police. The flies and maggots wouldn't help her house sale or her peace of mind.

'I'll ask if it's happened before.' Bella hastened up the brick path. It was a warm day, and Mary's oak front door was open, though her windows were closed.

Carys kept pace with her, taking books out of her satchel as she went. *Spells, Curses and their Origins, The History of Incantations*, and more besides. Perhaps Mary wanted to research the chanting she'd heard. It didn't have to mean she believed in its power but Bella had a nasty feeling she might.

She stood aside to let Carys enter the cottage first so she could put down her load. Through the open doorway she could see the beautiful oak dresser. It was the last normal thought she had that morning.

Carys came to a halt the moment she'd crossed the threshold, bringing Bella to an abrupt stop.

She knew something awful had happened from Carys's complete stillness. She tiptoed forward to see over her shoulder.

Mary's sitting room, with its tiled floor and saggy sofas, was visible through the rustic doorway. On top of the rug Bella had admired the previous day was Mary's body, a look of utter terror on her face.

6

THE MISSING STATUETTE

Bella and Carys stood staring at Mary's lifeless body. She looked heartbreakingly vulnerable in her worn blue nightdress.

Bella knew she'd cry if she didn't do something drastic. She dug her nails into her skin and focused on the facts for all she was worth. Her father would have been moved too, but his desire for justice would have taken over.

Mary wore no dressing gown or slippers. It made Bella think of putting Cuthbert out that morning. Even she'd had a wrap on, and she was only opening the door to the shared entrance hall. It was hard to imagine Mary opening her front door dressed like that.

She was distracted by Carys, who put the books she'd brought on top of a pile on a side table. She was moving mechanically.

'We need to call the police.' Bella took her phone from her bag and dialled.

As she waited for the call to connect, swallowing hard, she ran her gaze over the room. Something glinted from inside a shoe, close to the door. She crouched to get a better look. The key to a deadlock. Wouldn't Mary have left it in the keyhole if she'd just turned it herself? It seemed more likely that an intruder had dropped it as they ran to escape.

Her call was answered, and she told the handler what had happened. Adrenaline had kicked in now and she was breathless.

No, there wasn't any clue as to how Mary had died. The house seemed deserted. But no, she couldn't be sure there was no one else inside.

'They want us to get out,' she said, after she'd rung off. 'And leave everything just as it was. We should probably take the books away again.'

Carys blew out her cheeks, her eyes still wide with shock. She moved towards the books very slowly, still staring down at Mary. A moment later she'd picked them up and put them in her satchel.

As they waited outside, her face contorted. 'I can't believe it. Poor, poor Mary. I don't think I've ever seen anyone look so petrified.'

Bella texted John, who responded collectedly, despite the horrifying situation. He insisted on opening Vintage Winter while she and Carys spoke to the police. She felt rotten, dragging him in on his day off. So much for the carefree bike ride Leo had seen him and Gareth set off on that morning.

It took half an hour for the police to arrive, though paramedics got there sooner. There was nothing they could do, of course.

DS Barry Dixon spoke to Bella and Carys at a garden table to the front of Springside Cottage. He nodded at Bella, having met her before. He'd have a vague notion of Hope Eaton, but he was no substitute for a proper local officer who knew the relationships in the town.

Dixon looked just as Bella remembered: like an overgrown

schoolboy who was surely too young for the job. She guessed he was in his early thirties though his babyface might be deceptive. It would make her around ten years his senior, but she felt at least twice as mature.

She sighed. She shouldn't pre-judge him. He hadn't solved the last murder in Hope Eaton but there were extenuating circumstances. He'd been desperately overworked and permanently sleep deprived, thanks to a spate of jewellery robberies, his umpteen children and his wife's job as a vet.

She couldn't help noticing he had a piece of dried rusk stuck in his hair.

Bella tried not to stare at it as she and Carys told him everything. Not just why they'd been there and what they'd seen, but what had happened on May Day, the story of the hooded figure and the presence of the rotting meat.

'Hooded figure?' Dixon looked depressed, and even more so when Bella told him about the legend. After that, he went to view the rotting meat, then sighed and wrote copious notes. 'We'll call out the pathologist. Get the coroner involved.'

At last, he told them they could leave.

Almost as bad as finding Mary's body was meeting Fiona Fitzpatrick as they returned along the Sacred Way. She was en route to Springside Cottage to meet Mary and they had to tell her what had happened.

Fiona's hand flew to her mouth. 'What? I don't understand.' She gaped at them. Bella remembered the feeling of disbelief when she heard her father was dead. How could there be any mistake? Yet still your brain told you that the truth was impossible.

'The police are there now.'

'The police?'

Bella wondered how much to say. 'I think the coroner normally gets involved if there's an unexplained death.'

'You think there's something... something suspicious about it?' Fiona's eyes were wide.

Bella thought of Mary's mouth stretched with fear, like a gash in her face. The oddity of her key, dropped into one of her shoes. Her lack of dressing gown. 'I hope not.'

'What is it?' Fiona sounded desperate. 'What did you see?'

Bella couldn't help wondering if she knew or suspected something. *Leave her alone.* 'Someone had left rotting meat in her garden. And her front door was open.' Mary's face filled her mind's eye. 'She looked terrified.'

'I've just realised, her carving was missing!' Carys's tone was urgent.

'Wait a minute, what?' Bella turned to her.

'Mary had a wooden statuette of Sweet Agnes at the Sacred Spring. It was precious to her. I knocked it over once and she grabbed it and clutched it to her chest.' Carys's eyes were dark as she remembered. 'I felt quite uncomfortable. It was as though I'd physically wounded her. She set it back on its stand on the dresser. It was always there, but not today.'

Bella remembered it herself now. 'I saw it when I visited. It was interesting: saleable, but not all that valuable. Or not on the face of it. Do you know where she got it?'

Carys shook her head and Fiona frowned.

'I asked her once, but she changed the subject; I knew not to mention it again. But I can't believe anyone would have... would have, well, killed her for it. Or for any reason.'

But Bella thought of Mary's terrified expression and her stalker and couldn't agree. Someone had been tormenting her and her death felt like the next stage in their campaign. But if she'd been killed, then who had done it, and how? There'd been no sign of violence. She must find out the truth.

When she looked up, Fiona's eyes were on her, as though she knew exactly what Bella was thinking. Once again, Bella wondered why Noah had treated her with more civility than her husband.

It was early afternoon by the time she joined John at the shop.

She dashed in to be greeted by the smell of brewing coffee. She blew him extravagant kisses, partly because she knew it teased him but also as a defence against the shock and upset.

'You're a prince amongst men. Coffee is just what I need. But now you must go and make the most of what should have been a day off. You're owed. Let me know when you want to take the hours back and I'll arrange it.'

John met her bustling onslaught with his usual composure. 'I'd rather not leave until we've talked about what's happened. I don't want to sound like my mother, but you can't just dash from reporting a dead body to running the shop without breaking your stride.'

If John had been brutal about it, she'd have managed to maintain her stiff upper lip. His kindness got under her armour. She felt her eyes prickle as tears threatened again. 'I probably can, actually.'

'Even so, I rather think you shouldn't. If you won't bite my head off, I'd suggest sitting down, drinking your coffee, and telling me about it.'

Nine out of ten people would want to know out of curiosity, but Bella knew John. He really wanted to lend a listening ear. The thought made her even more emotional. She turned her back on him to fish for a tissue before things got out of hand. After she'd blown her nose, she twisted to face him. 'Thank you.'

Ten minutes later, she'd filled him in on everything, from Carys asking her for help to what Tony had said, the scene at Springside Cottage and Fiona's reaction afterwards. Offloading combined with coffee helped.

John polished a beautifully inlaid mahogany writing box as she spoke. A casual onlooker might think he wasn't listening, but she knew better.

'Now, you really should go,' she said as she finished. 'Come on.' She took the box from him then forcibly tipped up his chair, so he had to get out of it. 'Go home and have tea and cake or something. Gareth will never forgive me if he has to leave for work before you get back. And you know I find his dark brooding stare hard to take.' She remembered John's partner had had the day off, but was due at the Blue Boar that night, ready to delight Jeannie and Peter's customers with his inspired cooking. Jeannie always said he was the best cook they'd ever had. 'It's almost closing time anyway.' She shut Vintage Winter early on Sundays, as well as opening later.

'What will you do afterwards? Call your godfather?'

She met his knowing look. 'That is on my to-do list, now you mention it.'

She was on the phone to Tony Borley the moment she'd locked up the shop.

'*To what do I owe this pleasure?*' Tony's gravelly voice came down the line. '*Got something fresh?*'

'I'm afraid so, and it's not good.' She filled him in.

'*Blimey O'Reilly. I hadn't heard.*'

'Any chance you'll be able to find out more?'

His rumbly tones were reassuring. '*Don't you worry about that. Leave it with me; I'll be in touch.*'

7

A MEETING WITH THE GODFATHER

Bella had heard nothing further from Tony by Sunday night. The following day, she prepared to head to Vintage Winter. It was normally closed on Mondays, but Bank Holidays were an exception. Day trippers were too good an opportunity to miss. John still had the day off though – she could cope on her own. Between putting up her hair and doing her make-up, she peered at her mobile. Even if Tony hadn't got updates, he might at least text to say that. After the initial shock, the town was buzzing with speculation. Several people had decided that Noah had killed Mary, based solely on the way he'd treated her on May Day. Did they really imagine he'd flag himself as a suspect like that? Though Bella wasn't discounting him. Something could have cropped up to force his hand after his display of nastiness. She swigged more coffee as she dashed to her living room to grab her bag before exiting her flat.

Outside Vintage Winter, Bella saw John's former boss, Sienna Hearst, striding towards her. She was wearing a well-cut summer suit, but in her mind's eye, Bella always visualised her in Dalmatian fur. Sienna produced her standard wintery smile, followed by a derisive sneer as she surveyed Bella's window display. But it was all a pantomime. Her foul behaviour was driven by fury at Bella for poaching John. He'd worked at the Hearst House Museum when Sienna's aunt was still in charge, and very happy he'd been there. When the old lady died and Sienna took over, John quickly realised he'd like to move on. Bella smiled to herself. He was a gem and knew just about everyone in Hope Eaton, thanks to his previous job. It was Sienna's fault she'd lost him.

'Terrible news about Mary Roberts, isn't it?' Sienna eyed her. 'I hear she was planning to sell some furniture through you. You must be devastated that she died before you made any money from her.'

An inventively rude reply flashed in Bella's head, but it would be more of a triumph not to rise.

Sienna laughed lightly and moved on as Bella wished she could throw something at her.

Her adrenaline had just about returned to normal when her mobile rang an hour later. She'd been filling in time between customers writing a label and jumped, sending her pen skidding across the smart cream card. It was Tony.

I've got news. Probably best to fill you in in person.

'All right then. What about coming to the Steps at five?' She was following Sunday hours and closing early. She could easily make it by then. She'd invite John and Carys, and Leo would want to listen in of course. Tony had met most of the Jenkses, though not the elusive Matt.

He hesitated.

Please don't insist on the Mitre instead. The smell of disinfectant overlaying stale beer did nothing for its ambience.

'All right. The Steps it is. Come prepared. I don't think you'll like what I have to say.'

He could be very irritating at times. She wanted to know now, of course, but she wasn't going to amuse him by showing it.

. . .

Five o'clock came at last. Bella swept into the Steps to find Tony had beaten her to it. He was sitting at a corner table with a view into the valley, the River Kite running far below. Captain rose the moment Bella appeared in the doorway. She rubbed the black Labrador behind the ears, appreciating his liquid-eyed gaze and warm solidity.

Tony heaved himself from his seat to embrace her as Leo bounded out from behind the counter.

'I asked what's afoot, but Tony refused to say until you got here. I'm going to join you. Poppy will serve.' He glanced at the young waitress who was busy spilling hot chocolate over the shoe of a woman near the counter. 'Or her version of it, anyway.'

'I texted Carys too,' Bella said. 'She'll be here in a minute.'

Carys and Leo's teenage daughter Lucy was there as well, at a separate table, deep in a book about fungi. It was her latest passion.

'As I said on the phone, you're not going to like it.' Tony shook his grizzled head as he greeted John, who'd just arrived.

Carys bustled in next, looking harried. 'I'm glad you've got news; I haven't been able to get poor Mary out of my head. It still feels unreal. The distraction will be welcome. I've been surrounded by six-year-olds playing Ginny Greenteeth all day. They've been obsessed with her ever since May Day morning. One of the little darlings managed to colour her face with green felt tip, fifteen minutes before home time. Her mother was not pleased. I'd only turned my back for a minute to tell Jack Dawkins off for snarling. My patience is at an end.'

It was Carys's catchphrase.

Leo patted her arm soothingly as Poppy arrived to take their order.

'It's the wretched fundraiser meeting tonight too.' Carys

asked for a cappuccino and sank into a chair.

'It's still going ahead?' Leo looked surprised.

'Apparently. Adrian messaged the WhatsApp group to say he'll hold the event in Mary's memory.'

Bella asked Poppy for a hot chocolate and hoped most of it stayed in the mug. 'What's all this?'

'The Hope Eaton Combined Schools benefit do. I'd hoped they might cancel it. I promised them a second-hand clothes stall in a moment of madness.'

Bella's ears pricked up. 'Will there be bric-a-brac too?' It was amazing what you could find when people cleared out their cupboards.

'Oh yes, the whole shebang.' Carys put her head in her hands. 'So what's the situation?'

Tony leaned forward, elbows on the table. 'Pathologist says Mary Roberts's death was natural causes.'

There was a collective gasp.

Bella caught his eye. 'A hundred per cent certain?'

He nodded. 'Undiagnosed heart problems. Fright could have brought the death on, but no intruder could bank on that, even if they'd spotted her symptoms and guessed their cause.'

Bella took out her favourite notebook with the blue marbled cover and edges. 'What kind of symptoms would she have had?'

'You are your father's daughter,' Tony said, grinning for a moment. 'The answer is shortness of breath and swollen ankles.'

'Oh Sweet Agnes!' Carys put her head in her hands. 'I noticed she was out of breath quite recently, when I bumped into her on the Town Steps.'

There were several routes in Hope Eaton connecting the area by the river to the higher town. Bella had found the ascent testing when she'd arrived from London. Even now, she wasn't fully acclimatised.

'I should have realised.' Carys drew in a heavy breath. 'She's been going up and down them all her life and she's active. She shouldn't have been breathless.'

'Now, now.' Tony could be surprisingly sensitive on occasion. 'Don't you go taking on. I'm sure she had plenty of friends who saw something similar and thought nothing of it.'

Carys frowned. 'Come to think of it, her best friend Fiona's a former nurse. She can't have put two and two together.'

She had a point. In fact, perhaps it was a bit odd that it hadn't struck Fiona. Bella made a note which was seen by Leo, who was craning shamelessly in her direction.

She pulled the notebook to her chest but that wasn't enough to quell him.

'Why are you writing down suspects when Mary died of natural causes?'

Tony was smiling, as though he'd known she would. *Annoying.*

She leaned forward. 'Whatever happened, I'm certain she had an intruder on Saturday night. It looks as though they stole her carving, but I don't think theft was their goal. They'd have broken in during the day if it had been. Mary's movements were predictable.' All the same, it was a puzzle. They must have taken the statuette for some reason. 'I believe they were there to scare Mary, and that they let themselves in with a key. I saw one inside her shoe by the door.' The pitiful sight of the abandoned footwear came back to her. 'I think the intruder dropped it, then bolted in a panic when they couldn't spot it on the floor. Assuming the key was for her front door.'

Tony glanced at some notes. 'It was. Careless of the intruder, if that's what happened.'

'They'd have got an awful fright.' She imagined the scene. 'Perhaps Mary heard them and came downstairs. Her heart could have given out in front of them.'

Carys had her hands to her face again. 'I've just remembered. Mary talked about her belongings moving around on their own. She'd leave them in one place, then find them in another. I put it down to absent-mindedness, but if someone had a copy of her key...'

'They could have sneaked in and done it to convince her she was losing touch with reality.' Bella could hardly credit it, it was so cruel. 'Letting themselves in on Saturday night implies they were upping the ante. Why risk it when Mary was at home otherwise?'

'Hold up!' Tony frowned. 'There's no proof anyone was there, don't forget. And as I said, it's natural causes.'

Was he being sceptical just to irk her? She turned to Carys. 'You told the police about the missing statuette?'

She nodded. 'I called them after I left you.'

Tony frowned. 'Was it valuable?'

Bella shook her head. 'I'm sure I could have sold it to a local, but not for more than twenty or thirty pounds. I saw it when I visited. I'd say it was done by an amateur and within Mary's lifetime.'

'I can show you.' Carys pulled out her mobile and scrolled through her camera roll. She handed the phone round. The photograph showed Mary Roberts in her sitting room, her smile sparky, eyes alight. She'd looked full of vitality there. How quickly things could change.

The missing carving was in the background, sitting on Mary's beautiful dresser. You could still see the chisel marks; they hadn't worn in the way you'd expect with an antique. Bella enlarged the photo with her thumb and forefinger and showed it to John.

His eyes met hers.

It had a certain something. 'Maybe someone gave it to her as a present, and she treasured it for that reason.' Now she looked more closely, it reminded her of George Frederic Watts's sculpture of the ocean nymph, Clytie. The unhappy story from Greek mythology flitted through her head. Clytie fell in love with the sun god, Apollo, and after he deserted her she was turned into a sunflower, her head endlessly twisting to follow the sun on its daily course.

Watts had sculpted the nymph's beautiful human head and upper torso partway through the change, her lower torso already metamorphosing into a sunflower. In the case of Mary's statue, the artist had Sweet Agnes's head and shoulders disappearing into rock and ferns. The base was the pool by the Sacred Spring.

'So it's objectively low value,' Tony said. 'In which case, it probably wasn't stolen. Perhaps she lost it.'

But Carys shook her head. 'She was really attached to it. If it had fallen down the back of some furniture or something she'd have returned it to its place straight away.'

'I wonder if the intruder stole it purely to upset her.' The more Bella thought of them, the more furious she got.

'Or perhaps she moved it.' Tony stretched back in his seat. 'Either way, you can't expect the police to mount a statue hunt. They haven't got the resources.'

Bella knew how stretched they were, but this mattered. 'They could at least check if it's in the house.'

Tony shook his head. 'Wouldn't alter their approach, even if they couldn't find it.'

'What about the rotten meat in Mary's garden?'

'That made them wonder.' Her godfather laced his fingers and twiddled his thumbs. 'Perhaps it was someone *outside* who gave Mary Roberts a fright. She could have opened the door to look, then pulled out the key and dropped it as the pain in her chest took hold.'

A grim thought. 'What time did she die?'

'Between two and four in the morning, according to the doc.'

In that case Bella didn't believe Tony's theory. 'I wouldn't have opened the door at that hour.' Not even dressed in the velvet and satin kimono. 'And even if she did, why wouldn't she layer up first? There were coats by the door.'

'Just as tenacious as your old man.' Tony was smiling again.

Bella felt like a pet poodle sometimes. She gave Captain a sympathetic look and ignored Tony. 'I believe that Mary was being terrorised by at least two people, possibly with multiple motives, convincing her she was losing her grip being one of them. That would fit for the hooded figure – look how they ducked out of sight when Mary tried to show me. In which case, it was probably they who moved Mary's belongings while she was out, like Carys said, and let themselves in on Saturday night.'

Tony looked thoughtful. 'Using the dropped key on both occasions. Why make her feel she was losing her grip?'

'To raise her anxiety to fever pitch so her heart was under constant strain? Or simply as a punishment? Few things would be more terrifying. Or perhaps to convince her friends or lawyers she was no longer competent to organise her affairs. I'm sure there are other possibilities too. It's pretty ironic that her death seems to have prevented a police investigation rather than triggering one. You seriously think we should let it lie?' She had a fighting chance of working out what had happened, and no one else was going to do it.

Poppy, who was passing, had the look of someone who'd just woken from a long nap. Bella must have raised her voice.

'I didn't say that,' Tony replied, mildly.

She moderated her volume. 'Dad wouldn't have left it.'

He gave her a significant look. 'He'd have been all over it like a rash. No one should get away with making someone's life intolerable.'

8

ASSESSING THE SUSPECTS

The rest of the gang had been watching Bella and Tony.

'We'll start investigating who was responsible for tormenting Mary then,' Bella said, her heart rate starting to calm down.

Everyone was nodding. 'I'm in.' Leo's voice was the loudest, which was no surprise.

Bella scribbled Mary's time of death in her notebook before she forgot it and turned to Tony. 'So, what about the people who might have wished her ill? Noah's an obvious one. Did the police take his May Day stunt seriously?'

Tony's look turned dark. 'The local team devoted some time to him. Sounds like a cocksure young so-and-so. They were glad to have the excuse to focus on him again, I reckon, not having got the full truth last time.

'As far as this business goes, the police are willing to believe someone was mucking around *outside* Springside Cottage, thanks to the planted meat. It would take a while before it went maggoty, but someone could have let it rot beforehand. That's most likely in fact. If it had been there a while, a fox would probably have taken it.'

Bella shuddered at the thought of handling the meat when it was already in that state.

'In any case,' Tony went on, 'my old colleagues paid Noah a visit, in case he was responsible.' He looked at his notebook. 'Noah "smiled knowingly" according to the report – a bit leading, but the bloke who wrote it's only human. From what I hear, you'd need rhino hide not to let Noah get to you. Anyway, he insisted he was home all night. Says he's got into the habit after the curfew.' Tony raised a bristly eyebrow. 'A likely tale. And no one can vouch for him. His dad's away. Common occurrence apparently. He's high up in some development charity. Lots of trips abroad.' He looked at his notebook again. 'His sister, who's sixteen, was sound asleep, and his stepmum, Olivia, was out walking. Says she hasn't been sleeping well. Problems with her business.'

Which fitted with what Mary had said. Still, it was interesting that she'd been absent. 'Olivia's got a beef with Mary too. They were arguing over something Noah might or might not have done.' Bella described the scene. 'Olivia was telling her where to get off.'

Carys was frowning. 'Remind me what she said.'

Bella flipped to the page where she'd recorded it in her notebook. 'Something like: "How many times do I have to tell you? He's done nothing wrong! Haven't you done enough to my family?"'

'I'm surprised she hasn't lost patience with her stepson,' Tony said, then chuckled. 'From the police report, I'd say the PC has a crush on her.'

'Half the town does,' said Carys drily, 'including Leo.'

Leo looked scandalised.

'She was a model when she was younger,' Carys went on. 'An It girl in London. Related to the royal family and at least two senior Members of Parliament, so they say. Leo claims he's not shallow enough to be taken in by anything like that.'

Her husband sat up straighter.

'Oh, do stop trying to look dignified,' Carys said. 'If you got your hair cut you might possibly manage it. Otherwise, you haven't a hope. So, Olivia and Noah were both down on Mary and neither of them has an alibi.'

'That's right. Though on reflection, I'm not sure Olivia would respond to Mary's questioning by trying to frighten her. It could have driven her to go to the police, which wouldn't help. They'd probably suspect Noah – the very last thing she wanted.'

'Fair point.' Tony's brow furrowed.

Bella sipped her chocolate. 'All the same, any new information Mary had on Noah needs uncovering. And we need to know who put pondweed on the doorstep of Springside Cottage, whether or not it was the hooded figure. If that wasn't Olivia, then I wondered about Mary's ex-husband.'

'Oh yes, Shane Sadler has to be a candidate.' Carys leaned back in her chair nervously as Poppy delivered her coffee, the young waitress's eyes fixed on a handsome youth who'd just entered the café.

'When did they divorce?' Bella asked.

'Oh, around ten years ago? The marriage didn't last long.' There was a twinkle in Carys's eye. 'It was a work of perfection when Mary outed him for having a fling with that woman from the estate agents. Shane's punishment was richly deserved, but not diplomatic.'

It sounded like quality entertainment. 'What happened?'

Carys sipped her cappuccino. 'Shane and one of Olivia's employees had been using an empty property as a love nest. Mary got wind of it and arranged a last-minute viewing when she knew they'd be there.' She shot Bella a look. 'She'd invited several friends to join her. She told them she wanted second opinions.'

'And I saw it too,' Leo said eagerly. 'I happened to be passing and heard the commotion, so I poked my head in.'

'Nose, more like,' Carys said.

Leo looked affronted. 'I needed to talk it through afterwards, with my delicate disposition. It was hard to unsee.'

'I couldn't help admiring Mary's style.' Carys smoothed her swishy skirt over her knees. 'She said afterwards that humiliation would get Shane to change his ways, but it marked some indelible battle lines. A whole gang of their friends saw Shane and this woman in flagrante. He was livid.'

'He was wearing a leopard-print posing pouch!' Leo was laughing. 'And holding a—'

'Yes, thanks,' Bella interrupted. 'That's quite enough detail. And I see he might want revenge, though ten years would be a long time to wait. What surprises me is him and Mary getting together in the first place.'

'We thought it was odd, didn't we?' Carys glanced at Leo, who nodded. 'Mary was always quite serious and introspective, not a bit like Shane. He's the sort to see that as a challenge, so I got it from his point of view. It was her reaction that threw me. When he made a play for her, she responded with abandon. It was like watching someone diving into a deep pool with no thought of how they'd get out. The moment they were married, I think she came up for air and realised what a mistake she'd made. She started to act stiffly and dress more conservatively at that point, as though she wanted to distance herself.'

It was bizarre. 'Was Shane ever really in love with her, do you think?'

Carys looked cynical. 'I heard he was about to lose his home. I imagine Springside Cottage was a tempting proposition. He certainly bragged about it once he was living there. Being chucked out must have been difficult financially, as well as bruising to his ego.'

It went some way to explaining the situation. She visualised the two-timing muscle-bound man she'd seen at the spring. It still seemed odd that someone as self-possessed as Mary had fallen for him to start with. It sounded as though she'd been acting out of character, but why?

'I got the impression she blamed herself for the relationship with Shane,' Carys added. 'As though she recognised her moment of weakness. There's always been a bit of a question mark over him. He's a hardened gambler, from what I hear, and people hint that he's not quite honest.'

'I think there's some kind of link between him and Noah, too.' Bella reminded her about the glances the pair had exchanged on May Day morning. 'What happened to Shane's lover at the estate agents?'

'Olivia had to sack her,' Carys replied. 'She must have been livid with Mary, but she moved to Cardiff.'

'I doubt she's involved then.' Tony swigged his tea noisily. 'Reckon we're after someone local.'

Bella agreed. 'Noah and Shane both seem possible. And I can't help wondering about the Fitzpatricks too, after the intruder graffitied their house the night Mary died.' She'd already told him the story.

'"Leave her alone?"' Tony said.

Bella nodded. 'What if the intruder was addressing both of them and talking about Mary?'

Her godfather looked thoughtful. 'The Fitzpatricks never reported their intruder or the graffiti. Plenty of reasons why they mightn't, of course. Doesn't have to relate to a campaign against Mary. Any idea why they'd want to frighten her?'

Bella was stumped on that one. 'No, but it was odd on May Day morning. It looked like Fiona was telling Noah off and he was letting her. Maybe there's a connection between them. She could have been worried about him drawing attention to himself. And the way Adrian didn't come down when I knocked at their door on Saturday night bothers me. He's not backward in coming forward.'

Tony's interested eyes rested on hers. 'What are you thinking?'

'That he wasn't there, and Fiona was covering for him.' Bella would have to find a way to prove it. Him being out the night Mary died unnerved her.

Carys leaned forward. 'Just so you know, Fiona inherits Mary's house.'

'What?!' Bella had startled Poppy again. She dropped a plate of toast.

'For heaven's sake,' Leo muttered.

Carys nodded. 'Mary told me in confidence. She made some reference to "a room of one's own".'

A room was all well and good, but a whole house was generous. 'It was just her property, not her money and so on?'

'I believe that's right. She mentioned any funds going to charity but I don't think she had much.' Carys's gaze was steady.

'So there was no one else in competition for the house?' Unless someone wanted to challenge her will, an attempt to show Mary lacked mental capacity seemed less likely.

'That's right. Mary had no family left. She said she hadn't told Fiona about the bequest. I wonder if she knows now.'

Bella's eyes met Tony's and he nodded to her. 'An interesting little set-up, I'll give you that.'

'Especially as Fiona could have spotted Mary's heart symptoms. Perhaps she and Adrian predicted she might die if one of them entered her house without warning.'

Tony raised an eyebrow. 'Going in with that in mind's a bit of a stretch.'

He was even more annoying when he was right.

He drained the last of his tea. 'So, we have Noah who might have wanted to scare Mary for revenge, Shane Sadler, ditto, and the Fitzpatricks, with plenty to gain, but not much hope of getting it by scare tactics. And Olivia Elsworth, who was begging Mary to leave her family alone, but would only draw attention to herself and Noah by creeping around Springside Cottage. Beyond that, we know that although Noah put the effigy at the spring, he didn't leave the pondweed on Mary's doorstep.'

Bella nodded. 'All true. If any of them entered Mary's house to frighten her then they probably caused her death. They're guilty of murder morally, even if they're not technically.'

What to do next? Bella needed a way to talk to the key players casually, without drawing attention to herself. Only then could she start to answer some of the most urgent questions. She wrote them in her notebook:

- Was Adrian really away from home on Saturday night?

- Was there something that could have prompted Shane to take revenge on Mary now, after all these years?

- Was Noah working with anyone to scare Mary?

- What is the new secret that Noah's keeping, that Olivia and Mary argued over?

A potentially fruitful but unpleasant possibility entered Bella's head. 'I don't suppose the combined schools' fundraiser needs extra volunteers?'

'You want me to get you into Adrian Fitzpatrick's inner circle?' Carys's eyes were bright. 'I like your thinking.'

9

THE SHOW MUST GO ON

Carys and Bella met again that night in the Blue Boar, ready for the fundraising meeting. Leo and John were there too, and Lucy was behind the scenes in her grandparents' private quarters.

Jeannie sailed towards them like a galleon, hugging them each in turn. 'Someone mentioned something extraordinary about rotting meat in poor Mary's garden. Can it be true? What did you see, Bella?'

Bella confirmed it.

'The whole thing sounds very worrying. Did someone bump her off, do you think?'

Leo raised his eyes to heaven. 'Such a way with words, our mother.'

'There's no point in pussyfooting around. Well, Bella?'

'Her heart gave out. She was ill, but no one knew it.'

Jeannie let out a long breath. 'Well, that is a relief. Though tragic of course. I was worried in case there'd been foul play and your godfather encouraged you to get involved again. What was he thinking of, last time?'

John had got into terrible danger previously. Bella's heart

still raced at the thought of it. She'd felt horribly responsible. She decided not to share their plans going forward.

As Jeannie left them, Adrian and Fiona Fitzpatrick entered the room.

'Getting involved with the fundraiser should be a good gambit,' Carys said, as they took their places at the bar. 'Olivia Elsworth is involved too. Her stepdaughter attends Hope Eaton High. And of course, Noah *did*.'

Bella was interested. 'I thought Olivia might have taken against Adrian after the school's involvement in reporting Noah. She was very sharp with Mary, though Tony said Adrian wished they'd dealt with the theft informally.'

Carys looked cynical. 'That won't have been for Noah's sake; he's all about protecting the school's reputation. But he's good at managing people's impressions. He probably made Olivia feel he was on her side and blamed everything on Mary.'

It figured. Either way, Bella was glad of Olivia's involvement with the fundraiser. She might secretly know about Noah's latest wrongdoing, and her stepson had definitely victimised Mary. If Bella could prove he and an accomplice had been at it repeatedly, the police might take action. 'What will tempt Adrian to invite me to join in?'

'Oh, that's easy,' Carys said. 'Matt mentioned you're a singer.'

'A singer? How would Matt know—' The answer came to her before she could finish the question, along with a sinking feeling. He'd commented on her shower recitals a few months back. She'd moderated the volume a little afterwards but gradually forgotten. He'd probably heard her many times since.

Carys looked surprised. 'Haven't you performed before?'

'Not since I was a teenager.' There'd been the awful time when her mother's boyfriend's band had played at a party and put her on the spot. It hadn't really counted. It was a houseful of motley guests. She hadn't wanted to join in, though she'd been singing to herself, away from the makeshift stage.

Once she was up and performing, she'd forgotten why she was so angry with him. She'd felt warm. Buoyed up. But a couple of songs later, he'd given a friend of her mother's a look that should only have been directed at her mum. She'd flung the microphone down on a sofa and stalked off to her room.

She hadn't sung in front of anyone since. Well, not knowingly. Accidental bathroom performances didn't count.

'Matt says you're a natural and the fundraiser *really* needs people. One of the regulars has dropped out. You wouldn't be on your own.' Carys said that doubtfully, as though it might put Bella off. 'They want a group of backing singers so that obnoxious teens and drunk parents can do karaoke over the top.'

It sounded awful, but she'd get to talk to lots of people afterwards. For the sake of the shop, it would be worth it, to say nothing of finding out more about the Fitzpatricks and Olivia Elsworth. And supporting the fundraiser, obviously. 'All right. I'll offer to do it. If they want me.'

Carys patted Bella's shoulder. 'They'll want you. The group might be a mixed bag. Just so you know.'

Bella was wondering again if it was worth it when Adrian Fitzpatrick approached them. 'Thank you for coming, Carys. How's the second-hand clothes stall coming along?'

'Fine, fine.'

Bella knew Carys well enough to know that her airy tone meant she hadn't started work on it yet. She could help her knock for donations door to door. It would be another opportunity to meet her existing customers and make friends with the yet-to-be converted.

'And who's this?' Adrian smiled at her, all charm and bonhomie in his well-cut trousers and crisp shirtsleeves.

Carys introduced them and explained Bella's interest in

volunteering. Adrian looked as appreciative as if she'd donated diamonds to his bring-and-buy sale.

'We'd be delighted to have you with us.' He twinkled at her and lowered his voice. 'Our other singers are a bit hit and miss. You'll be invaluable.'

He went on to ask about her business and how she'd come to be in Hope Eaton. As usual, she explained about the antiques shop she'd managed in London and her desire to run her own place. She left out the scandal which had catapulted her move to Shropshire. Adrian was just the type of smooth-talking operator who'd think her boss was in the right, and she shouldn't have kicked up a fuss. Bella thought back to the discovery that one of their best clients was trying to con a nice elderly lady. He'd hoped she'd sell him a vase at a bargain price, thanks to a friend of his who'd deliberately undervalued it. Bella had ensured the client ended up in court, which had caused some of their other buyers to distance themselves. Presumably ones who were also involved in dodgy dealings. They were better off without them, but that hadn't cut any ice with her boss. She'd walked out in a fury. The Adrians of this world could take a running jump as far as she was concerned.

'Good-looking and knows it,' Bella said to Carys, when Adrian left them to schmooze someone else. 'A smooth talker too.' Bella liked polished, not smooth.

'He was being more honest than you might imagine about your fellow singers. I hate to break it to you, but Edwina's tone deaf.'

'Why have her then?'

Carys gave a wry smile. 'I don't know, but it's almost always political. Her husband's on the board of an educational trust.'

Adrian *was* an operator, just as Bella had thought. She decided to ignore the fact that she was too, in a small way. That was different. The friendships she formed were a genuine delight, even if improved sales *were* a by-product.

The group involved in the fundraiser assembled around a couple of large tables in the front bar. Bella and Carys joined the fray, taking their glasses of Gareth's signature summer cup with them. He'd refused to divulge the recipe so she had to guess the ingredients: a mix of mint, melon and strawberry but with a twist of something delicious she couldn't place.

Adrian Fitzpatrick began with a tribute to Mary Roberts, talking about their old friendship and her sterling work as school secretary. Bella watched Olivia's tense face as he spoke, her fingers fiddling nervously with her glass.

'We need to make this fundraiser special to honour Mary,' Adrian finished. 'Half the proceeds this year will fund a school award in her memory.'

After that, he complimented and flattered his way around the tables as he discussed the various acts, stalls and entertainments. Bella was introduced to the woman Carys had said was tone deaf, Edwina West. She was probably fifty or so. Very good-looking and curvy. Bella had a feeling she regretted the prospect of another woman on the team. Her smile didn't meet her eyes. They were to sing with the music teacher, an earnest young man who looked terrified by the whole thing.

Fitzpatrick was talking to Olivia Elsworth now. She'd agreed to do the teas and coffees.

After he'd finished, a man to Olivia's left spoke to her. 'It must feel very odd for you, after marketing Springside Cottage all these months. I suppose you knew Mary quite well. Perhaps the new owner will want to get rid of the place too, though it's hung around, hasn't it? It's as though you'd cursed it!' He laughed.

'That's the high school's PE teacher,' Carys hissed. 'Always extraordinarily tactless.'

Olivia stared ahead, stony-faced. 'The idea of Mary's building work at the bottom of the garden was putting people off. I tried to persuade her to change her mind, but it was a no-go.' She put her hands to her face, took a deep breath, then removed them and looked around the tables. 'In any case, someone was trying to prevent the sale.'

The person who'd left the rotting meat? Bella leaned forward to hear better.

'Seriously?' The PE teacher sounded incredulous.

Olivia nodded. 'They left disgusting things in the garden. Dog muck. Dead rats. They must have crept into the grounds when my back was turned. I'd taken to checking before viewings, but they still managed it.'

The culprit had had a negative impact on Olivia as well as Mary.

But it was Mary who must have felt unnerved. Bella watched Adrian and Fiona. Could they have known about the bequest? Delaying the sale made sense if they had realised Mary might die soon, leaving Fiona Springside Cottage. The combination of terror tactics to induce death, with dead rats to stop the sale, equalled a lot of effort with little hope of reward. But perhaps one of them had visited her on Saturday to take the next step... It could be a case of attempted murder.

It was quite possible that they'd found out about the will. Mary had been Adrian's right-hand woman. He was as likely as anyone to have got wind of it; he might have overheard her call her solicitor in work hours. It would be useful to know the layout of the school offices, and she must find out if Adrian had been home the night Mary died. She'd tackle that this evening. A plan had come to mind.

'How very disturbing for you.' Adrian frowned. 'I'm surprised you didn't go to the police. Have you told them now?'

If he was responsible for the campaign, he'd want to know what the authorities knew.

She looked up. 'I thought about it, but it doesn't seem relevant any longer.'

Bella wondered why she hadn't reported the incidents

earlier. Unless she thought it was someone with a grudge against her, not Mary. She might want to keep that quiet.

Adrian sighed. 'Anyway, to business. What about a talk from you, Olivia? You know how interested our guests will be by your experience as a model, hanging out with popstars in Paris and London.'

Olivia's face contorted.

'She hates talking about "the old days", as she puts it,' Carys hissed. 'We all find it fascinating, of course, however much we'd like to rise above it, but Olivia sounds glad to have left it behind. I think she feels more fulfilled now she's running her own business. Or she did, until it started to go downhill.'

Bella could understand that. She liked being in charge too.

Adrian was smiling at Olivia expectantly. 'You could find some old photos.'

She nodded at last. It would help shore up her place in the town, of course, which was important for any businesswoman, and she'd be supporting her stepdaughter's school. All the same, Bella was sure she'd been tempted to refuse.

When the meeting broke up, Bella buttonholed Adrian again to quiz him. She was about to launch in subtly, but it was he who brought Mary up.

'I'm sorry, I didn't make the connection earlier, but my wife tells me it was you who discovered Mary's body. She was one of my oldest friends, there for me through thick and thin. Fiona mentioned the rotting meat you saw in her garden too. What can you tell me about it?'

'The death was shocking. I guess the meat could have been left by someone like Noah, after what he did on May Day. Not meaning to harm her, of course.' She was keen to disguise her thoughts on attempted murder. 'I imagine she went to see what was going on but her heart gave out before she got any further.' If Adrian was guilty, she wanted to induce a false sense of security.

His penetrating gaze was steady. 'I expect you're right.'

Bella paused a moment before fishing for information herself. 'When I visited Mary last week,' she said at last, 'I noticed she had an unusual statuette. A representation of Sweet Agnes at the Sacred Spring.' She watched his eyes as she spoke and saw the very slight flinch as she mentioned the artefact. *Interesting.* 'I wondered where she got it from, and who the artist was.' She wouldn't labour the fact that it was missing. If he'd taken it, she'd rather he didn't think she was trying to track it down.

'I know the one you mean.' He sounded deliberately airy. 'But I don't know the answer. Picked it up at a second-hand stall most likely. I hear it wasn't in its usual place when you found Mary.'

'I didn't notice, but the friend I was with mentioned something. I suppose Mary must have moved it.' Bella had a strong feeling he knew more than he was saying, though why he'd hold back was a mystery. Unless they'd had an affair and he'd given it to her as a present. He'd naturally want to keep any relationship secret, and if he'd had the statuette inscribed, it might give him away. But they made unlikely lovers. They'd worked together for a long time, but Mary was a very different type to Fiona. And besides, her sense of morality seemed uncompromising.

Now to get the other information she wanted. 'I'm sorry about your graffiti artist, by the way.'

He didn't flinch. 'It was good of you to knock and tell us what had happened.'

She smiled. 'I wasn't sure if I should have waited until morning. I don't make a habit of waking people up at half past three. That's antisocial behaviour in itself.'

Fitzpatrick smiled back without missing a beat. 'Not at all. You were being neighbourly.'

His reply was telling. And how did he know she lived around the corner from him? She didn't like the idea very much.

As one of the fundraiser gang made to leave the inn, Adrian broke off to call out to the group. 'So, tomorrow evening at school, for a rehearsal. After that, you're all invited to drinks at our place. Singers, we'll be wanting you, and you too, Olivia, for an initial stab at your talk. And can you bring the clothes donations you've had so far, Carys? Let's see where we're at.'

Carys looked horrified and Bella shot her a look of sympathy. With that timescale, she'd probably have to buy some from the charity shop on the high street.

As Bella left the inn, John joined her. Leo and Carys had gone to find Lucy. 'How was the cosy chat with the headteacher?'

Bella turned to him as she did up the buttons on her swing coat. 'Worrying. When I claimed I'd called on him two hours later than I really did, he didn't bat an eyelid. I'd say that means he wasn't there when I knocked at half past one, or at three thirty either. And Mary Roberts died between two and four in the morning. That makes him a firm suspect.'

10

HANGING OUT AT THE HANGED MAN

'So, where are we at?' John said.

Bella was ahead of him as they walked up the high street. 'I've been thinking about the methods Mary's tormentors used again, and how different they are. The rotting meat could have been designed to stop the house sale but the Ginny Greenteeth references and demon dress-up look like terror tactics, designed to mess with Mary's mind. Perhaps the Fitzpatricks are responsible for both. They could have been trying to hasten Mary's death and put off buyers at the same time. Or there could be more than one perpetrator and motive. Either way, it made her life hell and whoever was behind it mustn't get away with it.'

John nodded. 'Have you got a plan?'

'Yes. A top priority is to find out where Adrian was the night Mary died. We must see if we can prove Fiona knew about her bequest too. That could be enough to convince Barry Dixon to open an investigation into the death. If they've been tormenting her all this time in the hope that her heart would give out, Adrian might have reached desperation point by Saturday. He could have gone in to kill her, only for her to die right in front of him.'

John frowned. 'I see it for Adrian, but Fiona? She used to be a nurse, dedicated to saving lives, and now she works for a charity. I know nothing's certain, but she visited the museum every few months. I liked what I saw of her.'

Bella nodded grimly. 'But as a former medic, she could have spotted Mary's symptoms.'

John still looked disgruntled, so she moved on. 'I want to go after Noah's secret too. As I said, frightening Mary to try and keep her quiet seems counterproductive – it would only draw attention, whether he or Olivia did it. But it still feels very convenient that Mary had something on him and now she's dead. Leaving that aside, the way he tormented her with the effigy looks more like revenge for reporting him last time. And on the topic of retribution, we need to know more about the humiliated Shane Sadler.'

'I know where you'll find Shane.' The voice made Bella jump. She spun round to see John's brother Matt behind them, walking with glamorous brunette Debra.

He smiled, his eyes glinting in the lamplight. 'He'll be in the Hanged Man.'

The dodgy pub down by the river, close to St Luke's Bridge. A very different affair from the Blue Boar, it was too rough possibly even for Tony's tastes. 'Thank you. John and I can go and find him.'

John looked deeply uncertain about this plan. 'I told Gareth I'd be home when he finished work.'

'And the pair of you would raise eyebrows in any case.' Matt peered at them critically. His girlfriend was smirking, which was especially annoying.

'He's right,' John said quietly.

'Whose side are you on?' But it was probably true. She'd never seen anyone in high heels and swing coats slip in there. The very name seemed intended to deter patrons not confident that they could fight their way out again. She could use her heels as a weapon, but she'd rather not have to.

John was frowning. 'Is Shane a serious suspect? Mary made a fool of him, but it was years ago.'

Bella folded her arms. 'He was smiling to himself when Noah laid the effigy at the spring; they have some kind of connection. Whoever entered Mary's house frightened her to death, don't forget, even if they didn't do it on purpose.'

John's look of discomfort increased. 'All right, we'll go. Just let me call Gareth.'

His loyalty made her emotional, but she couldn't do it to him. 'No, don't worry, you're right. You go on home. You shouldn't let him down.' Bella would still go though. She could change first to look less conspicuous. She wanted to hear Shane talking casually to his friends. He was bound to mention Mary after what had happened. She just needed to think of an excuse to—

At that moment, Boxer, Gareth's sous chef, appeared in the Blue Boar's doorway. The Brummie looked more than equal to the Hanged Man. His nickname reflected his physique.

'Perhaps I'll engage some alternative help though. Have a good evening, everyone.' Bella turned on her heel, ready to do some sweet talking.

Half an hour later, Bella and Boxer were sitting near the bar in the Hanged Man. Not that it was possible to sit far away. The place was even tinier than it looked from the outside. Bella had changed into her least self-advertising outfit, a figure-hugging black dress, and was carrying her coat over her arm. The evening was cool so she wouldn't dispense with it altogether.

She wasn't the only one not in the Hanged Man's standard uniform of jeans and biker jackets. Shane Sadler had a woman with him who appeared to be stuck in office clothes. Her hair was smartly cut – a gleaming blonde bob.

Shane had a hand on her waist and grinned. 'Don't you ever get out of that get-up?'

The woman arched an eyebrow. 'You know I do, on occasion. Tonight I didn't get the chance.'

'What did you tell hubby?'

She quirked a smile. 'Said I was working late. Which I was, until I came to meet you.'

He pulled her close. 'Always better to stick to something like the truth, in my experience.'

'That's what you do, is it?'

He laughed. 'Best you don't ask. How about coming back to my place? Slip into something more comfortable.'

'My goodness you're corny!'

He laughed again.

'But I can't. Not tonight. It's already late.' She downed her drink. 'I'd better go. People will talk after what happened to your wife.'

He shrugged. 'Not in here they won't. And it's ex-wife, thank you very much. Very ex now.' He laughed again and grabbed her hand. 'Another time then. Go on! Life's for living.'

A sentiment Bella adhered to, but she had some standards.

They leaned together and engaged in an off-putting display of physical attraction.

Bella couldn't help imagining Shane in the posing pouch Leo had mentioned. *Eww.* She turned towards Boxer. 'I can barely keep my gin and tonic down.'

He laughed.

She'd been surprised to hear that Boxer had visited the Hanged Man before. Then again, the Blue Boar was where he worked. If he stuck around, Jeannie might commandeer him for something. 'Is it always like this?'

He swigged his beer. 'Quite often. The people-watching's

as good as cabaret. And I like to see what the competition's up to.' He grinned. 'Not that this place is any. They serve reheated mass-produced pie and chips. Enough to send Gareth into a faint. Horrible stuff.' His last words were said with relish and a deep laugh.

She'd explained why she wanted to visit the pub. She trusted him. He and the Jenkses were like extended family.

Shane hadn't turned around since she and Boxer had come in. He'd been too involved with his companion. As Ms Blonde Bob left, Bella considered him afresh. She guessed he might be in his mid-fifties, like Mary had been. He was good-looking in a devilish sort of way, with his thick grey hair cut in a rakish style and his chinful of stubble. He leaned on the bar, laughing raucously with the barman.

'Seems in a good mood.' Boxer swigged his pint again. 'Seen him in here before in various states of highs and lows. Often loses a packet on the horses, then asks for credit. Reckon he props up the bar most nights.'

'Nah, mate,' Shane was saying to a guy next to him. 'Life's good. I mean there's no point beating around the bush. It's not like we were friends.' He turned to the barman. 'Yeah, another. Thanks, Steve. And whatever you're having. Drinks all round!'

'That'll be his latest winnings gone,' Boxer muttered.

Bella hadn't expected Shane to be drowning his sorrows, but his upbeat mood was extreme.

'Cheers, all!' He grinned from ear to ear.

He must have really hated Mary, unless he was celebrating for another reason. And if his feelings were still so strong, he could have been one of her tormentors.

He was clapping a friend on the back when his mobile rang. Bella leaned forward as though she was listening to Boxer, who seemed to be enjoying the game. It sounded as though Shane's caller was a friend or relation. Shane asked after someone called

Ellie, but the social chit-chat didn't last long. He went from hazily merry to sharp as he listened.

'Right.' He'd taken a notebook from his pocket and set it on the bar, scribbling as he pressed the phone to his ear. Anxious not to be overheard, Bella reckoned.

'Another drink?' She indicated Boxer's empty pint. She wanted to look at Shane's notepad.

'Don't mind if I do, babs.' Boxer gave her the thumbs up and she was at the bar in a second. The barman seemed to have accepted her because she was with a known customer, though he was still peering bemusedly at her dress. 'Same again, thanks.'

He nodded.

'Got it.' Shane was still scribbling. It was just a jumble of numbers, yet he moved to block her view. 'When? Yeah, of course. You'll get it. My overheads have gone down now.' He grunted. 'You too, mate, you too.'

As Bella paid, Sadler hung up. In seconds, he was smiling at her. 'Wait a minute, I know you! You were in the vintage gear on May Day morning, like something from a film.'

John always said her clothes were conspicuous, almost as though he suspected that was the point. 'That's right.' She smiled back, then let her face fall. 'Oh, Sweet Agnes, I'm sorry! I've just remembered what my friend told me. You were married to poor Mary, weren't you? Not any more, I know, but it must still hurt. I'm sorry for your loss.'

Shane heaved a sigh. 'It was a big shock.'

His friend by the bar raised an eyebrow and looked as though he was trying not to laugh.

Bella felt anger rise inside her, like water coming to the boil. But she'd wanted to act when she was younger. Keeping her true feelings hidden was satisfying. 'It must have been.'

'I know it's crazy,' Shane went on, 'but knowing she's gone, I'm feeling lonely again.'

Bella bet he had plenty of company, if blonde office woman was anything to go by. 'That's hard. So you were still on good terms then, after the split?'

The friend *was* laughing now. 'It would be a turn-up for the books if they were, after Shane's affair and the way Mary paid him back.'

Shane wheeled round. 'Shut it!' He looked defensive as he turned back to Bella. 'People always go on about my affair, as though I was to blame. From the moment me and Mary got hitched, she had someone else. I'm sure of it. Passionate as a cat she was, when we were courting. But a week after the wedding she was slipping out on her own. Went to meet someone at the spring, I reckon. Looked emotional and came over all distant when she got home.'

'Poor old Shane.' The friend was still sniggering, but Bella was interested. Shane's self-pity seemed genuine.

'It doesn't sound easy. You never found out what was going on?' She leaned on the bar and kept eye contact.

He shook his head.

That seemed odd in itself. If he'd been determined, you'd think he'd have managed to catch Mary out. Perhaps he was wrong. After all, Mary had been a stickler for the rules.

Shane was looking twitchy now. He glanced at his watch, but Bella caught his eye again.

'Do you remember Mary's statuette? The one of Sweet Agnes at the Sacred Spring?' She might get a reaction if he'd stolen it on Saturday night.

Instead, he grunted, eyes down. 'What about it?'

'I was just curious. It looked unusual. Do you know where she got it, or who the artist was?'

He gave an irritable shrug. 'No idea. Thought it might have come from her bit on the side. I asked, of course. She made out it was a present from an old friend but the writing on the base had been scratched out. Tell me that's not suspicious!'

Interesting. 'Did you hear that someone put nasty things in her garden recently?'

He stared back at her, unblinking. It reminded her of her younger sisters when they were about to lie. 'No. I didn't.'

'There was some rotting meat apparently. It might have been put there the night she died.'

Shane folded his arms. 'Wish I'd've been there. Mary and me, we had our fights, but I'd have socked anyone who tried to upset her. I still saw her now and then.'

Hmm. He'd looked delighted when Noah brought the effigy to the Sacred Spring. It was time to test him. 'You must have been furious with Noah on May Day morning.'

Shane drew himself up. 'That little waste of space? You're right there.'

He sounded totally convincing, but Carys said he had a reputation for dishonesty. Bella bet he was well practised. The pair had definitely been up to something; their connection was so close they could communicate in the subtlest of ways.

Shane glanced at his watch again. 'I'd love to chat, but I've got to dash in a minute.'

He shouted over the bar in the direction of an open door marked 'staff'. 'Tonya! Can you do us some sandwiches, love? Two rounds. And a coffee to go?'

There was some grumbling off-stage.

He turned back to Bella. 'You've got sympathetic eyes.'

How lovely. Her acting must be even better than she'd thought. Perhaps she should join the Hope Eaton Players.

Shane leaned towards her and reached for her hand. 'Can we talk when I've got more time? We could go somewhere quiet.'

Bella smiled. 'Sure. But I'd probably have to bring Boxer.' She indicated him. 'He'd be hurt, otherwise.'

A flash of irritation crossed Shane's face. 'Ah. Let's leave it for now then.'

'What a guy!' Bella said under her breath as she sat back down.

When she and Boxer were halfway through their drinks, a woman appeared from behind the bar with a couple of foil-wrapped parcels and a take-out coffee.

Shane leaned forward to smack a kiss on her cheek. 'Cheers, love. I'll settle up next time. I'm in a hurry.'

'One of these days, Shane Sadler...'

But he was already halfway out of the door.

'I'll just nip to the ladies'.' Bella had spotted them off a lobby by the front entrance. She moved casually, as though there was no hurry, and no one looked up.

The moment she was alone, she peered through the window. Shane Sadler was settling himself in the driver's seat of a white van. She watched him set off along Maid's Lane, then over St Luke's Bridge.

She was about to return to Boxer when she caught movement, just to the left of the window. Someone was out there. So close she could have touched them if it hadn't been for the glass. The shock made her jump and she hit her head on the pane. The person looked round but they wore a hoodie and she couldn't see their face.

Had they talked to Shane Sadler as he'd left? She'd swear their eyes had been on his van. If they'd arranged to meet, it was cloak-and-dagger stuff. Bella should have got there quicker. She might have been able to eavesdrop. The hooded figure continued to look in her direction; she wasn't sure if they'd seen her.

She stood back in the shadows, keeping absolutely still. She'd dash through to Boxer if they entered the pub. But they didn't. They were on the move, heading up the road, and as Bella stared into the night she saw Shane Sadler's tail lights disappear up Raven Climb and out of Hope Eaton.

11

DRAWING CONCLUSIONS

Bella thanked Boxer profusely before they parted at the end of Kite Walk. He assured her he'd enjoyed it and volunteered for any similar missions. In fact, he made it clear he'd be up for another drink whatever the circumstances. She smiled and nodded. He was good company but not her type. Besides, he had known downsides. For one, he was on the rebound and Bella was sure he was still in love with his ex, Alison. And for another, Gareth had told her he owned a pet python. She couldn't bear to watch him feeding it dead mice, knowing it would rather feast on her.

She bumped into Matt outside her flat.

'Productive trip to the Hanged Man?'

'Very, thank you. Boxer was the perfect decoy and an excellent drinking companion.'

'I'd expect nothing less.' Cuthbert had appeared and Matt scooped him up. 'What did you think of Shane Sadler?'

'He was in high spirits following his ex-wife's death, with an attractive woman on his arm. After she left, I expressed my sympathy and he claimed to be lonely and sad. He can't have realised I'd been watching him flirt. He could be faking sorrow because he was in Mary's house when she died, but it's just as likely he hoped I'd keep him company in the small hours.'

'Don't tell me you weren't tempted.'

'Somehow I managed to resist. He cooled off when he saw Boxer.' Bella told Matt about the things which had been found in Mary's garden. 'Perhaps those and the pondweed were him. He said he still saw Mary from time to time, but it might have been through a window.' He'd told his blonde friend it was always best to stick to a partial truth.

'Just before we talked, he took a phone call, then a short while later, he left town with a takeaway coffee and sandwiches.'

Matt raised an eyebrow. 'I've seen him do something similar before.'

She would have asked more, but Debra called his name at that moment. 'See you around, Bella.' He disappeared into his flat.

Before Bella went to bed that night, she left a voicemail for Barry Dixon. She appreciated the one-sided conversation, because she knew what he'd say if he were able: that her suspicion that Adrian Fitzpatrick had been away from home when Mary died was both flimsy and irrelevant. The death was natural causes. And the statuette could be anywhere. Blah, blah, blah.

The following morning at Vintage Winter, Bella filled John in on the visit to the Hanged Man.

'Did Boxer mind being recruited?' John was rubbing boiled linseed oil into a mahogany lamp base.

'He didn't seem to.' She was checking the displays for dust. 'And it was well worth the visit. What Shane told me about Mary cooling towards him immediately after their marriage ties in with what Carys said.' She sighed. 'He's convinced Mary was having an affair, but I find it hard to imagine. Though the obliterated inscription on the statuette is intriguing. Put that together with her secrecy about who carved it and it makes you wonder.'

'You said you had a hunch that Adrian knew something about it?'

Bella nodded. 'He went consciously breezy when I asked. I suppose it's not impossible the pair of them were involved at some point.'

John frowned. 'It's hard to see Mary betraying Fiona Fitzpatrick like that. She's her best friend.'

'True, but all sorts of things go on behind closed doors. And if Mary did fall for Adrian, it would give Fiona an extra motive.' At best to torment her, at worst to engineer her death.

John shook his head. 'But Carys said Mary was quite conservative normally, and that she couldn't bear wrongdoing. Would she really give up on her marriage within days? And take revenge on Shane for an affair if she was guilty of the exact same thing?'

Privately, Bella thought he had a point, but what else would explain what she'd discovered so far? 'I'd love to know where Shane was going in his van.'

'It's curious, though I don't see how it might relate to Mary.'

'Nor do I – yet. But after she made such of fool of him, he's got to be worth considering. The intervening ten years could have allowed his resentment to build, not dissipate. It would just take a trigger to send him over the edge now.' She could imagine him enjoying her fear. 'And I'm having second thoughts about Olivia Elsworth. I'd been discounting her because menacing Mary seemed counterproductive. I still doubt the rotting meat was her – it looks like an attempt to sabotage the sale of Springside Cottage – but what if she wanted to frighten Mary off her land? It might end the talk of the chalet and help

the sale go through. The demon and Ginny Greenteeth references could have been her.'

'So two miscreants at work, one trying to promote the sale
and one trying to thwart it?'

Bella shrugged. 'It's possible. Adrian and/or Fiona Fitzpatrick still seem the most likely saboteurs, if they knew about
the will. I know what you think about her character, but Fiona
could certainly have spotted Mary's weak heart.' She needed to
get to know her, to see if she could imagine her being ruthless
enough to act on it. 'In that scenario, it's like I said: perhaps the
Fitzpatricks lost patience, waiting for Mary to die. Adrian could
have gone into Springside Cottage on Saturday to help her on
her way.'

She visualised him creeping inside, caring nothing for
Mary's life, only focused on what he could gain. Bella closed
her eyes for a moment and took a deep breath. She needed to
keep her emotions at bay. 'But I don't know why he'd take the
statuette. It can't have been to upset Mary if he knew she'd be
dead before the night was out. And Shane says any distin-
guishing marks had been scratched out, so even if he gave it to
her, I don't see why he'd worry about it.' There was something
she wasn't getting.

'I'm going to Springside Cottage at lunchtime to look round
the grounds. If one or more people were out to cause problems
before Mary died, they'll have left clues.' Locard's law, or the
exchange principle. Her dad had taught her about it. When a
crime is committed, physical evidence will be left at the scene,
and the perpetrator will take evidence away with them. 'If I can
find proof of a determined campaign of terror, I hope I can get
the police involved.' She ought to be able to crack this.

John looked fidgety.

'There's no need for you to come.'

He sighed. 'It doesn't rank highly amongst my preferred
entertainments. But Mary used to visit the museum, just like

Fiona.' John chewed his lip. 'She appreciated the exhibits. I'll come.'

As Bella was locking the shop, ready for their lunchtime excursion, she caught movement out of the corner of her eye. Someone darting away? She glanced up to see one of her regular customers hurrying off.

Odd. Bella had been expecting her to come in for a paperweight she'd told her about. She'd been enthusiastic. Rather than doing so, the woman had almost run past. And surely she'd sped up as Bella exited the shop. It was almost as though she was avoiding her.

The thought was worrying.

12

THE WATCHER

Bella reluctantly accepted John's suggestion that she should borrow Leo's bike from outside the Steps to reach Springside Cottage. They could take Holt Lane, where Leo, Carys and Lucy lived, which skirted the north side of the woods. It was the long way round, but still quicker if you were on wheels, according to John.

She felt misgivings as she clambered aboard. Why were the Jenkses wedded to cycling in such a hilly place?

But, in fact, the journey was mostly on the flat. The only trouble was Bella's full skirt. She had to do complicated things to it for decency's sake thanks to the bike's crossbar.

'I wish Leo's bike wasn't quite so... garish,' Bella said, as they passed a dog walker who seemed to be staring at her. The frame he'd chosen was lime green and orange.

John glanced at her over his shoulder. 'There's nothing anonymous about him. But the same could be said of you.'

Long ago, a fashion-student lodger of her mother's had used Bella as a dressmaker's dummy. During days when she was constantly dressed in hand-me-downs, it had been fun. She hadn't looked back. Her clothes weren't usually expensive or new, she just made sure they had that certain something. Life was for living, you might as well do it like you meant it. The one time she'd prefer to fade into the background was when she was wobbling along on two wheels.

They arrived at the point where Holt Lane met the woods and Bella and John locked their bikes to the nearest lamp post.

'This isn't going to involve trespassing, is it?' John looked uncomfortable as they walked between the trees.

Bella had assumed he'd have reconciled himself to that idea. 'We won't get a true picture without veering off the right of way.'

'What if someone sees us?'

'We can pretend we got mixed up about the route. It'll be quite all right.'

As soon as they'd slipped through Mary's gate, Bella led the way to some trees and shrubs that would give them cover. She found the pussy willow where Mary had appeared to see something in the branches. She pointed it out to him. 'Carys talked about her seeming spiritual.'

They walked along a row of fruit trees, a small orchard.

'Her bond with the spring must have been something special. I saw the listing for the cottage. It was on for over half a million. She could have bought a comfortable place in town and had plenty left over. Yet she wanted to build a chalet here.'

'Only the cottage never sold,' John pointed out, his voice quiet. 'Maybe Olivia Elsworth overvalued it.'

They'd come to a hawthorn tree, and underneath there was some pondweed. What was that doing there? Bella pointed and John raised an eyebrow.

'Or maybe it *was* all down to someone trying to stop the sale.'

Bella shook her head. 'Pondweed's quite different to the rotting meat we saw and the dead rats Olivia mentioned. It would only spook locals who know about Ginny Greenteeth. I'd guess it's part of the campaign to frighten Mary, not her buyers.' Something about it was making her skin crawl. Suddenly, she realised what it was. 'It's still wet, as though it's only just been put here.' Yet the threat of the sale was over, and Mary was past being frightened.

A moment later a drip fell from the hawthorn just above the weed. The tree was a tall variety, at least twenty feet high. Bella thought of Ginny Greenteeth up in the boughs. Perhaps John was thinking the same. He shivered.

But it couldn't really be that. Bella shook herself and peered into the spiny branches festooned with creamy white flowers. They were too spiky to move with bare hands, but she found a stick and used that to shift them.

What on earth? There was something up there. It looked like the bag of a medical drip. It was out of reach, a tube pointing downwards with a nozzle at the end. 'Have a look at this.' She pointed and John shifted position to see.

'We've got some of those.' He turned to Bella. 'For watering our houseplants while we're away. We used to ask our neighbours but they always killed everything.'

'You can adjust the flowrate?'

He nodded. 'There's a dial. They can keep watering for a week.'

'Sophisticated.' Bella felt more than ever that at least two people were at work. Poor Mary. A small patch of damp pondweed would instantly make her tense. Hopefully she'd have investigated, just as Bella had, but the discovery that the scene was rigged wouldn't have been comforting. She'd have known someone was out to menace her.

Bella took a photo for reference. 'We need to work out where the hooded figure might have hung around. She saw them from her kitchen when I visited.' She wandered around the perimeter of the cottage until she found the right viewpoint. 'Looking from here, she could have seen someone in the trees where we found the plant waterer, or beyond in the nearest bit of wood.'

John nodded his agreement.

They re-checked the area near the hawthorn but found nothing. It was a shame. If anything might increase the likelihood of trace evidence, it was a spiny tree. Bella was quite sure she'd left drops of her own blood on it.

As they let themselves out of the garden gate, Bella heard John catch his breath.

'What?'

'There's someone over there in the shadows. I'm sure of it.'

'You saw movement?' How could she have missed it? She'd been keeping a close watch.

But John shook his head. 'No. They're completely still.'

That was worse. It implied they'd been monitoring them for a while. 'Where?'

John inclined his head very subtly and Bella looked, peering into the dark thickness of the trees.

He was right. She could just see a partial outline.

'Any ideas what to do now?' John was looking at her with a hint of desperation.

'There are two of us and one of them, as far as I can make out. I think we should talk to them. I'd rather know what we're dealing with.'

13

A QUESTIONABLE WITNESS

John was still staring at the figure in the woods. 'All right,' he said. 'Let's see if we can get near them.'

'We can act as though we're heading back to town along the Sacred Way, then cut across to them quickly, before they can run.' She doubted they'd be any keener to be caught than she and John were.

John nodded. He kept glancing at his watch as they walked. 'We'll be late reopening at this rate.'

'Needs must.' Bella thought of the client who'd seemed to be avoiding her. What had that been about? She needed to nurture her customers, but she couldn't ignore the watcher. It was too important.

Bella faced forward and made small talk with John but all the while she monitored the figure, flicking her eyes right. She still couldn't see them clearly. They were keeping to the cover of the trees. When they were level with them, she caught John's eye and they turned as one and marched over. Bella didn't want to run, in case they scared their quarry, but the watcher ran anyway, darting out from behind their cover. It was a woman dressed in dark-green velvet, her long dyed hair streaming out behind her. For a moment, Bella wondered about the Fitz-patricks' intruder, but the hair was too long and not quite the right colour.

'I should have known.' John's voice was shaky as he ran after her. 'This isn't to do with us.'

'What? How can it not be? She was watching our every move.' Bella put on an extra burst of speed and called out, 'Excuse me! We just wanted to talk to you.'

The woman had picked up her long skirts and was tripping over the rough ground. Now she stopped and peered at them over her shoulder.

'It's Opal.' John was breathless. 'Everyone in Hope Eaton knows about her. You would, if you'd been in the woods more often.'

'If that's the case, she might know something useful.' And John should work in their favour. He looked ridiculously trust-worthy in his quiet, traditional suit and white shirt. 'You remember John from the museum,' she called out. 'He works with me now. You probably know his parents. They run the Blue Boar.'

The woman gave a crooked grin. 'Oh, I know him all right. I knew him afore you said all that.'

John looked anxious.

The woman turned to him. 'I seen you come through here every May Day. Have done since I was a little girl. And all the others of course. But you stand out.'

'You live near here?' Bella asked.

The woman nodded. 'Took over my ma's place on the east side of the holt when she passed on. I'm always out in the trees.'

John was fidgeting as though uncomfortable. He wasn't the sort to enjoy being singled out. 'What made you notice me?' he said at last.

'My ma used to say you were a peacemaker. She said your ma was fire but you were earth.'

This was all very well, but not particularly enlightening. Bella decided to move the conversation on. 'Did you know Mary Roberts?'

'I knew who she was.' Opal looked suspicious. 'She saw the spirits.'

Bella caught John's eye, then focused on Opal again. 'She told you that?'

She gave a scornful laugh. 'She didn't have to. Anyone could see it. She was brought up on it, like I was. Her old da used to bring her to the woods to teach her. Threatened to leave her by the spring once for old Ginny to take acos she'd been bad.' Poor Mary, no wonder she'd grown up scared of the legend. 'When her ma died, her da told her she was taken by the demon. She wasn't as good as Sweet Agnes.'

For Pete's sake! What an appalling way to bring up a child. She wished she could go back in time and give him a shake. 'How do you know all this?'

Opal drew herself up. 'My gran told me. She watched, and now I do.'

'People call her the guardian of the holt,' John murmured. Bella suspected it wasn't just kindness that stopped him from making fun of her, but slight nervousness too. He might not believe the same old legends that she did, but her conviction was disconcerting.

'Do you wear a dark cloak?' Bella asked.

'No!' She sounded cross.

Not the hooded figure then. Probably. 'You chatted with Mary?'

She frowned. 'No. We didn't talk. But I knew her from watching. She was water. But you, you're fire.' She turned to Bella.

Bella still had no idea what that meant, but she quite liked being the same element as Jeannie. No one's pushover. She hoped she had a bit more appreciation for nuance though.

'Did you ever see the hooded figure?' Given the strange conversation, it seemed fine to come straight out with it.

'Oh yes. I seen him.'

'You think it was a man?'

Opal looked at her as though she'd said something very ridiculous. 'It was the demon.'

Ah.

'He only came recently. It was her he was after.' She nodded towards Mary's house, still and silent in its clearing. 'And now he's took her, he won't come back.'

'What about the person who painted a message on the wall of the Fitzpatricks' house?' She pointed in the direction of their place. Opal could have seen them too, if she roamed about at night. The Fitzpatricks' garden backed onto St Giles's Holt and the intruder had climbed the back wall to escape.

Opal shook her head. 'Don't know. Unless that was the clatterer.'

'Clatterer?'

'There was such a clattering, the night the demon came for her. It started over there.' She waved towards the Fitzpatricks' place too, then turned away.

John let out a breath as she picked up her skirts again and took long strides through the trees.

Bella turned to him. 'Did that just happen?'

'It really did. It's the first time I've actually spoken to her, but I've seen her a few times. D'you think *she* could have graffitied the Fitzpatricks' house? Is that why you mentioned it?'

Bella shook her head and explained about the mismatch in hair colour. 'Besides, I think Opal's someone who observes but doesn't get involved. And paint daubing seems a bit ordinary for her, if you know what I mean.'

John nodded.

Bella could imagine her burning a sacred root or something,

but not getting busy with some Dulux. 'I must look up what fire, water and earth symbolise when we've finished here.'

'Fascinating. But perhaps not pertinent.'

She hadn't meant to say it out loud. 'No. What is relevant is that Opal saw the same hooded figure that frightened Mary. It can't have been a figment of her imagination. I'd say we definitely have two people at work, or one person with two motives: to torment Mary by dressing up as the demon and leaving Ginny Greenteeth calling cards, and to frustrate the house sale.'

'What about Noah and the effigy he claimed was meant to be Ginny?'

'I think that's a red herring. He wasn't using Ginny to frighten Mary, just making a preposterous claim to stop anyone stating the obvious – that the effigy was modelled on Mary herself. But he had a massive grudge and some kind of link with Shane. I'll bet he's involved somehow.'

'Right. Good. Now, shall we dash back and open the shop, before we go bankrupt?'

It was important, but Bella hadn't finished yet. They'd been side-tracked by Opal. 'Would you mind making an advance party? I want to see if I can find any physical sign that someone was here. Something tells me Opal won't make the perfect witness if I go to the police.'

'You have a point. You'll be all right?'

'I'm sure I shall.' *Almost certainly.* 'Tell Leo I promise to return his bike soon.'

Bella didn't like leaving John to get on with it, but Tony always said you had to act quickly to catch a crook. Besides, she knew John was more than capable. After he'd gone, she went back to the area of wood nearest Springside Cottage. The trees grew densely and there were plenty of them. She peered at the house to make sure she was still facing the kitchen window.

After that, she paid particular attention to hawthorns, holly and blackthorns where anyone wearing a long cloak might get snagged up. It took another forty minutes, but she was rewarded. Black fibres, stuck to a particularly long thorn. It looked like polyester or some such. Nothing a real demon would have been seen dead in, she was sure. A cheap dressing-up item, but perfectly serviceable.

She looked around for other traces. If she could find more, she might get an idea of the direction the hooded figure had taken. That in turn could hint at where they'd come from. But after another twenty minutes she'd only found one more fibre and she wasn't sure it was the same stuff.

After photographing it and noting her position, she gave up. She'd taken a step towards the edge of the wood when she paused again, a twig sticking painfully into her left shoe. As she bent to remove it, she looked at the ground rather than the trees around her.

There, under a low-growing blackthorn, was a stick. Hardly shocking in the middle of a wood, but it looked unnatural. Like a cudgel. It was partly embedded under old leaves. She pushed them aside with her shoe and revealed a length of thick black twine. What was that all about?

She skirted the blackthorn, pushing more leaf matter aside and after a moment, she found a flint. Evilly sharp.

As she bent to look more closely at the stick, she realised it had notches on it. And the cord had been cut – with a penknife perhaps. It was frayed where it had been sheared off, a tight knot still in place further along its length.

She looked again at the cudgel-like stick with its notches near one end and the shape of the flint. Then she picked the flint up and fitted it to the cudgel. If you placed it so its sharp edge stuck out beyond the wood, it fitted exactly between the notches.

She was convinced it had been tied in place by the cord.

Someone had been here and left black fibres behind, but also a deadly looking homemade weapon. One which they'd dismantled and tried to hide before leaving the wood, presumably in a hurry. They hadn't paused to undo the knot or make a better job of burying the thing.

Bella thought of the key she and Carys had seen, dropped into one of Mary's shoes, and felt ice at her very core. Here was evidence of the darkest of crimes. It looked as though someone had walked into Mary's house, fully intending to kill her. Faced with a hooded figure, holding a terrifying medieval-looking weapon, she wasn't surprised poor Mary had collapsed and died before they managed it. She'd read about a similar case once, where a would-be killer had scared a householder to death. The intruder had been convicted of murder.

Bella photographed the components of the weapon, then put them back so the police could see where they'd been left – if only they agreed to investigate.

She needed to talk to DS Barry Dixon.

14

PLOTTING, PLANNING AND CHILDCARE ADVICE

Bella dropped Leo's bike at the Steps, flew into Vintage Winter to update John, then ran home to fetch Thomasina, her electric ex-London taxi.

On the way to Shrewsbury, she plotted her approach to Barry Dixon, dreaming up argument upon argument, because she knew what he'd say.

Half an hour later, he was busy saying it, looking at her through bleary half-closed eyes, the dregs of a vat of coffee at his elbow.

'It's very good of you to let us know, Ms Winter, but look at it from our point of view. Mary Roberts's death was natural causes. That's a given. Even if what you found was once bound together to form a weapon, who's to say it has anything to do with her death? Most criminals would pick something they already had to hand, like a hammer or a crowbar. What you found was likely left by kids playing.'

Bella shook her head. 'It was definitely more than a prop. Someone made sure the flint was lethally sharp.'

He shrugged. 'Or a poacher after an animal then. Illegal in which case, but we don't have the staff to tackle it.'

Someone knocked on the door, came in and handed Dixon a note. He read it, put his hands over his elastic face, then stuffed it in the pocket of his rumpled trousers. His socks were coming down. Bella longed to tell him to pull them up.

'But the stick, the cord and the flint had clearly been dismantled and hidden in a hurry. That would fit with someone who'd planned to kill but had been overtaken by events. They weren't thinking straight.'

Dixon shrugged as two messages flashed up on his phone in quick succession. 'They could have been disturbed while they were hunting.'

'The flint looked sharp and clean.' Bella doubted it had ever been used to kill anything. It was prepared and ready. She showed him her photographs.

'I'm sorry, Ms Winter, but it doesn't prove anything.'

But when you took it together with everything else... She fell back on her least convincing bit of evidence.

'I've found someone who saw the hooded figure Mary mentioned.'

Dixon raised an eyebrow.

'A woman called Opal who lives on the east side of St Giles's Holt. It might be worth talking to her.'

Dixon winced as though she'd shone a torch in his eyes and leaned back in his chair. 'This would be the palm reader who owns thirteen black cats?'

It sounded possible. 'I'm not sure. She didn't say.'

'Did she have any idea who the hooded figure was?'

The demon. 'I don't think so.'

'So it won't really get us any further. The DI won't consider her a reliable witness anyway. My wife has come across her. She's been in to treat the cats. She says they've taken control of the house. Four of them were sitting on the dining table when she visited, and Opal's never been known to pay a bill.'

Bella leaned forward so Dixon could see she was in earnest.

'I believe Mary Roberts was being terrorised before she died, and I'm now convinced someone set out that night, wanting her dead. It was pure luck she died before they got that far.' She knew he needed evidence, but she still felt the need to say it.

Dixon closed his eyes. 'Duly noted. But at the moment we're dealing with everything from a vandalised car at Standing Stones House to dodgy practices at Stockett's Farm.' He rubbed his furrowed brow. 'An impatient, entitled Audi owner and a dysfunctional farmer failing to dispose of dead animals in a bio-secure manner. What a life. Plus, the twins have stopped going to bed when I tell them. They played merry hell with me last night.'

'You have my sympathy.'

He raised an eyebrow. 'You've got kids?'

'Yes.' The response was automatic. 'Well, three younger half-siblings. I did a lot of the childcare. They're grown up now. Theoretically.'

'You don't have any tips, do you?'

'Barry,' the first name slipped out, 'you're a police officer. You arrest criminals. And these are your kids.'

He looked down and mumbled something.

Bella sighed. 'We had a family friend, Val, who sometimes mucked in at bedtime. She sewed pockets onto a blanket for my sister Suki. When she wanted to coax her to bed, she'd put secret things in them, only to be revealed when Suki was under the covers. That worked.'

Dixon frowned. 'I might give that a go, actually. What kind of things did you put in the pockets?'

'I didn't put anything in.'

'But you said—'

'I was telling you what Val did.'

'So what did *you* do?' Realisation seemed to dawn as he looked at her. 'Don't tell me. They went to bed when you told them to.'

Bella smiled. 'They did, actually.'

As she got up to leave, his phone rang and he suppressed a groan.

Before leaving Shrewsbury, Bella googled Barry on her phone. He seemed very helpless at times. Perhaps he was even younger than she'd thought. After a moment, she found his LinkedIn profile. *Sweet Agnes...* Judging by the year he'd done his A levels, he was thirty-eight. Only four years younger than her. Absolutely no excuse then.

Back at the shop, Bella was texting Tony an update when she caught sight of a couple opposite Vintage Winter, on the grass by St Giles's Church. They were staring at the shop. That ought to be good news, but Bella had an unpleasant sinking feeling. They weren't looking at anything in her window display – they couldn't be at that distance. But the man was pointing. Bella or her beautiful business were being discussed and the man's jabbing finger suggested negative comments. A moment later he turned on his heel, as though dismissing Vintage Winter from his mind. He and the woman marched away.

Bella pressed send on the text and turned to John. 'Did you see that?'

He was all unruffled calm. 'They were thinking of coming shopping but changed their minds.'

'No. They didn't look keen from the start. They were passing and paused to make a derogatory remark.'

'You don't think you're being a tiny bit oversensitive?'

'Not after another customer ran away earlier.' Why would any of them feel antagonistic towards her lovely shop? The trouble was, where one person took a dislike to a place, more tended to follow. She'd seen it happen. And if—

'What news, anyway?' John said.

Bella knew he wanted to distract her, but she decided to let him. 'We should use the drawing board again.'

Bella's beloved mid-century architect's board sat in the office of Vintage Winter. She used it to record plans for the shop, but it was perfect for case notes too. Bella liked its size; leaning over its large, sloping surface gave her a sense of occasion and control.

They went to the office. As John watched, Bella updated him on Dixon's disappointing response to her find, then jotted down key facts, from Mary's time of death, between two and four in the morning, to what Leo excitedly called 'persons of interest'.

They moved back to the front showroom when a customer came in, but the minute they were alone, Bella picked up where she'd left off.

'Finding the weapon makes a huge difference. Before, I'd wondered if Adrian Fitzpatrick might have gone into Mary's house on Saturday to scare her, or even with violence in mind. Now I'm sure someone went in to murder her. The weapon wasn't mocked up casually just to create fear, it was precisely engineered so that it could kill too.'

John frowned. 'I wonder why they went to so much effort, rather than using a cricket bat or something.'

'Maybe they were covering all eventualities. If they were accidentally seen, any witnesses would be thrown, including Mary if she'd somehow survived. The whole spectacle would have looked supernatural or like some crazy dressing-up game.

'The other new development to consider is the plant waterer in the hawthorn tree. I could see Shane or Noah depositing the rats and so on, but neither of them looks the sort to take an interest in houseplants. Though I imagine Shane's hobbies are quite earthy.'

John winced and gave her a quelling look. 'What about future plans?'

'I want to focus on the Sweet Agnes statuette for one thing. It beats me why any of the suspects would steal it. They can't have taken it to upset Mary if they planned to kill her, and even if they carved it, it sounds as though any giveaway markings have been removed.'

'And why would anyone think it came from Mary's would-be killer anyway?' John removed his glasses to polish them.

'Unless it was made by someone not usually associated with her, who no one would consider without that clue. Even with the obliterated inscription, they might worry someone would tie it back to them.'

'Suspect X.'

Bella closed her eyes. Not a good thought. She had no idea how they'd identify them in that case. 'We need to be certain the statuette really is gone from Springside Cottage. We should find out who Mary's executor is and see if we can sweet talk them into checking. If it's someone here in town, you probably know them. How are your connections with local solicitors?'

John looked resigned. 'Tom on the high street is a relation. His is the only outfit in Hope Eaton.'

'Perfect.' She doubted John agreed. 'Let's hope Mary used them.'

'You want me to call and ask?'

'Please. Just tell them we're concerned about the statuette. I'm sure they'll understand, and if anyone can sort it out tactfully, it's you.' She held up a hand as he opened his mouth to protest. 'You know it's true. Modesty is not required.' She rearranged some stock. 'Overall, I think we need a three-pronged approach. One focusing on attempted murder from hatred, with Shane as perpetrator, one from fear, with Noah and Olivia in the spotlight protecting Noah's secret, and one from greed, with the Fitzpatricks in the frame.

'I'm already convinced Adrian was out when I called on Saturday night. I need to track down their graffiti artist and find out what they know. I'll go and look for clues tomorrow morning.

'For the others, I'm going to ask Matt to contact me next time he sees Shane acting oddly so I can investigate further. And we need to talk to Noah's colleagues at the garage. They might give us a lead on his secret.' She turned and gave John her best winning smile. 'I don't suppose you know the management there? Only it would be so much easier with an "in".' Trust and connections were everything. Dealing in antiques had plenty of overlap with investigating. It was one of the reasons she was determined to keep pushing for clues. She had a sneaking suspicion she could do this.

John was looking twitchy again. 'Couldn't you just take Thomasina for a service?'

'Are you suggesting I exploit my beloved car?'

'You seem to be exploiting me.' At last, he sighed. 'But I do know them. Mum's been taking her Mini there for twenty years. I tend to drop it off for her. It's created a bond between me and the owner. One I'd like to maintain.'

Bella checked the motor repair shop's opening times. 'They close half an hour after us. We could nip along after work and observe, then catch your friend on their way out.'

'You remind me of my mother sometimes,' John said.

First it was Opal pointing out the similarities, now it was John. Of course, she loved Jeannie's positivity and bullishness, but she did dash into roomfuls of eggshells in hobnailed boots. 'In what way?' She'd aimed for neutral but realised she'd missed.

'You seize on things and run with them.'

'In velvet slippers though, not hobnailed boots.'

John just looked puzzled.

15

THE LOWDOWN ON NOAH ELSWORTH

The moment she'd shut up Vintage Winter, Bella walked with John along the high street then cut through to West Street, the location of Hope Eaton Auto Repairs. The atmosphere as they approached was pleasing, a sense of busy hubbub, the sound of someone hammering metal, the smell of oil and polish. A hive of activity. Someone was singing along to a radio.

Bella turned to John. 'Let's approach quietly. If we can see Noah in action it might tell us what he's like when he's not putting on a show.'

John looked depressed about being there at all, but nodded. They tiptoed to the corner of one of the workshops, then peered round.

Bella saw a portly man with grey hair and a bushy moustache, dressed in an oil-smeared boilersuit, bent over an open car bonnet. When he exclaimed in what sounded like triumph and straightened up she could see his grin. A man after her own heart. He clearly loved his work.

Beyond him, a pair of legs stuck out from under an elevated van. Curses emanated from their direction. A tough repair perhaps. She and John never swore when frustrated at Vintage Winter, but she could understand it might be restorative.

And there was Noah, also wearing a boiler suit, buffing a Volkswagen. Every so often he glanced over his shoulder as though he was monitoring the people around him. At last, after a third look, he disappeared down a passageway.

Bella suspected Noah had wanted to leave undetected, but the moustachioed man glanced after him and shook his head. Another, much younger, man who'd been tinkering with a Volvo put his head on one side.

'You cut him too much slack. He's got no focus.'

The older man shook his head. 'He's able, that's the shame of it. Bright. He could be a skilled craftsman if he applied himself; that or work his way up the business side.'

The younger man looked as though he'd swallowed a wasp. He and the older guy were alike. Father and son perhaps.

'Let's shift position,' Bella murmured. 'I want to know what Noah's up to.'

John looked less than keen, but Bella led the way, skirting around the far side of the workshop, away from the mechanics.

The passageway Noah had used was open to the elements, running between one building and the next. It was empty now, and Bella crept along it. If she went a little further, she might work out where Noah had gone. She held her breath and didn't check if John was following. It didn't matter.

She was only a few feet along when she caught sight of Noah through an open doorway, slouching against a worktop in a small room in the second building. There was a coat stand near where he stood and a kettle and mugs on a bench beyond. It must be the staff area. Then, as Bella watched, hardly daring to breathe, Noah looked around him very carefully and slipped his hand into one of the coat pockets. A moment later he'd pulled something out; she couldn't see what. He pocketed it and walked further into the room, out of sight.

Very interesting.

She slipped back to where John was standing and relayed what she'd seen in the lowest of voices. 'It was something flat. Bank notes, perhaps? Whatever it was, he's a thief.'

As they returned to their original position, John was fretting. 'Maybe we should tell Ted.'

'The moustachioed man? He's the boss?'

John nodded. 'Ted Ashcroft.'

'I think we should hold back.'

He raised his eyebrows.

'He and the other staff know Noah disappeared. If anyone finds they've been robbed, they'll guess who's responsible, and I'd rather not show our hand. If Noah realises I was following him, his guard will be up. We can always report him in a few days, once we've worked out what's going on.'

John sighed. 'All right.'

'Let's offer to buy Ted Ashcroft a drink at the Blue Boar when he leaves.' The inn was only just around the corner.

'Won't it seem odd?'

'If you introduce me, I'll manage the rest.'

His look spoke of grave misgivings. 'All right then.'

'Cheer up. You'll be able to pop in and see Gareth. Which way will Ted walk home?' She bet he knew.

'Towards the high street. But he might not go straight there.'

'Let's gamble that he will.' He'd probably head home for a shower. She walked towards the high street, then hid behind a shrub where John joined her. They could 'happen to be passing' when Ted appeared.

Bella took regular peeks around the corner to monitor the situation. Noah left first. He probably wanted to get what he'd stolen off the premises. Ted Ashcroft was the last to leave, out of his overalls now, dressed in jeans and a plaid shirt.

Bella talked busily to John so that Ted thought he'd taken them by surprise.

'Well, hello there, John!' He was beaming. Everyone loved her second in command as much as Bella did.

They exchanged news and pleasantries; John sounded more or less strained the entire time. *Oh ye of little faith.*

Ted turned happily to Bella and was introduced.

Now was her chance to form a bond. 'So *you* run the garage John told me about. He said you've been looking after his mother's Mini for years.'

Ted rubbed his hands together. 'That's right. It's a beauty. Got to love a Mini.'

'Absolutely. One of my sisters has one.' Bella had slept in it once. She was meant to have been in Thea's flat but her youngest half-sister had left her the car keys instead of the front-door ones. She'd been in Berlin at the time. Bella had felt less fond of Minis afterwards. 'I have an ex-London taxi now. Electric. She's called Thomasina.'

'Really? I like it!'

'I'd love to bring her in sometime. She could do with a service.'

As they talked, they'd been walking towards the high street. They were outside the Blue Boar now.

'John and I were just going to nip in for a drink. Won't you join us? It's so good to get to know everyone.'

They could hear laughter from inside the inn, and someone saying: 'Cheers.'

'I ought to go and get cleaned up really.'

'Just as you like, though you look very presentable.' It was no use sounding desperate. That never worked.

He grinned. 'Well in that case, perhaps I will. Just for one, mind, or the wife'll wonder what's happened to me!'

John looked a fraction more relaxed as they walked through the door.

Bella selected a table amongst the throng, where noise would equal privacy, and insisted on buying the round. Ted's bonhomie increased even further, though it had already been in good order.

Five minutes later, the three of them were shooting the breeze. Bella decided to get Ted to mention Noah first.

'Tell me about your team.' That ought to do it.

She got the full run-down and made a mental note of everyone he mentioned. She might run into them at the shop one day. She loved placing the townsfolk and unearthing unexpected connections. It was like working on a jigsaw puzzle, and finding a piece that linked two sections together.

But for the purposes of Mary's death, she focused on Noah.

'I heard about him getting into trouble,' she said. 'It's great that he's got work with you.'

'The least I could do.' Ted sipped his drink. 'Everyone deserves a second chance. And Noah's dad's a good man. Been a customer of mine for years.'

'So Noah's working out well?'

Luckily, Ted was too honest to lie and too polite to tell her to mind her own business. 'We're working on him.'

'We were a bit shocked at the way he behaved on May Day morning.' John put down his drink.

Ted shook his head. 'I spoke to him about that, and he told me it was Mary who'd reported him when he stole the quad bike.' He raised an eyebrow. 'I get that he's angry and hurt, but that's no way to behave. Though I don't think Mary was helping, God rest her.'

Bella leaned forward. 'How do you mean?'

'Well, not to speak ill of the dead, but I spotted her peering at him when he left work a couple of times. I think she was still on his case. She had that reputation, to be honest. If she thought someone was misbehaving, she wanted to know. Not for gossip, to be fair, but to steer them back towards the straight and narrow.'

It fitted with what Tony had said about Mary reporting

wrongdoing to the police. But what had she known in this instance? 'Do you think it's possible Noah's involved in something fresh?' Thieving, for one, though it might not stop there.

At last, the man nodded. 'Yeah. It's possible. He turns up to work tired and he took time off to "visit the dentist" the other morning, only my better half saw him skulking somewhere off Boatman's Walk.' Ted shook his head. 'I've started to teach him proper mechanics already, way earlier than most trainees. I hope it'll keep him interested, but I'm not sure it's enough. We'll see.'

'At least he's got his stepmum looking out for him, even if his dad's not around much.'

But Ted looked gloomy. 'They don't get on. He's a handful and he's too proud to accept her. Wants his real mum, I daresay, but she died six years back, so there's no help for it. Olivia's always tried with him, I know that. Our kids were contemporaries at school. But Noah won't give an inch.' He drained his pint. 'Ah well, I must be going, but I'm looking forward to working on that taxi of yours. I'll treat her like she was my own.'

She believed him, and watched as he exited the inn. 'What a nice man.'

John nodded.

'And a mine of information. Olivia defended Noah fiercely in my hearing. I assumed they were close. That's an anomaly that needs investigating. And what about Noah claiming he was off to the dentist? If theft is his game, it's not just opportunistic, if that's anything to go by. It sounds as though he wanted to be in a specific place at a specific time.'

Soon after, Bella walked home, cutting down St Giles's Steps, then along Boatman's Walk, past the corner with Friar's Gate where the Fitzpatricks lived. The leafy honeysuckle that clung to their garden's red-brick wall wasn't flowering yet, but it was alive with nesting birds and blue tits hunting for insects.

Why had Olivia defended Noah so vehemently and pulled

up the drawbridge when Mary tried to talk to her? Bella remembered her words. *How many times do I have to tell you, Mary? He's done nothing wrong! Haven't you done enough to my family?* Why was the matter up for debate if Mary had evidence? And why had she gone to Olivia, not the police as she'd done last time?

Bella could understand Olivia being upset, even if she and Noah weren't close. She'd probably had a basinful of town gossip, as well as Noah being under her feet during his curfew, no doubt in an appallingly bad mood. But she'd sounded heated and rattled.

If Noah was involved in something more organised than just petty theft, was there any chance she was in on it too? Her business was under pressure, according to Mary. Perhaps she was desperate enough to resort to crime to improve her finances. If so, she'd have a prime motive for murder, just like her stepson.

16

SINGING AND SLEUTHING

That evening, Bella reported to the high school for the fundraiser rehearsal as planned. Her goals included finding out if Fiona Fitzpatrick had spotted Mary's symptoms of a weak heart, and checking for any hint that Fiona (or Adrian) had known about her bequest.

Carys had been in full-scale panic mode about the evening. In the end, Bella had raided the back of her wardrobe and supplied her with an outfit or two for her second-hand clothes stall. As they'd collaborated, she'd filled her in on the latest developments.

When Carys put her clothes on one of the school's coat rails, Bella recognised a couple of Leo's loud jackets there. The headmaster's smile became fixed when he viewed them.

'I don't suppose anyone will buy them,' Carys said to her later, 'but I've been desperate to remove them from Leo's grasp for some time. If I tell him it's for charity, I might just get away with it.'

Carys had been right about Bella's fellow singer, Edwina West. She really couldn't hit a note, though she looked glamorous and her husband was watching her with fervent admiration. The music teacher was good, but not as loud as either Edwina or Bella herself, and not brave enough to call order.

'I think you should lead us,' Bella said to him, 'and we'll sing more quietly, so the parents and kids can be heard over the top.'

Edwina frowned but agreed. They went again and it wasn't *so* bad. Bella had to quell the desire to really go for it. Performing appealed, but this fundraiser was the start and end of it. Band members meant people like her mother's disastrous post-divorce boyfriend number three. And Matt, of course, who played guitar. Not a world she intended to inhabit.

When they paused for a break, Bella went to tackle Fiona Fitzpatrick. She opened the conversation by expressing her sympathy over Mary's death again. 'I heard what good friends you were. I'm very sorry Carys and I had to break the news to you so suddenly.'

'Thank you. Please don't apologise. You couldn't help it. It was a relief to hear it was natural causes after what you'd said. It's still so awful, but the idea of anyone deliberately harming her...'

Bella nodded. Fiona sounded genuine, but if she or Adrian had set out to kill then the relief made sense. 'Carys felt terrible when the news broke about her heart condition. She'd noticed her getting breathless on the Town Steps but she hadn't realised what it meant.'

Fiona put a hand over her face. 'I'd spotted her symptoms too, and I did worry. Her ankles were a little swollen. I suggested she should go for an examination but she refused. She said it was natural at her age. I told her it wasn't, but it was no good.'

Bella couldn't make up her mind whether the words tumbling from Fiona's mouth had been practised.

'I'd hate anyone to think I hadn't warned her out of self-interest,' Fiona rushed on. 'I had no idea she'd left me anything in her will, let alone her house. She never told me.'

People were bound to talk, and if Fiona was innocent, it was rough on her. Bella nodded. 'Don't worry. She told Carys, but she said she'd kept it secret in general.'

Fiona let out a long sigh. 'That's something.'

Bella would circulate the story. It should take the pressure off Fiona, and more importantly, if anyone knew different, they'd speak up. 'It's an amazing house. What will you do with it?'

'I haven't decided yet.' There was a gleam in her eye.

However close she'd been to Mary, Bella could tell she wanted Springside Cottage, despite her and Adrian's palatial pad. Was it greed? They could sell it or let it out. Just because someone had money, didn't mean they didn't want more. It was good that they'd been invited to the Fitzpatricks' after the rehearsal. Bella might do some snooping and see what she could discover. 'Did you find out who graffitied your house?'

Fiona tucked her dark hair behind her ears and sighed. 'I don't suppose we'll ever know. The police don't have the resources.'

But you didn't tell the police. Bella nodded and sighed too. 'I'm so sorry it happened. It must have made you anxious.'

'I'm trying not to think about it.'

She figured that was her cue to back off.

While Adrian and Fiona talked to the parent organising decorations, Bella seized the opportunity to slip out of the hall. The place was a Victorian rabbit warren and she had no clue where she was going. She made for the front entrance, hoping the administrative offices might be near reception. The layout mattered.

At last, she found a door labelled 'Headteacher' and 'School Secretary'. It was locked, but looking through a glass panel, she could see the arrangement. Adrian had an inner office and Mary had been set up to guard his lair, with a desk just outside it. Bella couldn't see into his room, but it told her what she needed to know: Adrian could easily have overheard Mary if she'd taken a call from her solicitor in her lunch hour, say. And he'd find it simple to pinch her door key from her bag if she left it unattended too. He could have nipped to the hardware shop to get a copy.

Back in the hall, Olivia was running through the talk she hadn't wanted to give. Adrian was pressing her for more photographs. 'Didn't you have one of you and Robbie Williams? We really need to big this up, so don't be shy!'

'She told me it made her look like a groupie,' Carys hissed.

Bella could see Olivia wasn't pleased. She agreed, but her eyes were on a tall man with sandy hair that flopped forward. In his forties maybe, but the hairstyle made him look boyish. 'Is that her husband?'

Carys nodded. 'Harry. I often think his height reflects his outlook on life. He's focused on the horizon, dreaming big dreams, doing noble things for his charity, but not always noticing problems under his nose.'

'Noah?'

She nodded. 'And Olivia's feelings. They were on the rocks for a bit when Noah was arrested, but things have got better now. You can tell just by watching.'

It was true. The moment Adrian had finished putting Olivia through the mill, she all but ran to Harry. He'd been deep in animated discussion but she inserted herself into his small circle, pulling him close. He seemed surprised and delighted, like a teenager who realised he'd just found the love of his life.

'They're definitely going through a renaissance,' Carys said.

Olivia's eyes were emotional as she rested her head against Harry's chest, nodding and smiling at the people he'd been talking to.

'The way she defended Noah to Mary is starting to make more sense.' Bella turned to Carys. 'I could imagine her doing it out of loyalty to Harry. That looks like true love to me. And not just the relaxed easy-going sort, but something more intense.'

'I know what you mean,' Carys said. She sighed. 'I'd settle for Leo just looking at me with the same adoration he has for an Eaton sausage sandwich. Though I suppose I can just about put up with him.'

Her words made Bella smile. She knew how strong their bond was.

Back at the Fitzpatricks' house, Fiona was being the hostess with the mostest, dishing out savoury biscuits topped with mushroom pâté and cream cheese.

Bella reached for a plate of the mushroom canapés. 'These look so good. I'll take some to the sitting room and join the others.' It was important to plant that idea in Fiona's mind. In reality, she was headed elsewhere. She'd already warned Carys not to ask after her whereabouts and to tell anyone who enquired that she'd gone to the loo. She met Carys in the hall, handed her the tray, then stood for a moment, checking to ensure she wasn't watched. After that, she made for the stairs. The house was old and they probably creaked but the party below was so noisy she shouldn't be heard.

She wanted to get a look at Adrian and Fiona's bedroom. Whoever had been tormenting Mary owned a long, black cloak. They'd have jettisoned it after the death if they had any sense, but it had to be worth checking. Bella had already decided that was her job. The police weren't interested and at this rate someone would get away with intent to murder. She wasn't going to sit around eating canapés, knowing she hadn't done all she could to find out who. What if they did it again?

She crept along the wide landing, one floor up. The carpet was soft, and everywhere smelled of polish. It helped that the bedroom doors were ajar. She passed more than one guest room and a study, but then came to a likely looking space. She could see a dressing table with a bottle of scent and a hairbrush on it, as well as a pair of Adrian's brogues on the floor.

She looked about her again. There was no way she'd be able to explain herself once she entered the room, but everyone seemed busy downstairs.

In a moment, she was in and automatically assessing the furniture and ornaments. There was a vintage framed botanical print, and on the dressing table a beautiful Georgian mahogany mirror. But she mustn't get distracted.

In another second she was opening the couple's wardrobe.

She didn't find a black cloak. It had been too much to hope for. What she did discover, peeping out of a coat pocket, was a letter from Mary Roberts.

Dear Fiona,

I'm horrified at what you've been keeping from me. Why didn't you come clean?

I thought we were friends.

We should talk now. This changes things.

Tomorrow at six?

Mary

Bella checked for a date, but there was none.

17

IN SEARCH OF AN INTRUDER

Bella photographed Mary's letter to Fiona and returned home that evening with thoughts fizzing in her head.

This changes things. It did indeed. It was starting to look as though Mary had been a collector of damaging secrets. Perhaps she'd planned to disinherit Fiona because of what she'd discovered about her. Everyone knew she acted if she didn't like someone's behaviour. There was still no way of proving Fiona had known about the bequest, but the whole set-up looked sinister. Bella needed to pass news of the letter on to the gang. She hadn't had the chance to update Carys at the Fitzpatricks' gathering.

Back at her flat, she found Matt's cat Cuthbert had got shut inside again.

She picked him up, to be met with the usual intense purring. He was so loud. There was something life-affirming about the warm, solid, vibrating feline, but she needed to set some boundaries. She carried him into the hall, ready to return him to the shared entryway, where Cuthbert could access his cat flap. 'What's the matter with your own home, eh? Is it Matt's endless girlfriends? Can't stand the constant changes in personnel?'

'There aren't that many.' The low, muffled voice came from beyond her front door.

Disaster. He must be right outside. Nothing for it but to brazen it out. She opened up.

'There seem to be *quite* a few.'

'I hadn't realised you'd been counting.'

'Good observational skills. It comes with working in antiques.' Carys had told her Matt's tale of woe: how his child-hood-sweetheart fiancée had left him for another man. That was supposed to account for his reluctance to commit but it had been years ago now. She had the distinct impression he was enjoying the ever-thinner excuse to endlessly play the field.

'What about Boxer?' Matt said. 'Seeing him again? I hear he's been talking about you.'

Whatever happened on that score, being spoken about spurred a warm feeling. 'Perhaps.' In reality, no. Not when he was still in love with his former girlfriend. And there was the snake to consider. But Matt ought to be kept guessing. 'Speaking of after-hours activities, might you visit the Hanged Man again soon?'

'It's always possible. Want me to keep an eye on Shane Sadler?'

'Yes, please. I'd like to know if there was any reason for things to come to a head between him and Mary before she died.'

Matt looked thoughtful. 'You really think someone was in her house on Saturday night?'

Bella nodded. 'And that they went in to kill her.' She told him what she'd found in the woods that lunchtime. 'The police insist it's not conclusive, but I don't like it.'

'Fair enough.'

'By the way, is there any reason you prefer the less-than-salubrious surroundings of the Hanged Man to the Blue Boar?'

He leaned against his door frame, Cuthbert in his arms. 'Don't take this the wrong way, no one loves my mother more than me, but if I enter her territory she tries to fix me.'

Bella hated being steered too. All the same, someone needed to ensure Matt grew up.

That night, Bella slept soundly, as she always did, but Mary's letter to Fiona was topmost in her mind when she woke. What had Fiona been keeping from her friend?

It made Bella's trip to investigate the Fitzpatricks' intruder even more urgent. The graffiti might relate to what Mary had discovered. All the same, Bella baulked at leaving her comfortable bed so early. Luckily, she was 'helped' by hearing someone depart from Matt's place shortly after her alarm went off. For a moment, she lay there, determined not to peer from behind her curtain, but ultimately she gave in.

Interesting. It was Matt himself. It wasn't the first time she'd seen him leave his flat so early. He came back in the middle of the night sometimes too. She was more than curious to know what he got up to.

Once she'd watched him leave, she went to shower, and plotted her approach to the Fitzpatricks' intruder. She planned to sneak round the back of their house and look for clues as to who'd climbed over their wall. She badly wanted to know what they knew. She'd be relying on Locard's principle again, but she thought she might be lucky. They'd been carrying a pot of paint. They were far more likely to leave a trace than if they'd used a spray can. She still thought it was interesting that they hadn't. If they'd planned ahead, they could have made their life easier. Something must have triggered their actions at the last minute.

She walked along the river, the route lined with lush linden trees and hazels. It was no use trying to access the rear of the Fitzpatricks' place via Boatman's Walk, thanks to the high brick wall. Instead, she followed the River Kite out of town. At last, she crossed the lower reaches of Kite Hill, then doubled back towards the rear of the Fitzpatricks' home through St Giles's Holt.

She was glad she'd worn her walking shoes – 1930s-style lace-up Oxfords with a low heel. As she headed towards her goal, she passed a lone cottage, just visible through the trees. That must be Opal's place. The thought of her monitoring the townsfolk was creepy. From what she'd said, she was probably out in the woods now, watching.

At last, Bella found herself behind the high brick wall she'd seen from Boatman's Walk. It was side-on to the Fitzpatrick's back wall, which was tall, with anti-climb spikes on top. The intruder must have been determined.

Bella looked at the ground. The long grass had been crushed as though something four or five feet wide had been resting on it. All at once she remembered the crash she'd heard, which had made her peek through the knothole in the Fitzpatricks' gate. A clatter as though something had fallen. But Opal had talked of clatter*ing*, not just a single clatter – something that *started* in this corner of the holt. As Bella thought, the answer came to her. She searched and found what she was looking for in a patch of rust-coloured earth. Tyre tracks.

The intruder had arrived by bike.

Bella visualised the scene. The woman must have leaned her machine against the Fitzpatricks' brick wall. Perhaps she'd used it to give herself a leg up. She could have trodden on the saddle, but it would have been precarious. The bike had probably crashed to the ground a short while later.

The intruder had been lucky to get out again before she was caught. Bella remembered she'd climbed on some garden furniture to help her back over the wall.

All that racket, yet still Fiona hadn't investigated. Either she hadn't known what she was dealing with, or she had, and it had filled her with fear.

The knowledge of the bike was useful. Unless the intruder had brought it solely to climb on – which seemed unlikely – she must have used it for a quick getaway. And that would only work if she'd escaped alongside St Giles's Holt, not through the trees. It would still have been rough going, but doable. No wonder her bike had clattered. After some intense scrutiny, she spotted a drip of dried green paint which confirmed her theory.

After that, she followed the track the intruder must have taken, which was straightforward enough, but eventually it joined a lane beyond the wood. To pursue her, Bella needed to know which way she'd fled. South-west, towards Springside Cottage; east, in the direction of Kite Walk and the river; or north, to the isolated houses at the foot of Kite Hill?

Just when Bella was about to risk her Oxfords by kicking a stone in frustration, she spotted more of the pale green paint.

It was pleasing, the way she got her eye in. Once she'd seen one small splash, she caught sight of another. It showed up better than a darker colour would have, but who used pale green paint to graffiti a wall? She must have had it around the house. Bella followed the trail north towards Kite Hill.

Did the intruder know something about Fiona? Or had she seen Adrian Fitzpatrick outside Springside Cottage that night, tormenting Mary? She could have left to daub the message before Adrian entered the house with his homemade weapon. But if she had, you'd think she'd have gone to the police when Mary's body was found.

Either way, it was essential to track the woman down. Her knowledge could be crucial. And if Bella could work out where she lived, she might find her at home at this hour. Her stomach told her it was breakfast time. She promised herself something from the Steps when she'd finished her mission.

The drips of paint became fewer and further between as she walked on. *Inevitable.* She was holding her breath as she spotted two last drips. After that, they gave out completely. It left her with a handful of remote houses to investigate at the foot of the hill. It certainly looked as though the intruder lived on Mary's side of Hope Eaton. She could have seen the person who'd tormented her.

The lane to the hamlet took Bella uphill. The elevation would give anyone who lived there a decent vantage point to view Mary's house. To Bella's left stood the mound of Kite Hill, the stone circle just visible on its flank. She walked along a track which led to Standing Stones House, according to a sign. The name rang bells. Who had mentioned it recently?

But there were other places to investigate first. To her left was a tiny stone dwelling: Lilac Cottage. The lilac tree in the garden was just coming into bud. It would smell glorious soon. She guessed the house must date back to the 1700s and it was for sale. It was full of character, but so remote. She'd never put down roots that far from the town. All the same, she itched to see inside. She'd snoop at the estate agents' details later. It was being sold by the Nest, just like Springside Cottage. She could enquire about it in person and see what she could pick up about Olivia.

Of course, if you were selling your place, you might be redecorating... It was entirely possible you'd have some pale green paint on hand. The shade of the drips was unfortunate, but each to their own.

Bella needed to check her hunch. The cottage's windows were dark, but she knocked anyway. The 'For Sale' notice was the perfect excuse for a chat.

But there was no reply. Bella stood looking at the front door. It would be a shame to go home without any information.

Unlike the Fitzpatricks' place, the tiny cottage wasn't protected by high brick walls. It would be interesting to know if one of the rooms had recently been painted green. She glanced over her shoulder to check for onlookers, then began to investigate.

She struck gold on the third window she peered through. Pale green walls. And then, through a chink in the door of a lean-to outhouse, several pots of paint including – by the light of her phone torch – one with pale green drips down the side.

Not proof, but highly suggestive.

She'd come back, and soon.

18

BOOK LEARNING

Bella nipped into the Steps for a takeaway Eaton sausage sandwich. She'd asked John if he'd like one but he'd informed her that he'd already had breakfast in a controlled and non-indigestion-inducing manner.

At the café, Leo pressed her for updates excitedly. With a minute and a half to spare before Vintage Winter opened, she filled him in. Leo interjected with various theories and comments.

'Carys already told me you thought someone made their own weapon,' Leo said as she finished, his eyes like saucers.

'I'm afraid so. It would have been terrifying; it fits with the way someone tormented Mary before she died. But the police won't do anything. They don't have time to follow leads based on hunches. We need proof if we want them to act. Update Carys on everything, would you?' Leo nodded eagerly, like a schoolboy who'd been made exercise-book monitor. 'And don't mention any of this to Jeannie. You know how she worries.'

. . .

As Bella dashed into Vintage Winter, her takeaway swinging in its paper bag, she caught a woman glancing at her from across St Giles's Close, then turning away quickly.

Her appetite evaporated as she reported the incident to John. 'I'm sure there's something going on.' On impulse, she propped the shop's door open to try to make it look more welcoming.

John poured her a black coffee. 'I'll ask around. If you're right, it shouldn't be hard to find out.'

That was probably true. The Jenkses had contacts everywhere and people talked to John. He was that sort of person. It made her think of his solicitor cousin.

'Did you call Tom, by the way?'

He groaned. 'Yes, and I'm sure I sounded shifty. But it turns out he is Mary's executor.'

'Well done! You asked about the statuette?'

He raised an eyebrow. 'Of course. He's going to have a look.'

'You're one in a million.'

After that, she filled him in on what she'd discovered the evening before. He looked horrified at her excursion to the Fitzpatricks' bedroom. She cocked her head. 'Tell me it wasn't worth it. What do you say to Fiona as a suspect now?'

He bit his lip. 'I'd never have thought she had something to hide.'

'Everyone has, John. Except perhaps you.' After that, she recounted that morning's efforts. 'I'm going to visit the Nest at lunchtime. Pretend I'm interested in Lilac Cottage.'

John stiffened. 'Lilac Cottage? I know the woman who lives there. Beatrice West. Bea. She volunteers at the Hearst House Museum. Or she did when I worked there.'

'I wouldn't be surprised if Sienna's frightened her off.' She'd heard that visitor numbers had plummeted. 'What's Bea like?'

His brow furrowed. 'Quiet. Diligent. Good to work with. I

didn't know she was moving. Her day job is at the high school. She's an English teacher. First job since qualifying.'

She didn't sound like your average vandal. But the connection with the high school was interesting. Bella needed to know if it was significant. 'I think she could probably see Mary's cottage from her upstairs windows.'

'But not in detail, surely?' John had gone back to the clock he was working on. He was sitting at one end of the refectory table they used as a cash desk.

'Perhaps not, but if she'd heard rumours about Mary's hooded figure, she could have used binoculars.' Bella would have. 'Maybe she spotted them, went closer and realised it was Adrian Fitzpatrick. I'm pretty certain it was Bea who daubed his walls with paint. It has to be worth following up.'

They were discussing theories when Bernadette, the bookseller from the Steps, dashed in as though someone was chasing her.

She arrived at the refectory table red in the face. 'I'd missed something crucial to do with Mary!' She gulped for air and put an old clothbound tome in front of them. A legal reference book.

Bella picked it up and read the title. 'What's tort law got to do with anything?'

Bernadette shook her head vigorously. 'Nothing, as far as I know. But it's a book Carys must have taken from Springside Cottage by accident!'

'How do you mean?'

'She went off to Mary's place on Sunday morning with the books Mary'd ordered, but she came back with one extra.'

Bella thought back to that terrible day. 'Of course. We were both so shocked we were on autopilot. I remember Carys put the books down on a side table on top of some others. When we left again I said she should take them with her, because the police wanted the scene just as we'd found it.' And all the while, Carys's eyes had been fixed on Mary's body.

Bernadette nodded. 'That would explain it. Carys returned the books to me as Mary hadn't paid for them yet and I put them in a box for sorting. I suppose I was in shock too; I only remembered them today. When I didn't recognise this one, I opened it and look what I found!'

At last, she drew breath and flipped it open. There was a handwritten note inside.

> I imagine you regret it now, but it's too late. It's time to pay your dues.

Bella photographed it. 'A blackmail note? Someone was extorting money from Mary?' How would that fit in?

But Bernadette looked at her, her eyes round. 'That's just the thing. It wasn't that way round. Carys was there when I found it and she says the handwriting's Mary's. Now you know someone was tormenting her, I wondered if—'

The sound of movement behind her made Bella jump. It was Olivia Elsworth. She'd entered the shop without them noticing; Bella shouldn't have propped the door open after all.

Olivia's eyes were on the note. It hadn't been sent, clearly, but that didn't mean the message had never gone out. It looked like a partly completed draft. It was entirely possible a final version had reached Mary's target. Or maybe she'd ended up issuing the ultimatum in person instead. In her note to Fiona, about her secret, she'd asked to see her.

But perhaps it had been Noah she was blackmailing. Olivia was still staring at the note, her eyes wide, as though she understood the contents. She might be wondering if her stepson was a murderer. Or, with her business failing, she could have bought into his illegal activities. She'd sounded desperate when Mary accused him. And she'd been out, the night of the death. Perhaps it was she who'd entered Springside Cottage, ready to strike the fatal blow.

19

HOUSE HUNTING

When Bernadette left, taking the note and book, Olivia Elsworth stared after her.

Bella had to raise her voice to get her attention. 'Are you looking for anything in particular? How can we help?'

At last, she dragged her gaze back to Bella, though her eyes remained anxious. 'I wanted to talk to you about the possibility of hiring some of your stock to accessorise the houses on our books.'

Bella had come across estate agents doing that before, but mainly those who were doing well. For expensive London houses, it could pay dividends. Bella could imagine the fun of it – like setting a stage. Positioning her stock at Vintage Winter was one of her favourite activities.

'Some of the houses just need a characterful item or two to help people imagine what they could be like.' Olivia bit her lip. 'The only thing is, I wasn't sure about cost. I want to invest to help our clients, but there's a limit to what we can afford.'

Olivia probably guessed her financial struggles were common knowledge. Bella felt for her, but what if she'd killed over it?

'We've got insurance which would cover anything we hire, but I know you need to make a living too.'

She must be used to negotiating house sales, but she seemed shy about the money side of this minor deal. Bella remembered her hugging her husband. Or clinging to him? She suspected her confidence was at a low ebb.

From Bella's point of view, the arrangement could work. And maintaining contact with Olivia could only help when it came to uncovering what had happened to Mary. 'I'm sure we can work something out and the publicity could be useful.'

Olivia blushed and nodded. It was hard to imagine her stalking Mary, let alone entering her house with a weapon. But if she'd got desperate and made money illegally, it could have happened. An arrest and the news that she'd abetted Noah would threaten her marriage and Bella sensed that was everything to her.

They agreed to talk further. Bella wanted to help; it was at least 70 per cent altruism, but the more locals who were on her side, the better.

'I'll be popping in a bit later anyway,' Bella told Olivia, before she left. 'I'd like more information about Lilac Cottage.'

She brightened, which made Bella feel guilty, but you couldn't make an omelette without breaking eggs.

Once she was gone, Bella texted Barry Dixon a photograph of the draft blackmail note with an explanation. Surely he must see it would have made Mary a target? But she could guess what he'd say: there was no proof the message had ever been sent, and her death had been natural causes. Twenty minutes later he replied, saying just that, but Bella bet the note had made him think. She just needed something to tip the balance and get him onboard.

. . .

As Bella dashed to the Nest that lunchtime she ran rapidly through her aims for the visit. If Olivia was in, she'd build on their chat that morning and find out more about Noah. Bella would drop the auto repair shop and Thomasina's service into conversation, then probe for information and identify sensitive areas. She'd already seen him stealing. The operation would need careful handling though, with Olivia also a suspect.

Bella wanted to arrange a viewing of Lilac Cottage too, so she could talk to Bea. The meeting would feel more coincidental than if John introduced them and there were plenty of ways to slip the Fitzpatricks into conversation. She just needed to make sure Bea showed her round personally.

In the end, it was another woman on duty at the Nest, not Olivia, so Bella focused on her feigned interest in buying a new home.

'I love my place, but Lilac Cottage is in such a peaceful location. I'm very conscious of my neighbours in Southwell Hall.' She was definitely more conscious of Matt than she should be.

The woman leaped into full-scale sales mode, laced with desperation. Bella's feelings of guilt increased. She'd have to put the word around about Lilac Cottage. Try to drum up some genuine interest.

'I'll give the owner a call now,' the woman said, after waxing lyrical for some minutes.

Bella thanked her and strolled around the reception area, pretending to look at other property details as she listened in.

'Ah, good morning, Ms West, this is Gail Hughes from the Nest. I wonder if you could give me a call back about a viewing? Though I'll try your mobile as well.'

She didn't get any reply on that either.

She tutted and Bella agreed. Though to be fair, Bea was probably teaching.

'As Ms West isn't at home, I can take you for a viewing right now if you'd like?' She looked very eager indeed.

'It's kind of you, but I'd rather visit when Ms West is there. It's so useful to talk to the current owner about the area.'

'You won't find a quieter part of Hope Eaton.'

Complete with weapon-brandishing hooded figure, graffiti-daubing intruder and thirteen-cat-owning palm reader. Bella nodded. 'I'm sure you're right, but just the same, I'd rather wait.' She gave Gail Hughes her number. 'I wasn't sure if I'd find Olivia here. She popped into my shop this morning.' She hoped Hughes would assume they were friends.

'She should be back any minute.'

'I might be visiting her son soon, to get my car serviced.' She met the woman's eye. 'It won't be him leading on it, of course, but I've heard he's very good.' If Hughes had doubts, the claim might tempt her to share them.

Sure enough, she was frowning. 'I couldn't comment, I'm sure.'

'Ah. I see.' Bella gave her a look to show she understood. 'But the job's a great springboard I suppose. It must have been hard for Olivia, dealing with all the trouble over his arrest.'

The woman folded her arms and sighed. She was definitely about to crack.

'The poor woman,' she said at last. 'Noah would try the patience of a saint.' She shook her head. 'He's a wrong 'un and he'll stay wrong, you mark my words. Between ourselves, I wouldn't let him within ten feet of my car. Sorry, but I felt I had to say it.'

Bella nodded earnestly. 'Thanks for the advice. Though his days of dodgy dealings are over, I presume. Unless you've heard otherwise?'

'I haven't...' The woman sounded disappointed. 'But as I say, I'd be surprised if that's the last trouble he causes. He's that sort.'

Bella leaned in. 'Of course, he was horrible to poor Mary Roberts on May Day.' Linking the pair might trigger some relevant memories in Hughes's mind.

'Yes, that was Noah all over. No love lost between them, of course.' She must have heard about Mary reporting him; Olivia had probably let it slip. 'Truth to tell,' Hughes went on, 'Mary caused us a few problems too. She would insist on keeping some of her land. We had to be honest with buyers and tell them the bottom of their garden would be a building site for a while. At least she'd decided to put a chalet up in the end, not bring in a caravan. We had her friend to thank for that.'

'Her friend?' That needed exploring. 'Fiona Fitzpatrick, you mean?'

Hughes nodded. 'Fiona persuaded her she'd be more comfortable in a chalet. She suggested having a cottage built at first, but Mary refused. Still, a chalet would have been more attractive for the new owners than a caravan. The one she had her eye on was a grotty old thing.'

The chalet would have made a better inheritance too, though not quite as good as the cottage Fiona had suggested initially. Very interesting indeed. Perhaps she *had* known about the will.

20

TONY'S WORDS OF WISDOM

Bella updated John when she got back to Vintage Winter, and they continued to discuss theories between customers, who were few and far between. A little after four, John's solicitor cousin called back to say there was no obvious sign of the statuette at Mary's cottage. They couldn't be sure though. The place was stuffed with things.

After work, Bella dashed through to the Steps to update Leo and Bernadette and found Carys there too, so a full-scale catch-up ensued. After that, she went home to commune with some Italian meats, breads and cheeses from the less heinously expensive deli in town.

Feeling pleasantly full, she poured herself a Crodino to continue the Italian theme and called Tony.

'*Talk to me,*' he said without preamble.

'How extraordinary. That's just why I was calling.' She started to fill him in on what had happened. Every so often they paused to examine her new information in depth. 'The blackmail note is interesting. It sounds as though Mary had proof of someone's wrongdoing.'

She heard Tony slurp. She bet he was drinking Hobsons Twisted Spire. *'Have you talked to Carys about it?'*

She had, during the after-work catch-up at the Steps. 'She said she'd never have believed Mary would stoop to blackmail if she hadn't seen the note. But then she pointed out that Mary was unconventional. She might mete out justice in whichever way seemed fitting. Maybe she decided blackmail would put her victim off misbehaving in future.' That had been her idea when she'd humiliated Shane, according to Carys.

'Or her evidence wasn't something the police could use.'

'Possibly. Or perhaps the person had been in trouble with them before and official sanctions hadn't worked.'

'Pointing to Noah?'

'That's what I wondered. The fact that Mary talked to Olivia about him, rather than the police, might imply she planned to deal with the matter differently this time. When Olivia wouldn't hear her out, she could have decided to relieve Noah of any cash he was making illegally. Either way, Carys reckoned Mary wouldn't have done it out of greed. She said she'd probably have given the blackmail money to charity.'

Tony grunted. *'But she was short of cash. We know that.'*

She'd known he'd be sceptical.

After that, they reviewed the letter she'd found in Fiona Fitzpatrick's bedroom.

'I know I said you're a chip off the old block,' Tony said, *'but that sounds more like the kind of thing I'd do.'* Bella was secretly pleased, though she wouldn't dream of saying so. *'Of course,'* Tony added, *'you are the product of two parents.'*

She couldn't imagine what he meant by that. She was nothing like her mother. Bella read the words from the photograph she'd taken of the letter:

'"Dear Fiona, I'm horrified at what you've been keeping from me. Why didn't you come clean? I thought we were friends. We should talk now. This changes things. Tomorrow at six? Mary."

'Leo's still very excited about it.' It was another topic they'd hashed over when she'd dropped in after work. 'He said it implies Fiona knew about the will and that she'd done something to change Mary's mind. I'd had much the same thought.'

The phone rustled, as though Tony was shifting position. '*Imply is the operative word. You can't tell Mary's tone from the letter and there are an awful lot of unanswered questions.*' He paused. '*But it certainly makes you wonder.*'

'The bottom line is, we're still left with three main motives.' Bella put her feet up on the sofa and stretched out. 'Fear, on the part of a blackmail victim; greed, on the part of someone with an interest in Mary's bequest; and hatred, on the part of anyone with a grudge. So far, Noah seems most likely as the blackmail victim, though Fiona's nipping at his heels after the letter I found. And there's still a chance Olivia teamed up with Noah in some way. She looked stunned when she saw the draft blackmail note.

'As for Noah, I've seen him pilfering, and his boss says he's made excuses to leave work during the day. Whatever he's up to, some of it is planned and time-sensitive.

'Then there's Fiona and/or Adrian for greed. I need to catch up with the graffiti writer.'

Tony rumbled his agreement.

'We think we know who she is at least: Bea West. John knows her. And now I've had time to think, I wonder if she's any relation to Edwina West.' She of the curves and the pitchy notes. Bella explained their connection and Tony laughed.

'I might have hoped for a little more sympathy.' Of course, Bea and Edwina sounded like chalk and cheese, character-wise. Bella remembered John saying Bea was quiet, diligent and good to work with. 'We haven't managed to track Bea down yet. But she's a teacher at the high school; she's bound to be busy. We'll keep trying.'

Tony grunted. '*Right you are.*'

Bella's thoughts ran on. 'Now we come to hatred, with Noah as a suspect once again and Shane Sadler too. Though in Shane's case, there's still the question of why now?'

'*Yes.*' Tony sounded thoughtful. '*There's usually a trigger.*'

She wondered if it had anything to do with Shane's mysterious late-night van rides. 'The hatred motive fits especially well with the terror campaign that began before Mary's death. It could have been a way to draw out her suffering before the end. But the torment fits for the greed motive too, if it was a half-hearted attempt to frighten Mary to death before the Fitzpatricks decided they were being unrealistic.'

'*True, but it jars if the would-be killer was a blackmail victim,*' Tony said. '*Can't think of any reason for them to dress up and frighten Mary before entering her home.*'

'I agree. Unless Noah began acting from hatred, then killed for practical reasons when he got her note.'

Tony sighed. '*It's a quandary. The greed motive is strong, but it would be a whopping coincidence if the blackmail's unrelated to what's happened. It's a classic motive for murder. Course, the other stuff like the rotting meat could be separate. And it's always best to keep an open mind.*'

'One of the most curious things is why Mary's would-be killer wanted her statuette. It doesn't look as though it's in her house.' She explained about the rough search the solicitors had done. 'Why complicate matters with an objectively low-value object when they were on such a desperate mission?

'Anyway, Noah and the Fitzpatricks are the top suspects in my eyes.'

'*Thought about how they'd get a copy of Mary's key?*'

'Adrian could have managed it easily.' She explained the

school layout. 'But I bet Noah would have succeeded too. He's a thief after all.'

'*Fair point. Next steps?*'

'To find out what Bea West knows. I'll knock again early tomorrow and ask. If she's not there, I'll contact Edwina. If they're related, she might know Bea's routine. I need to find out what Noah Elsworth is up to too, to see if it's blackmail-worthy. I'll follow him if necessary.' She couldn't think of a better way.

After she'd said goodbye and rung off, she texted John to explain her plans for another visit to Lilac Cottage. He messaged back to say he'd come too. He knew Bea, which would certainly help. A moment later, her phone rang.

Matt. She picked up.

'*I'm outside the Hanged Man. I've just heard Shane Sadler take a call like the one you overheard. He's asked for a round of sandwiches.*'

'Right, thanks. I'm on my way.'

21

A WILD GOOSE CHASE

If Bella was going to find out what Shane Sadler was up to, she'd need Thomasina. The taxi was a mixed blessing. Being electric, she was very quiet, which would be handy if she ever wanted to approach someone in stealth mode, but in all other ways she was noticeable. Bella parked her south of the Hanged Man on Maid's Lane. If Shane did as he'd done on Monday night and hopped into his van, she could follow him at a distance.

She texted Matt to let him know she was keeping watch. A moment later he appeared like a shadow, next to Thomasina. She put the window down and he crouched to her level.

'Would you like company?'

The thought of Matt in the taxi next to her brought on a rapid heartbeat, which was all the more reason to say no.

'I'm fine. I wouldn't want to keep you from your adoring fans. But thanks all the same.'

He laughed and walked off into the night.

He never took offence, whatever she said. She hoped that wasn't because he could guess what she was really thinking. But her reactions were off, surely. Matt wasn't her type, any more than Boxer was. He was a directionless, A1 scruff.

She was distracted by movement. Someone was emerging from the Hanged Man. It was Shane Sadler all right. The evening was cool now. He was wearing a bomber jacket and clutching something, hunched over it as though it was slightly too much to carry. Probably the sandwiches and a takeaway coffee again. He somehow managed to open the passenger door to his van, looking like a flailing octopus, then dumped the refreshments. After that he glanced over his shoulder. Bella shrank down in her seat. She could see his eyes glint in the streetlight. It was still fascinating to think of him and Mary as a couple. He'd said how passionate she'd been during their courtship and Carys had said her abandon was out of character. Bella longed to know what had caused it, and why it had ended so soon after they'd married. If she could deduce why errant dealers and siblings behaved as they did, surely she could work it out.

But it was no good speculating now. Shane's van's lights were on and he was pulling out of his parking spot.

The roads were quiet this time of night and there was no traffic to cover Bella's move. She let him get partway across St Luke's Bridge before she set off. As before, she could see his tail lights heading out of town, up the steep and narrow Raven Climb – a channel of road between massive slabs of sandstone rock. Bella drove after him, accelerating a little. She needed to know which way he went when he reached the outskirts of Hope Eaton.

She was just in time to see him go north. He'd followed a tiny road, rather than the more logical A-road he could have taken. Maybe he was headed for a local farm.

But no, he didn't stop. There was one other vehicle on the road behind them – a motorcycle – but it didn't catch them up.

Bella wished Shane *had* taken the main route. It would have sped up their journey. She'd like to get home, put her feet up and listen to Edith Piaf. There was nothing like vinyl. But this was important. Who drove off into the night after a suspicious call? What if Shane was involved in something illegal, just like Noah? He could have been taunting Mary for sport, then decided to kill her when the blackmail started. But why wouldn't she have gone to the police? How could she know enough to threaten him, yet not enough to convince the authorities to make an arrest?

Whatever the truth, she doubted Shane's antics would add to the happiness and safety of Hope Eaton, and no one else was going to discover his game. The old adage came to her: if you want something done well, do it yourself. Though here it was a case of if you want something done at all.

Eventually, Shane gave up his rural routes and headed onto the M6 motorway. Bella followed, and got as far as Stoke-on-Trent before she gave up. She needed answers but this wasn't a practical way to get them. She could be on the road for hours – longer than Thomasina's battery would last. Besides, if the route got lonely, she might be driving into danger. She had another idea. Next time Matt saw Shane in the Hanged Man, she'd make for his house and search for clues there. He had no live-in partner that she knew of. She'd hopefully have the place to herself.

As she signalled to exit the motorway, the motorcyclist was still on her tail. She held her breath as she waited to see if they followed her, but they carried on in the same direction as Shane.

She turned for home. She wanted to get enough sleep before visiting Lilac Cottage again. Bea West's absence was starting to bother her. The estate agents hadn't called back. Presumably they hadn't succeeded in contacting her, even after the school day had finished. What if she'd dropped out of circulation?

When Bella arrived outside her flat in Southwell Hall, Matt greeted her. Did he never go to bed? Cuthbert was in his arms, purring extravagantly.

'How did it go?'

'Frustratingly. I got as far as junction fifteen on the M6, then gave up.'

Matt whistled.

'He left Hope Eaton using back roads, so I assume he's trying to put anyone local off the scent. Do you know what he does for a living, officially?'

'A jack of all trades. The Fitzpatricks asked me to lay a new carpet for them but I hadn't the time. I heard later that Shane had ended up with the work. He did it all right, from what I hear, but Adrian reckoned some cash went missing the day he visited. He had a go at him, shouting the odds so all the neighbours could hear.'

'Could you let me know next time he's in the Hanged Man? I might try snooping round his house to see if I can find out anything there instead. Do you know where he lives?'

Matt nodded. 'I'll text you the address. I wouldn't go alone though. Safety in numbers.' He looked at her, his mischievous blue eyes behind unreasonably long lashes. 'You must be knackered. Do you want a drink?'

Could Matt possibly be without company tonight? She thought of her mother and pulled up short. She wasn't going to fill the gap in his schedule. 'Very kind, but no thank you. Bed's calling.'

He nodded and grinned, his eyes still on hers. At that moment she heard a voice from inside his flat. 'You going to play your hand or not, mate?'

She let herself into her quarters feeling irritated. He'd wrong-footed her. He'd got a friend or friends round. The drink had been a disinterested offer after all.

22

TROUBLE AT LILAC COTTAGE

Bella met John at seven o'clock outside Southwell Hall, ready to take the same route Bella had used to reach Lilac Cottage the previous morning.

During the twenty-five-minute walk, Bella filled John in on Shane Sadler's activities the previous evening. 'It's hard to imagine him being up to anything honest.' She detailed her plan to visit his house and grounds next time he was safely in the Hanged Man.

John closed his eyes for a moment. 'I do wish you wouldn't tell me things like that.'

'What? Why?'

'It's not a good idea to go trespassing on someone like Shane's land. I saw him in a fight once. He's handy with his fists.'

'But the whole point is that he won't be there.'

'And what if he comes back?'

'I'll listen out for him and be out of there in no time. His van's old. You could hear it a mile off.'

'So it's no use telling you not to go ahead?'

'Not when he might have been doing something blackmail-worthy, no. I'll need to take my chance when I get it.'

John was twisting his hands. At last, he sighed. 'Give me a call when you go. I'll come with you.'

As ever, she thought how incredibly lucky she was to have him. She could see very well that he didn't want to come. 'You don't have to. Honestly. I won't take any risks and your repro-bate brother will probably offer as well. Of course, if he does come, I expect he'll have some glamorous brunette in tow.'

'As well as you, you mean?'

'You say all the right things. I could always take Boxer, as an alternative. I bet he'd come. He's up for adventure.' Besides, they needed to talk about his love life. She'd have to tell him he should get back together with Alison; it would stop things getting compli-cated. The pair of them belonged together. Anyone could see that. She just needed to look at the psychology of the situation.

They were still thirty feet from Lilac Cottage but Bella was already convinced they'd get no reply. The place looked just as dark and unoccupied as the day before.

Her eyes met John's.

'I'll give her a try, anyway.'

'What will you say if she answers?'

'That we were passing and I'm interested in her cottage.'

John looked unhappy. 'No normal person would call at this hour. It's antisocial.'

'I'll be so delighted to see her that I won't care if she's put out.' Bella approached the front door. Just to her right, half hidden behind a shrub, were two bottles of milk. *Sweet Agnes, were they today's, or yesterday's?* She bent to touch them. They matched the air temperature. The foil lid was bulging slightly.

'They weren't there when you called yesterday?'

Had they been? It would be too awful if she'd missed them. 'I don't think so. But they could have been delivered soon afterwards. They're not cool enough to be today's. If I'm right, Bea West's been away overnight, and it was unplanned.'

'And the woman at the Nest said she wasn't answering her phone?'

Bella nodded. 'Neither the landline nor her mobile. I don't like it. If the graffiti was about Adrian or Fiona tormenting Mary, she might be a threat to them. Perhaps that's why she's missing.'

'Why wouldn't she go to the police?'

'Maybe she wasn't confident they'd do anything when she heard Mary's death was natural causes. I'm going to look through the windows again. See if anything's changed since yesterday.'

Even John rushed to peer in.

Bella hadn't really expected to see anything enlightening, which was why the sight of the room next to the one with the green paint came as a shock.

'What is it?'

She must have gasped. 'Look.' There was smashed crockery on the floor – only the remains of a plate or two, but here, there and everywhere, as though someone had flung them in anger and they'd hit the wall. 'There must have been a row. Perhaps she hurled accusations and the other person hurled plates. I don't know when it happened. I didn't look in this room yesterday because I'd already seen the paint but I'm going to call Barry Dixon.' He needed to know. It all added to the picture they were building, though whether he'd do something was another matter.

He sounded tired when she got through: in general, probably, and with her, quite possibly. When she gave him Bea's address, he sounded slightly more awake.

'*It's just around the corner from where that Audi I told you about was vandalised. West. That's the same name as the couple at Standing Stones House. A relative perhaps. Have you tried asking for your missing friend there?'*

'Not yet.'

'*Might be worth a go.*' His sigh sounded like air leaking from a leather sofa. '*Either way, I'm sure her friends, family or employers would have reported her missing if she's really gone AWOL.*'

'But she's selling her house. Doesn't that make you wonder why she'd leave it in such a state? I've been trying to reach her through her estate agents, the Nest in Hope Eaton. They'd drawn a blank, last I heard. Couldn't you talk to them? See if they're concerned?'

There was a significant pause. '*All right, I'll try to get to it – just to be on the safe side.*' He sounded resigned. '*Call me if the people at Standing Stones House know anything.*'

She could tell from his tone that an extra mystery was the last thing he wanted. Still, at least he'd heard her out.

'Let's go and ask at Standing Stones House now,' Bella said, when she'd rung off. 'Perhaps that's where Edwina the songbird lives. Maybe she's Bea's mother.'

'We're bound to interrupt her breakfast.'

'I'm sure she'll cope. Best-case scenario, she'll offer us some.'

John put a hand across his eyes.

As they approached the large, modern house with its expansive driveway, Bella spotted a figure flitting across one of the picture windows. Someone was in, at least. There was a Jaguar in a double garage to the right. The Audi was nowhere to be seen. Perhaps they were fixing it at the Hope Eaton garage.

Bella told John about the vandalism.

'It's a lonely spot. I can imagine they're vulnerable.'

'You'd think they'd have security cameras or something.' Bella looked and spotted some. 'That might have made our boy

Barry's job easier. Though I had the impression they hadn't caught anyone.'

John was hanging back. Bella strode ahead and knocked at the door.

It *was* Edwina. She greeted them in a silk kimono. Bella didn't like it as much as her own mustard-yellow one, but Edwina wore it with total confidence and that was always attractive, of course. Her auburn hair fell in loose waves and she looked the picture of rude health, her skin – of which plenty was visible – tanned and smooth.

'Bella! Not here about singing practice at this hour, I presume?'

Bella introduced John. 'No, nothing like that. We're sorry to bother you. We were looking for Bea at Lilac Cottage. I've tried twice now with no luck.' She wouldn't explain further. If Edwina was Bea's mother, it wouldn't be necessary. 'There's milk outside her front door from yesterday, so we were worried.'

Edwina laughed. 'She's a grown woman. She stopped telling me her plans when she turned eighteen, and I've stopped asking!'

So much for motherly concern. 'You don't have any idea where she could be?' Bella plucked an excuse from the air. 'Only John needs to ask her about one of the Hearst House exhibits. He doesn't work there any more of course, but he's investigating something as a favour. He knew Bea would be able to help.'

If they'd been sitting at a table, she had a feeling John would have kicked her under it. Unfortunately, ad-libbing had been essential. An interest in Bea's property wouldn't go far enough to explain the urgency.

Luckily, Edwina looked bored by her explanation. Bella doubted she'd mention it to Sienna Hearst.

'Simply no idea at all,' she said cheerfully.

Why didn't she care? Bella would have been anxious if it was one of her sisters. Irritated, certainly, but anxious as well.

A tall, thin man with greying hair appeared behind Edwina. 'What's all this? You're looking for Bea?'

Bella nodded.

'She should be back soon.' The man's blue eyes were concerned, though. 'She sent me a text,' he said after a moment, with a quick glance at Edwina. 'She was after a couple of days to herself, I believe.'

A text. It wasn't proof that Bea was all right and it was odd to take off if she was meant to be teaching. 'You haven't spoken to her?'

He chewed his lip and shook his head.

What to say about the mess in Bea's house? It was only a smashed plate or two, but she'd want to know if it was one of her sisters. She explained what they'd seen and how she'd alerted the police, just in case.

The man looked a good deal more concerned than Edwina, who tutted. 'She's always been clumsy. I expect she dropped a tray and couldn't be bothered to clear up.'

She'd have to have dropped it in a very energetic way to achieve the results Bella had seen, but discussing it further with someone like Edwina felt like a waste of time. As she turned, she caught sight of the couple's garage again. 'I was sorry to hear about your Audi, by the way.'

Edwina's smile vanished. She cared about the vehicle all right. 'Who told you about that?'

'I'm afraid I can't remember. You know what Hope Eaton's like.'

'All too well. You were lucky, weren't you, Bob?' she said to her husband. 'I expect they'd have started on your Jaguar next. Presumably something disturbed them. Well, if you don't mind, I'd better get on and have some breakfast. I'll see you at singing practice.'

On their way back to town, Bella turned to John. 'You'd think Edwina would at least wonder if Bea's okay.'

'Perhaps they don't get on.'

'If that's the case, why do they live a stone's throw from each other?'

John shrugged. 'To be fair, Bea's house is up for sale.'

He had a point. 'We need to find her, make sure she's all right and discover what's behind all this.'

23

ONE MISSING, ONE DEAD

Bella texted Barry Dixon to relay her conversation with Bea West's parents. 'I wonder where Bea's moving to,' she said to John. 'If it's outside Hope Eaton she might have connections there, or maybe she's moving in with a partner. We need to find someone who knows her well. What about a fellow volunteer at the museum? Did she have any close friends?'

John nodded. 'Good thought. There was another woman her age. Danielle.'

'You have her number?'

He shook his head. 'And I doubt Sienna will give it to me. All the same, I'll try. If Danielle's volunteering today, she might even answer the phone.'

He called as they neared the Steps and Vintage Winter. She listened to his monosyllabic replies and thought dark thoughts about Sienna.

'No joy, I take it?' she said when he'd rung off. Bella would have been tempted to give his arm a comforting squeeze if she didn't know he'd hate it.

'Sienna says it's against data protection. Which it is, of

course. But she refused to ask Danielle to call me instead. She said she wasn't my secretary.'

Bella could feel her blood pressure rising. She bought a breakfast bap from Leo and tried to eat it without getting indigestion.

Matters weren't improved when Barry Dixon returned her text mid-morning thanking her for the update and pointing out there was no need for him to contact the estate agents if Bea's dad had heard from her. Bella texted back immediately.

Could you at least leave Bea West a message and ask her to call you in person?

After a considerable pause, she got a reply:

I think it's pointless, but I'll see if someone can get to it.

Then a follow-up message arrived:

Your friend Val's solution to the going-to-bed problem has helped, by the way. Thanks for that.

She hoped he'd remember that one good turn deserved another...

There was one other development that morning. Carys rang to say she'd been gossip-gathering after Leo had passed on the latest news.

'Bea West has handed in her notice at the high school.'

'Really? Is this to do with her moving house?'

'I don't think so, because her written resignation only arrived on Monday. She hasn't been in school since before the weekend.'

The feelings of urgency intensified. Bea had resigned the first working day after she'd graffitied her boss's walls – assuming the resignation letter was genuine and not sent to disguise her disappearance. Had what happened on Saturday night made up her mind? If she'd seen him tormenting Mary, she could have felt strongly enough to quit. Especially if she suspected he was involved in her death. Bella guessed Bea had no evidence – she hadn't gone to the police – but she could still imagine Adrian feeling threatened. People would say there was no smoke without fire. For a horrible moment she imagined him deciding to silence her, but then shook herself. She was getting worked up over pure speculation.

At lunchtime, Bella went back to the Nest as planned to ask if they'd managed to reach Bea West yet. Luckily, she got chatty Gail Hughes again.

'Some people just won't help themselves,' she said in response to Bella's question. 'I mean, here we are trying to sell her house and she's barely contactable at all. Just a text. I ask you! So if you want to speak to Ms West yourself, then I'm afraid you'll have to wait. And even if you'd like us to show you round there'll be a delay. She says she dropped some plates before she left and she wants us to book a cleaner to tidy up!'

That sounded above board, but Bella was still suspicious. There was no way those plates had simply been dropped. 'Of course, I understand.' She did plenty of sympathising, combined with admiring the woman's necklace. It was all going swimmingly until Bella mentioned Vintage Winter. She'd thought the woman might be a potential client, but she stepped back at the name of the shop.

'Oh yes, I've heard it mentioned.'

Sweet Agnes, that tone wasn't encouraging. 'All good, I hope?'

'Of course.' But Bella could tell she was lying. She needed to talk to John again. See if he'd found out what people were saying.

She was about to press Hughes for more information when a man in a suit came in. His glasses were in one hand, and he clutched at his hair with the other. He made straight for Hughes, and Bella guessed they were colleagues.

'I can't... I can't... it's horrible. So horrible.'

Hughes dashed from behind the counter. 'What is it? What's happened?'

'It's Olivia. Our Olivia.' He was almost gagging over his words.

Hughes gasped.

'They're saying they found her on Blackthorn Lane. Sprawled in the road. All grazed and her head all...' He stumbled to a temporary stop. 'Her bike was in a ditch. They... they think she must have been killed by a driver. A hit-and-run.'

24

MEDITATING ON MOTIVES

Back at Vintage Winter, Bella found a customer had just arrived. She had to hold in her feelings and postpone giving John the awful news as he welcomed them. She went through the motions of watching them stroll around the shop and judging how best to help them, but her mind was full of what had happened. Poor, poor Olivia. Visions of her flung down on the country road rose up. She imagined her long, ash-blonde hair surrounding her head like a halo, her limbs splayed at awkward angles. Defeated. And then she thought of the times she'd met her. How vulnerable she'd seemed when she'd asked about hiring Vintage Winter's stock. And how she'd clung to her husband, as though for dear life. He'd be going through hell.

As soon as Bella and John were alone, she told him. She watched as his lips parted, wordlessly, and his expression changed, moving from normal, to blank, to a look of pain.

'Who would have done such a thing? To knock her off like that and not even stop...'

Bella met his gaze.

He swallowed. 'You're thinking this is related to Mary?'

'The pair of them were closely connected. They argued the

day before Mary died. They were probably both aware Noah was up to something fresh. And Olivia was here when we found the draft of Mary's blackmail note.'

'But why would that make her a target?'

'Remember how shocked she looked? Her eyes were fixed on it. I think she knew what it was about. Maybe she guessed Mary was blackmailing Noah and that he'd gone to kill her on the back of it. Bernadette was talking about someone tormenting Mary when Olivia came in – that could have been news to her too. If she said something that betrayed her suspicions, I could imagine Noah deciding to kill her. He could go down for murder if his intent to kill Mary triggered her heart attack. He'd have had a lot at stake.'

John sighed. 'It's possible, I suppose.'

'And look at where Olivia was killed.' The spot had been pinpointed on a local news site. She showed John. 'Blackthorn Road, just near the stile that leads to the spring. It might be coincidence, but I can't help feeling it's all connected. I'm going to ring Tony. Tell him what's happened and see if he can give us any updates.'

She got through and managed to get him to agree to meet them in the Blue Boar that evening. After that, she called Carys, then nipped out to tell Leo, who'd already heard. Everyone in the café was talking about it. Bernadette had gone into a back room to have a good cry. Leo was putting on a brave face, but his eyes were red too. He gave Bella the hug of someone who realises life is never certain.

She patted him on the shoulder. 'Come along to the Blue Boar this evening at eight if you feel up to it. Carys says she'll be there.'

He nodded, lost for words, which was vanishingly rare.

Back at the shop, it was quiet. John was cleaning a beautiful square painting of the mill on Hope Clee Hill. Bella loved to watch him work, so absorbed and grounded. It would be a soothing activity in the current turmoil and it was coming up beautifully.

'I'm still concerned for Bea West.' She sat on a stool nearby. 'Dixon's team will never get round to contacting her now. Curse Sienna Hearst for not giving us her friend's number.'

John nodded. 'I'm going to watch the volunteers leave the museum later. See if I can intercept someone who doesn't hate us and pump them for information.'

The rest of the afternoon was unusually quiet. It made her think of Gail Hughes's strange reaction when she'd mentioned Vintage Winter, but she hadn't the heart to ask John about it now.

Given the lack of customers, Bella needed something to distract her. She got to work creating certificates with information on new items, but it was hard to focus. Thoughts of Olivia filled her head. When John's mobile rang, she jumped.

'Hello? Oh! Yes. That was kind of her. If you can help us, that could make all the difference. We're worried, you see.'

Bella stopped work and listened intently.

'Upper Bewley? Well, if you don't mind, that would be—Right, right. That's good to know. No, I've got a pen. Thank you. Ah, yes. I've heard a few people feel that way. Thanks very much again.'

Bella raised an eyebrow as he rang off.

'That was Danielle, the volunteer who's friendly with Bea.'

'Don't tell me Sienna passed on your message after all.' Bella was prepared to fall off her stool dramatically with shock.

'No. But a friend of Danielle's overheard Sienna's end of the call. She worked out it was me, and that Sienna was being obstructive, so she called Danielle herself.'

'What an exemplary human being!'

'Indeed. Danielle said she and this other volunteer were considering resigning, only they love the house so much.

They've stayed to try to keep old Mrs Hearst's vision alive, but it's proving difficult.'

'I imagine that's an understatement.' She knew John had found it a wrench to resign for similar reasons. 'So what does Danielle say?'

'That Bea has a close friend who lives in Upper Bewley. The sort you message daily with updates. Danielle's met the woman a few times. She says if Bea was worried about something she'll probably have confided in her. And I've got her address.'

25

THE TRAIL TO UPPER BEWLEY

Straight after work, Bella drove John to Upper Bewley in Thomasina. The news of Olivia Elsworth's death was starting to sink in, like a horrible grey cloud you knew would never lift.

'At least Bea's friend in Upper Bewley feels like a firm lead.'

John nodded. 'Let's hope we find Bea safe and sound.'

'And if she can tell us what she knows about the Fitzpatricks, we might get Dixon interested.'

They were travelling past open fields now, cattle grazing, the road lined with an abundance of cow parsley. It looked so wholesome. Bella tried not to worry about the killer getting to Bea first.

'By the way, the woman at the estate agents was weird when I mentioned Vintage Winter. I'm not imagining it, John, honestly. Have you asked around?'

She glanced at him and he looked shifty.

'What is it?'

'I don't know, but people are clamming up.'

That was worrying. No one clammed with John. He was Hope Eaton's universal uncle. What on earth were they holding back, and how could she find out?

She put it to one side as they entered Upper Bewley. 'Where did you say this friend lives?'

'Beyond the church on a lane to the left. It's just past a post box, apparently.'

Bella followed his instructions and found the place, a white-washed cottage even smaller than Bea's home, with a low front door painted a glossy black.

She pulled up as close as she could and she and John got out. Nerves were knotting her stomach. What if the friend couldn't help? 'What's she called again?'

'Chloe.'

Bella knocked at the cottage and heard movement inside. That was a good start. Half a minute later the door opened. Bella didn't know the woman who answered, but she gasped and took a step back, her eyes on John.

'Bea!' John said the word on a huge exhale of relieved breath.

So this was her. Bella could see the physical resemblance to her mother, but it was amazing how a different approach to dressing created an entirely different impression. Bea was wearing a belted knee-length dress with puff sleeves. She couldn't look more presentable if she tried. There were shadows under her eyes. She was certainly troubled.

'What are you doing here?' She seemed utterly perplexed.

'We were worried about you.'

'We?' Bea looked at Bella, who stepped forward to introduce herself.

'Your friend Danielle gave John this address. It's a bit of a long story. Do you think we could come in, if Chloe won't mind?'

Bea shook herself and nodded, stepping back. 'Chloe's away. She lent me her key. Please.'

They entered the one up, one down with a tiny lean-to kitchen at the back. Where on earth could the loo be?

Bea offered them orange juice and directed them to a sofa where Bella and John had to sit very snuggly together. He looked uncomfortable.

'So tell me what's wrong,' Bea said, as she put their drinks on a small coffee table and sat on a ladder-backed chair.

John turned to Bella. 'It's your story, to begin with.'

So Bella explained how she'd seen the graffiti at the Fitzpatricks' house, how she'd worried initially that the 'her' might be Fiona, and how she'd later wondered if it was anything to do with Mary Roberts and her death. She detailed the way she'd tracked the intruder, following the green paint, then spotted the 'For Sale' sign at Lilac Cottage and put two and two together.

'I wanted to find out what you knew. I knocked on your door, but there was no reply, so I looked for matching paint and saw you'd redecorated.' John was squirming next to her, probably at the lengths she'd gone to. 'When the estate agent couldn't get hold of you in person, we were worried in case...' How to put it so she didn't frighten Bea? But perhaps Bea was already conscious of the threat. She'd decamped to her friend's cottage after all. 'In case you were in danger,' she said at last.

Bea's look was far away, as though she was struggling to take it all in. Perhaps she was shocked that they'd managed to follow her so easily.

'We'd love to know what led to the graffiti.' Bella leaned forward. 'Mary died of natural causes but I'm certain there's more to it.'

'And there's been another death now too,' John said quietly.

'What? Who?'

Bella filled her in about Olivia Elsworth. 'If you know anything relevant to either her or Mary, it would be best to tell the police. They can protect you.' She thought of Barry Dixon and hoped she was right. She doubted they'd have the staff for proper surveillance.

'We could see there'd been an argument at your place,' Bella went on. 'The smashed crockery made it obvious. We were worried in case you'd had a run-in with someone already.'

Bea closed her eyes for a moment before meeting Bella's gaze. 'The smashed crockery is separate.' She flushed. 'I had a row with my boyfriend on Saturday evening. I was the one who smashed everything. I wasn't throwing stuff *at* him. He'd gone by that stage. I was letting off steam I was so furious. It's embarrassing.'

'Okay.' That was reassuring in some ways, and sheepishness explained her telling the estate agents she'd simply dropped the plates. 'Did you come here because of the row?'

Bea hesitated, then clasped her hands together and sighed. 'No. I came here because I was scared. You're right. The graffiti did refer to Mary Roberts and I did suspect Adrian was up to something.'

'What had you seen?'

Bea paused again. Maybe she was scared to tell them. 'I saw him hanging around near her place. Watching.'

'The night she died?'

Bea bit her lip, then nodded. 'And— And other times too.'

'How did it come about? Were you walking in the woods?'

'No, but nearby. In fact, you can see Springside Cottage from my house.'

'And you're sure it was Adrian? You saw his face?' She must have gone closer to investigate.

She nodded. 'I was worried, so I went to look.'

'And when did you come here?'

'The morning after I did the graffiti.'

'You heard Mary was dead?'

Bea twisted her hands and inclined her head.

'But you didn't go to the police,' Bella said, 'even though you saw Adrian more than once?'

'I didn't know it was him at first.' She sounded uncomfortable. 'And even when I did, I knew it would be my word against his.' She looked down at the floorboards. 'And then, of course, the death was natural causes.'

'Was it seeing Adrian torment Mary that made you quit your job?' John asked.

She nodded again after a moment. 'What do you think happened to her?'

They filled her in on the hooded figure Mary had seen, and the discovery of the homemade weapon.

'That was Adrian in the cloak,' Bea said at last. 'I saw him when it fell back from his face.'

'Can you tell the police about it?' Bella asked.

John nodded. 'Please, Bea. You'll be safer that way. Do you want to come back to Hope Eaton? Mum would put you up at the Blue Boar and keep an eye on you. It feels lonely here.'

But Bea shook her head. 'Thanks, but I'd rather keep my distance.'

Bella and John spoke at once, urging her to think again, but nothing they said persuaded her to change her mind. They had to make do with exchanging mobile numbers, in case of emergency.

'Don't worry.' Bea walked them to the door. 'I'll call the police and tell them what I know.'

26

LINKING THE CASES

Bella drove John straight back to Hope Eaton so they could each grab some supper before going to meet Tony at the Blue Boar. On the way, John worried over Bea, and Bella worried over what she'd said.

'What do you think about the row with the boyfriend?' she asked as she pulled out to overtake a tractor.

'The timing seems unlikely.'

'I know. I mean, obviously, it's all possible, but I'd assumed the graffiti, the mess in her house and her decamping to Upper Bewley were related. She's trying to sell Lilac Cottage, yet she didn't clear up before she left. It suggests she made a dash for it immediately.'

'She could have had the row, chucked stuff about, then been distracted by the sight of Adrian.'

'Whereupon she went closer to identify him. Quite something, when she was in the throes of such upset. And why would she care so much about Mary, anyway?'

John cocked his head. 'Perhaps her blood was up, after the fight with her boyfriend. Then maybe she was so incensed by Adrian's behaviour that she biked over to the Fitzpatricks' place, painted the graffiti, then went to bed. It was late by then.'

'True, and emotional upset is exhausting. I suppose I can imagine her dashing off the following day without clearing up, the moment she heard Mary was dead. She was probably terrified.' But it was still two lots of high drama in quick succession, apparently unrelated. It continued to niggle in the back of her mind.

By eight, the gang was assembled in the Blue Room at the Blue Boar. It was the inn's snug, and perfect for private conversations. Bella suspected it was Tony who had commandeered it. He was good at getting other customers to move if they were cluttering the place up. He'd act oddly, muttering words at random or striking up conversations about bizarre topics. That tended to work.

He was at the head of the table now. The rest of them assembled on either side, perched on the room's Chesterfield sofas.

Suddenly, Leo sat to attention. 'Uh-oh.'

Bella followed his gaze. Jeannie had spotted them through the room's internal window. Bella could tell from her look that she suspected something. Sure enough, she bustled in to join them.

'I presume this cabal is nothing to do with poor Mary Roberts and Olivia Elsworth's deaths?'

'If you presume that, Mother dear, then why are you here?' Leo rose and tried to steer her back towards the door, which was never going to work.

'Because Gareth is being very tight-lipped about the whole thing. I sense he knows something but is keeping quiet out of loyalty to you, John. I applaud the devotion but if there's something afoot then I demand to know about it.'

Naturally. There was no point in arguing at this stage. Bella summarised what they knew so far.

Jeannie ruffled her feathers. 'I can't believe you didn't tell me sooner.'

Gareth had appeared. Boxer must be holding the fort. 'We didn't want to worry you,' he said in his soft Welsh accent.

'Dear boy.' Jeannie took his hand. 'But I must be involved. Where do we stand following this shocking attack on Olivia?'

Tony leaned forward. 'The thinking is, she was knocked down by a stolen car. The doc reckons time of death would have been between ten and twelve thirty today. They're appealing for witnesses to come forward. That should narrow the time down further.

'A breaker's yard just north of here is missing a wrecked Peugeot. An old model, so the thief could have hotwired it. The skid marks match. The driver was heading into town, which makes a joyrider unlikely. They normally go like the clappers into the countryside. Besides, the local youths don't tend to careen around on a Thursday morning.

'The killer did a U-turn after the collision and the car hasn't been found yet. Our boy Barry's desperate to identify the driver of course, though he's not convinced it was a deliberate attempt to kill Mrs Elsworth.'

'But the circumstances are odd.' Bella leaned forward to press her point. 'You said yourself that the driver wasn't behaving like a joyrider.'

Tony shrugged. 'He could have been speeding in case he got caught after stealing the car. But given what we know, I'd say we can assume this was murder. If so, the driver must have known where Mrs Elsworth would be and when.'

'Horrific!' Jeannie's eyes were huge, her voice loud.

'I noticed Olivia was found near the stile leading to the Sacred Spring,' Bella put in.

Tony nodded. 'But Barry isn't linking the death to Mary Roberts's heart attack. There's still no evidence anyone entered her house.'

'But Mary and Olivia are connected through Noah.' Surely Dixon's radar was pinging?

Tony held up a hand. 'True. But there's no proof it was him menacing Mary Roberts, the effigy aside.'

Bella sighed. 'Just the opposite, in fact. We've found someone who saw Adrian Fitzpatrick dressed in a cloak, hanging around Springside Cottage.' She explained about Bea. 'She's promised she'll report it to the police now.'

'I *knew* there was something off about him!' Jeannie's eyes were bright.

Tony sipped his pint. 'There you are then. But if it was Fitzpatrick who was trying to scare Mary to death for the bequest, how do you make him fit for Olivia Elsworth?'

'Maybe she found him out,' Bella said. 'After all, they're connected. Both Olivia's kids were at the high school, though Noah's left now. And she's taking part in his fundraiser. Was.' She closed her eyes for a second. She mustn't cry. 'They must have dealt with each other when Noah got into trouble too, given he was reported to the police by Mary.'

'It's always possible.' Tony opened a bag of crisps. 'Fitzpatrick would have to be careless to let something slip, though.'

'Well, alternatively, perhaps Olivia caught him in the act.' Bella thought back to her movements. 'She was out walking the night Mary died, wasn't she? Where did she say she went?'

Tony referred to the bundle of confidential notes he kept loose in his back pocket. *Honestly.* 'Out from Crow Cottage where she lives, along Moat Street, then Heartsease Lane.'

'No witnesses?'

Tony shook his head.

'So she could be lying if she was scared.' Bella made a note of the route.

'Why wouldn't she have gone to the police if she'd seen Fitzpatrick enter Mary's cottage?' Tony offered his crisps around.

Bella was about to take one when she noticed they were Marmite flavour. She suspected Tony had chosen them deliberately to avoid losing too many. 'Perhaps she wasn't sure she could convince them. She'd put herself in danger if she reported him and nothing came of it.'

Tony nodded slowly. 'And if Fitzpatrick's guilty and the motive was greed, then where does the blackmail fit in?'

'Blackmail?' There was a brief interlude as Jeannie demanded more information and was duly filled in.

'The blackmail's a sticking point when it comes to Adrian, unless he went to kill Mary with more than one motive.' Bella had to admit it felt messy. 'And I can't believe it's not relevant. Olivia looked horrified when she saw the note. I think she knew what it was about and it convinced her that the recipient was guilty of attempted murder. The next thing we knew she was dead.'

'But Adrian's an odious man.' Jeannie sat back in her seat. 'I don't like this muddying of the waters.'

Tony grinned. 'I'm sure.' He turned to Bella. 'You already reckoned there could be more than one person at work though. Who else looks likely now?'

Bella glanced at her notebook. 'Noah. I can imagine Olivia protecting him for her husband's sake. Especially at first, if she thought Mary's death was the result of a nasty prank gone terribly wrong. Harry looked like Olivia's life raft to me.'

'I thought the same,' Carys said. 'What on earth must he be going through?'

Bella's eyes were pricking. It was horrendous to imagine it, and thoughts of grief always brought back her father's death too. She took a deep breath and focused on her suspect list. 'Noah would fit with the blackmail note as well. We know Mary had something on him and despite Olivia's denials, she could have known Noah was keeping a dangerous secret.

'When it comes to Fiona and Shane, Olivia could have seen

either of them enter Springside Cottage too. It would make her a threat and, as with Adrian, she could have baulked at going to the police if she doubted they'd act.'

'But once again there's the blackmail note to consider.' Tony rubbed his chin.

'Yes. It's hard to believe Olivia would have understood it if it had been sent to Shane, for instance. They're not connected as far as I know.'

Tony nodded. 'Any alternative motives for Olivia's killing?'

'If she knew about an illegal business of Noah's, he could have decided it was too dangerous to leave her alive.'

Tony swept crisp crumbs off the navy jumper he wore. He was lucky that Jeannie hadn't spotted him. 'Next steps?'

Bella met his eye. 'Will you hear what happens when Bea West contacts Barry about Adrian Fitzpatrick?'

He rubbed his hands. 'I'll make sure I do. Might solve the whole case.'

But Bella couldn't forget the row Bea claimed she'd had with her boyfriend, just before the Adrian drama kicked off. Two tumultuous events in one evening. It was a big coincidence if it was true. Like the time her sister, Suki, had claimed a cat had broken a jug of their mother's, when Bella knew she'd been rolling drunk the same night. Something else was making her twitch too, but she couldn't put her finger on it.

She shook her head. 'If it's not wrapped up by Bea's evidence, then we need to know where the key players were between ten and twelve thirty this morning. It might be time to book Thomasina in for her service at last. I can find out if Noah was at work. I'm sure the police will ask him but I'd rather check myself.'

Worry lines crossed John's face. 'How will you—'

'I'll think of something. Is there any way you can check on Adrian's movements, Carys?'

She nodded. 'Oh, the bliss of having a challenge that doesn't involve getting small children to sit cross-legged in assembly.'

It wouldn't be easy to pinpoint Shane Sadler's whereabouts, but she could work on that. And on Fiona too. But perhaps Adrian would be under arrest within twenty-four hours and none of this would be necessary.

Before the gang left, she drew John aside. 'I'm going to visit the Sacred Spring before work tomorrow. I can go over the stile from Blackthorn Lane. I want to know if that's where Olivia was heading when she was killed.'

John raised an eyebrow. 'You think you'll be able to tell from visiting?'

'Perhaps not, but I might get lucky. I certainly won't learn anything if I *don't* go.' Deep down, she felt she had to. She needed to force herself to look at the spot where Olivia had died and face it head-on.

He frowned. 'All right. I'll come too.'

'Half past eight by the stile?'

He nodded.

After everyone dispersed, Bella disappeared behind the scenes to see Boxer. He was busy tidying. The last food orders had been served.

He greeted her with his crooked grin. 'Hello, babs. Wondered when I'd see you again.'

She smiled back. 'Have you got time for a quick drink out front? We need to talk.'

He glanced at Gareth, who nodded. 'I'll finish off in here.'

Bella knew he secretly went over everything one more time after his underlings had finished. As Jeannie often noted, he was a perfectionist.

'How're things?' Boxer leaned against the bar. 'Time for us

to have another outing? I don't mind if there's no sleuthing involved.'

Beyond him, Bella could see his ex, Alison, sitting at a table with a girlfriend. She'd spotted Bella and Boxer all right. 'I'd be very tempted, normally.'

Boxer raised an eyebrow.

'If I wasn't convinced you're still in love with Alison.' And if it weren't for the snake, obviously.

Boxer's shoulders sagged.

'I'm right, aren't I?'

'I need to get past it. And I like you, Bella. Genuinely.'

'Thanks. The feeling's mutual. But anyone can see Alison's still hooked on you. Don't look round.'

He stopped mid head-turn. 'Thanks for trying to make me feel better, but Jeannie's already tried to act as a go-between. Alison wasn't interested.'

No surprises there. 'Jeannie will have taken your side. She's very partisan. Not that I'm saying you were in the wrong. But she could have made Alison dig her heels in.'

A ray of hope lit his eyes. 'You reckon?'

It was a no-brainer. 'All I can say is, Alison's looking daggers at me right now.'

'D'you think we should kiss?'

'Too risky. Go over to her after I leave and say I asked you out, but you've only got eyes for her.' Alison would probably forgive Bella in the end, and it was in a good cause. 'She needs a grand romantic gesture.'

Boxer grinned suddenly. 'I'll do it. Thanks, babs. She needs to admit she was wrong about that shrimp paste though.'

Shrimp paste-gate had been much discussed by the Jenkses. Bella tended to agree with Alison that it was best avoided, but throwing it out of the window had been tactless. Bella would have limited herself to a frank discourse about its shortcomings.

'Maybe leave it as something to laugh about when you're old and grey?'

'P'raps you're right.'

Bella left the pub, the feeling of Alison's eyes on her back.

She walked home via the high street. It was as she passed Narin's superior kebab shop with its tempting smells that she saw Noah Elsworth. He had his back to her and was stuffing down a large doner he didn't deserve. He'd just taken a huge mouthful when his phone went, so he answered through his food.

'What? Yeah, no, it doesn't matter. Forget it. No, I'll still go ahead. I've got the day off tomorrow now. I'll be on the road by half seven.'

Bella walked on slowly. Ted Ashcroft had probably given him compassionate leave. The callous little tick was clearly planning to use the time productively. She wondered what he was up to, and who was paying him.

Back at her flat, Bella thought through everything she knew. Adrian Fitzpatrick had a lot of questions to answer, but so did Noah. And he and Olivia lived in the same house. He could have known she'd be on Blackthorn Lane at a particular time.

Steeling herself, she set her alarm for six thirty. The early start was essential if she wanted to be there when Noah left home. She needed to find out his game.

27

SKULDUGGERY AND STATUETTES

Bella decided to take Thomasina on her Noah Elsworth mission the following morning. She'd have to find somewhere to hide her, but she'd never make it to Blackthorn Lane afterwards to meet John if she didn't have wheels. And of course, if Noah left his house by bike or car, she'd need her taxi to keep up.

On her way, she passed ivy-coated red-brick walls on her left, the view uphill to Hope Eaton's castle ruins on her right. In the end she found a gateway and parked Thomasina there. The grass was high on the other side, the lock on the gate rusty. She guessed the entrance wasn't much used.

After that, she snatched up the coffee she'd brought with her, donned her Audrey Hepburn-style hat and retraced her steps to a handy bus stop, right by Noah's home.

A moment later, she'd checked the timetable. No buses due for a while; she could wait without it looking odd, under cover of her brim. Hats were endlessly useful; she was glad she had some for every season.

Just before half past seven, as predicted, she heard movement over her shoulder, from the driveway of Crow Cottage.

'You hated her!' A girl's voice. Young, passionate. Rising in volume and pitch.

'So?' That was Noah. 'What's it to you? She wasn't *your* mum either. I'm glad she's out of our lives.'

'Think what you're doing to Dad!'

'Dad's an idiot. He should never have hooked up with her! Now, leave me alone.'

Charming. Bella heard an engine start. A motorbike. She leaped up and dashed along the pavement towards Thomasina, glancing over her shoulder. Noah had appeared at the top of the drive. He flicked the briefest glance up the road in her direction, then took a right, gravel and dust rising in his wake.

Bella ran, unlocking her car with the key fob as she went, then dashing her coffee down in the cup holder. She swung out of her parking space and managed to follow Noah along Long Reach and the Causeway, crossing the river, but by that stage he was way ahead of her. His acceleration beat hers hands down and his nerve made anything possible. He flew along Hope Clee Road, and at the top of Raven Climb, she lost him. She had no way of knowing which way he'd turned.

She sighed. 'Come on, Thomasina. Time to go and meet John.'

As she drove, she remembered following Shane Sadler. There'd been a motorbike behind her then. Of course, there were plenty around, but it had been a lonely route. She had a creepy feeling it could have been Noah, following her. But he hadn't turned off the motorway when she did, and he probably wouldn't know her from Adam.

Then she thought of the figure she'd seen outside the Hanged Man, the first time she'd watched Shane leave in his van. That could have been Noah too. Perhaps he and Shane were business partners, leaving town separately to avoid discovery. Noah had had all that cash when he was arrested for stealing the quad bike. It must have come from somewhere. And there'd been that secret look he and Shane had exchanged on May Day.

She needed to explore Shane's place, the very next time Matt spotted him at the Hanged Man.

Bella arrived on Blackthorn Lane to find John already waiting. She checked her watch, but she was almost exactly on time. He must have got there early.

She found a place to pull up, tucking Thomasina in near the stile which led to the spring. As she manoeuvred, she watched John lock his bike to a fence post. It triggered thoughts of Olivia and her final cycle ride. The calculated way the killer must have rammed into her left her full of impotent rage.

'Are you all right?' John approached her car.

'Just thinking about Olivia.'

He nodded. 'I know.'

'Let's go and look at the spring. I can't imagine why she might have been going there, but it's odd that she was so close to a place that was central to Mary's life. And it was the subject of the stolen statuette too.'

As they climbed over the stile, the wood worn smooth after years of weathering, she told him what she'd seen outside the Elsworths' house. 'The stepdaughter was upset about Olivia, but Noah was brutal. I need to know what he's up to. Olivia could easily have found out, just like Mary.'

'But then where does Adrian fit in? Bea saw him.'

'I know. But he could still have been trying to scare Mary to death. I'll bet he's greedy and Fiona admits she spotted her symptoms. She could have lied and known about the will.'

John shook his head. 'I still find it hard to believe she's involved in any way.'

'I know, I know. She's a former nurse turned charity worker.' Bella suppressed an eye roll. 'But think of the note I found from Mary in her bedroom. "I'm horrified at what you've been keeping from me." It might have been a great relief to Fiona when she died.'

John sighed.

They were walking along a narrow not-much-trodden path now, cow parsley, red campion, nettles and oxeye daisies to either side of them.

'As for Noah,' Bella went on, 'for all I know, he and Shane are in cahoots.' She explained her thoughts.

'I could imagine Noah doing it.' John's gaze was on the middle distance.

'So could I. But that goes for Shane and Adrian too. And I can still see Fiona being involved, even if it was at arm's length.' Bella thought of her weary, angry look as she'd opened the door on the night of Mary's death. She'd have been tense and worried if she knew Adrian was out committing murder. As for Bea West's graffiti, referring to the very woman he'd set out to attack – that would have felt like a disaster. Especially when she realised Bella had seen it. The saving grace, from her point of view, would have been that Mary's name wasn't mentioned.

The smell of grass, wildflowers and earth intensified as the day warmed. They were climbing steadily, circling Kite Hill. John kept glancing at his watch.

'It's all right. We've got time.' *Just.* Though if someone had found fault with Vintage Winter and was putting the word about, punctuality was even more important. 'We're nearly there.'

At last, they could see the spring. Bella could still make out the remnants of the flowers Hope Eaton's children had left as offerings to Sweet Agnes.

She thought of Adrian, ruining the beautiful surroundings by menacing Mary in his cloak. She wanted to know what the police thought. It wasn't surprising that Tony hadn't reported back yet. It was still early. Bea might have waited until this morning to report what she knew, though Bella would have got in touch immediately if it had been her. Either way, the police would be snowed under, working on Olivia's death. She jabbed in a text to Tony to remind him of the urgency.

John was looking ahead. 'Why d'you think Olivia might have come here?'

'To remove evidence because she was protecting someone? Coming via Blackthorn Lane suggests a secret visit. She probably knew Opal lurks in the woods, watching comings and goings.'

John shivered at Opal's name. 'I'm sure she did, but if she was visiting in secret, how would her killer know where to find her?'

'Noah might, if she wanted to remove evidence that could incriminate him. Even if she was protecting him, he might decide it was safest to kill her. He comes across as utterly callous.

'But perhaps her presence on Blackthorn Lane yesterday wasn't secret after all and she mentioned her plans in front of the murderer.'

'I suppose it's possible.'

They were walking around the grass in front of the spring now. Bella was looking for anything that might indicate that Olivia had been there, but the route they'd followed didn't look as though it had been used recently. Perhaps they were on the wrong track.

She was close to the path which led down towards Springside Cottage when she found it. Sitting in long grass, almost hidden.

Mary Roberts's carving of Sweet Agnes at the Sacred Spring.

28

CURIOUSER AND CURIOUSER

Bella photographed the statuette in the grass, then got John to pick it up using a tissue so she could take shots from other angles. The base was as Shane Sadler had described it. Scores in the wood meant there was no way to divine the inscription that had been carved there. After that, she texted Dixon the pictures, explaining where they'd found the carving.

'I don't suppose it'll make any difference, but at least he knows.'

John was looking at his watch again. 'We must dash.'

'All right.' She took the carving with her. Unless Dixon sent forensics, which seemed out of the question, she might as well keep it for reference. They could pass it on to Mary's executor later.

'I wonder why Mary's attacker dropped it?' John was jogging along the path, making his voice wobble. 'You'd think they'd take care if it was important.'

'You would.' Bella strolled after him. 'And why not come back for it when they realised they'd lost it? One thing's for certain, the statuette was handled frequently.' It had the tell-tale marks, caused by the skin's natural oils. 'Carys said Mary always kept it on the dresser, but she must have picked it up repeatedly.' She was increasingly sure it had had huge emotional significance for her.

When they reached the road, Bella offered to put John's bike in the back of the taxi and give him a lift.

He gave her one of his austere looks and claimed cycling would be quicker.

She wondered if he might be right, then felt disloyal and patted Thomasina's steering wheel as she got in. 'You're still invaluable. Could John carry a large chest of drawers on his bike? I think not.'

Back at Vintage Winter, John examined the carving again. He was wearing the gloves he used for precious items. Neither of them had touched it bare-handed. It was still possible Bella could find something to persuade Dixon to take its discovery seriously.

Bella was interested to see the work up close. 'It's like I said, it reminds me of George Frederic Watts's *Clytie*. He sculpted her metamorphosing into a sunflower, but it looks as though she's rising out of the plant. And here, the artist has Sweet Agnes's head and shoulders rising from rock and ferns.' The similarities felt too close to be a coincidence.

John looked up at her, pushing his glasses up his nose. 'There's a painting of that statue at the Hearst House Museum.'

'What, that?' Bella pointed at Sweet Agnes.

'No, *Clytie*.'

'That's very interesting. Why didn't you say so?'

He put his head on one side. 'This is the first time you've aired your thoughts out loud. At least in front of me.'

Was it really? Bother it, perhaps he was right. 'Remind me to always tell you what I'm thinking. Your responses are invaluable. I wonder if whoever carved this statuette was inspired by the picture. They might be a museum visitor or, more helpfully, the person who donated the painting. Can you remember who that was?'

John frowned. 'Not offhand, no.'

'Think Sienna will welcome us in if we go and snoop?' Bella had visited the museum regularly when her dad lived in town. Each exhibit had an information label, which included the name of the donor, if it hadn't come from old Mrs Hearst herself.

John grimaced. 'I'll assume that was a rhetorical question.'

'Let's sneak in when someone else is on duty.'

He looked pained. 'She's bound to come back and catch us.'

'Well, what's the worst that she can do? I'm up for a confrontation if you are. So long as she doesn't interrupt before we get some answers.'

'Couldn't I just call Danielle and ask her to check for us?'

It was a bit of an anticlimax, but she nodded. 'All right.'

While he was busy on his mobile, Bella attended to a couple of customers, but the shop was still quiet. People were entering the antiques centre but giving her outlet a wide berth. Sometimes they strode past hastily, without looking in Vintage Winter's direction, but a couple had pointed her way before moving on.

She was distracted by John, who'd ended his call and looked unusually animated. 'What is it? Who donated the painting?'

'Adrian Fitzpatrick's father.'

Bella met his eye. 'Wow. Is it possible that Adrian carved Sweet Agnes and gave it to Mary? Perhaps they were lovers after all.'

John's brow furrowed. 'It would explain Mary removing any giveaway inscription on the base. Fiona Fitzpatrick was a frequent visitor.'

'But would Mary really be such a hypocrite? And why would Adrian carve something incriminating on the statuette?'

'I'm not sure, but there's more to find out. Danielle says

they've unearthed two more carvings that sound similar to Mary's. They were in a box which was meant to be sealed for fifty years, kept in the Hearst House cellar. Old Mrs Hearst had respected the donor's wishes of course, but when Sienna heard about it she told Danielle to open the box immediately. She said she had no time for people's "whims". Danielle had already noticed the likeness to the Clytie painting.'

'Now that really is interesting. And did the statuettes come from Adrian or his father?'

'She needs time to check. She hopes there'll be records somewhere that will tell her.' He sighed. 'She says we can visit tomorrow lunchtime to compare Mary's statue with the ones they've found. She swears that Sienna will be out then.'

'Excellent. We need to check Noah's alibi for Olivia's death next.'

He looked agonised.

'I'll sort it out. You mind the shop.'

She disappeared into the office and sat on the stool in front of her drawing board, her eyes running over the suspects she'd noted for Mary's murder.

'*Hope Eaton Auto Repairs.*'

'Is Ted Ashcroft available please?' She needed it to be him. They'd already built a rapport. 'It's Bella Winter. I'm calling about my taxi.'

'*One moment.*'

The line went muffled and she heard Ted's name being called.

Seconds later he was on the line. '*Bella! Good to talk to you again. You've decided to book your taxi in for that service, have you?*' He didn't show any annoyance that she'd dragged him to the phone. The power of a drink at the Blue Boar. Jeannie would be delighted.

'That's right. When would suit you?'

'*Let me see now.*' She heard him tutting. '*I'm afraid we're a bit pressed just at the minute. One of my mechanics has gone AWOL.'*

'Noah?' It was as good a chance as any to bring him up. 'I can imagine he needs some space to come to terms with what's happened.' *Like hell.*

Ted sighed. *'Ah, no, not him, poor lad. I gave him the day off, though the timing's tricky.'*

'He must be in shock.' Bella was thinking on her feet. 'Was he at the garage when the news came in? I remember exactly where I was when I heard my dad had died. It stays with you, doesn't it?'

'That it does.' Ted heaved another sigh. *'He'd just arrived back from his lunch hour when the news broke.'*

Normally, she guessed lunch might be anywhere between twelve and two, and the police said Olivia had been dead by twelve thirty. It would have been tight, but Noah could have done it if he'd left at twelve, and had the stolen car ready. And he might have asked to take lunch early. She needed to fish for that information. 'Were there plenty of people around to support him? It must have been horrendous.'

'Just me, in fact. Everyone else was still out. I'd stuck around to hold the fort, thank goodness.'

Noah could have gone early then – certainly ahead of the others. There was a definite possibility he'd been on Blackthorn Road when Olivia was killed. She'd have to check with Tony – see if he'd managed to glean more information.

'Yes, thank goodness,' she echoed Ted. 'But I'm sorry, I've got us off topic. You were saying you're a member of staff down.'

'Ah yes, Ant Philby's off at the minute. An urgent domestic problem.'

In the background she heard someone snigger and say what sounded like, *'The lecherous old goat. Bet his wife's giving him hell...'*

Someone else talked over them. *'At least we all know he's*

using his time off to pick up the pieces. Unlike Noah. I saw him this morning near Meadow End, grinning like the Cheshire Cat.'

The words quickly became muffled, as though Ted had put his hand over the receiver. She could just about hear him telling them to be quiet, then his voice came clear on the line again. *'Ant'll be back soon, but right now, we're thin on the ground.'*

'Well, there's no hurry for the service.'

They arranged a date three weeks hence.

'How was it going with Noah before this awful business with Olivia? Any more smoothly?' She was wondering about the theft she'd witnessed; you'd think it would have come to light by now.

'Nothing to report, but I'm not sure what effect the bereavement will have. We'll see.'

Bella replied on autopilot. 'I'm sure your support will make all the difference.'

After they'd said goodbye and rung off, Bella sat there stewing over what she'd seen at the repair shop. She'd been sure Noah would get found out without her help, but perhaps she'd made a mistake. Sometime soon, she'd need to tell Ted what had happened.

Half an hour later, as Bella chatted to a day tripper who'd bought a vintage slipware jug, she saw John snatch up his vibrating phone and retreat into the office.

As the jug woman left the shop and Bella waved her off, she could hear his voice faintly through the wall. He was sounding animated again.

A moment later he reappeared. 'That was my cousin Tom, Mary's executor.' John was barely suppressing a smile. 'He wants us to go and value her house contents. They don't go to Fiona with the cottage. I suppose Mary knew she was well off and wouldn't want for anything. We might be asked to sell the rest, which is good news. The profits will go to charity.'

'That's amazing. We'll get to investigate Springside Cottage to our hearts' content.'

He put his head on one side. 'I had a feeling you'd regard that as an important benefit.'

Bella was imagining all the missing bits of puzzle she might acquire. Perhaps she could work out what Fiona had kept from Mary, which 'changed things'. Or she might find a response to Mary's blackmail note, assuming it had been sent. And then there was her secret knowledge about Noah. Had she got evidence, squirrelled away? The possibilities were endless.

'When can we get in there?'

The small smile played on John's lips again. 'Tomorrow morning. We can go before we open.'

Another early start, but it would be worth it. She came down off her high at the sight of Adrian Fitzpatrick, crossing St Giles's Close. He was heading towards the Steps, smiling as though he hadn't a care in the world. You'd think the police would be interviewing him by now; he shouldn't look so relaxed.

She called Tony and demanded information.

'I've just got off the line from the nick, as a matter of fact.' Tony's gravelly voice reverberated down the line. 'Thought I'd get you an update at least. There was no one to talk to earlier. Too busy. But the news now is interesting.'

He really knew how to spin out a good story. 'Yes?'

'Bea West hasn't reported what she saw.'

'What? She's supposed to be too scared to stay in Hope Eaton.'

'Perhaps she's frightened of repercussions.'

'Maybe.' Bella planned to find out, the moment she'd rung off. She'd ask John to call Bea, as an old friend. 'By the way, any news on alibis for Olivia Elsworth's death?'

He grunted. 'That's an interesting one too. Apparently, the un-lovely Noah asked to leave work for lunch at half eleven. He *says he was meeting a mate, and said mate swears they were together, but the mate's got form, and so has he of course, so...'*

'Hmm.'

'For what it's worth, his boss at the garage says he often asks to take lunch at odd times.'

Not the clear-cut answer she'd been hoping for. 'What about the others?'

'No reason to question them, as they're not tying the cases together.'

It was deeply frustrating. They said their goodbyes after she'd made Tony promise to keep her up to date.

She went back to join John, who was dusting. 'Could you please call Bea and find out if she needs help going to the police about Adrian Fitzpatrick? She doesn't seem to be able to manage it on her own.'

He looked uncomfortable. 'All right, but we can't force her hand.'

He went into the office and Bella hovered outside, so she could hear.

But Bea didn't answer.

Bella folded her arms as John reappeared. 'Here we go again.' She was starting to feel less worried about Bea's safety and more bothered about what she was playing at.

29

OLIVIA'S LATE-NIGHT WALK

At lunchtime, Bella headed to Heartsease Lane. Olivia had claimed she'd walked there, the night Mary died. If Bella could find a witness to prove it, it would be less likely she'd been near Springside Cottage, watching Mary's stalker enter the house. Or indeed, entering the place herself, to silence Mary because she was involved in Noah's underhand dealings. If she'd done *that* then Bella could well believe Noah had killed her, to tidy up a loose end. Even if they'd cooperated for practical reasons, he'd clearly hated her.

Bella had leafleted most of the town about Vintage Winter over the course of the last few months. To begin with she'd knocked on every door and introduced herself too, but it had been too time-consuming. She'd taken to visiting just a couple of houses in person in each road, then leafleting the rest. Her hope was that neighbour would chat to neighbour and word would spread.

Now, she was glad she hadn't managed to speak to everyone. She could claim she was calling as a follow-up to the leafleting, then work Olivia into conversation.

She was still en route when her mobile rang. Carys.

'*Agent Jenks, reporting for duty!*' There was a note of hysteria in her laugh. '*Horrendous trip to the swimming baths with the small-but-vocal ones this morning. One of them managed to gum up the pool pump with a toy stegosaurus. Anyway, I bumped into a group from the high school in the changing rooms. One of the admins was with them and she says Adrian was in his office all yesterday morning, dealing with some accounts.*'

'Thanks. That's useful.' Jeannie would be disappointed, and it didn't help with solving the mystery. 'How did you manage to ask?'

'*I said I'd tried to call him about the fundraiser, but he didn't answer.*'

'Did the admin actually see him, do you think?'

'*I'd say not. Her office is across the corridor from his and he told her he mustn't be disturbed. She wasn't surprised he hadn't answered my call. He normally shunts them to voicemail if he's busy now Mary's no longer with them. So it's not conclusive, I'm afraid.*'

'Not to worry. It'll be even harder to work out where Fiona and Shane were. I wonder what they'll do about the fundraiser. They'll have to cancel it now, surely?'

'*I certainly hope so. The admin says they'll be in touch.*'

An end to the meetings would cut off one of Bella's sources of information, but it couldn't be helped.

After they'd rung off, Bella began her knocking. Heartsease Lane was a favourite of hers: full of quaint cottages with low front doors, set on a steep incline. At the end of the road, the houses gave out and you could walk up Gallows Hill.

Bella rapped a fox-head knocker on a red front door. Inside she could hear a child crying. That was positive. Anyone with a baby might have been up in the night, just like Olivia. She introduced herself to the woman who answered, carrying a toddler on her hip, and was relieved that her face didn't fall when she mentioned her beloved shop. As ever, she presented herself as a neighbour first and a businesswoman second.

'I love your door knocker.' Mustn't look covetous.

'Thank you!' The woman smiled. 'Not mine though, actually, I'm Granny – house-sitting and looking after this one while Mum and Dad enjoy a long weekend.'

Ah, less good news. She probably hadn't been here on the crucial night. Bella took out a fresh copy of her leaflet anyway, then moved into gossip-gathering mode. 'I was going to do Moat Street as well, round the corner, but I heard about the poor woman from there who died.'

'The hit and run?' The woman's eyes were wide. 'I heard about it too. I live in town, the other side of the river. Terrible, isn't it? You just don't know what's coming.'

'Too true. I'd met her. We were going to work together.' She explained about Olivia's proposal to hire some of her stock. 'She seemed so nice. Unassuming, too.'

'My daughter said she was friendly. Always asking after this little monkey here.' She nodded at her grandson and sighed. 'I only knew her by sight.'

'I think her business was struggling. She said she'd wandered up here in the small hours, thinking about things. I suppose your daughter or son-in-law might have seen her actually. I imagine they're up in the night half the time.'

The woman bit her lip. 'They might have. My daughter didn't mention it. But how sad that the poor woman was having a miserable time, as well. I'll tell you who I did see though. Her stepson, Noah.' She cocked her head. 'Everyone knows *him*, of course. He was near my place on Meadow End.'

The name rang bells. After a moment, Bella had it. Someone at Hope Eaton Auto Repairs had seen him near there too.

'I have to say,' the woman went on, 'I wondered what he was up to. There's only one house beyond where I live and that's

Shane Sadler's. Skulking along, Noah was. I remember thinking he must be going to Shane's. Birds of a feather and all that.' Her words echoed Carys's on May Day. 'But perhaps I'm being unfair. Noah might have changed.'

Highly unlikely, in Bella's opinion. She wanted to know what he'd been up to as well but she needed to focus on Olivia for now. 'Can I ask a slightly odd favour?'

The woman looked curious and leaned forward, tucking a stray strand of hair behind one ear.

'When your daughter gets back, would you mind asking if she noticed Olivia walking along this road last Saturday night? It was when Mary Roberts died, and I'm worried in case her death and the hit-and-run are related. The police aren't taking me seriously, but my dad used to be Hope Eaton's sergeant and I know he'd have been concerned.'

'Your dad?' The woman looked again at Bella's card. 'Winter. Of course! Douglas Winter. He was such a nice man. He helped us when we had some problems with a neighbour. The tenant before Shane, as a matter of fact. He knew the whole town so well.' She nodded at Bella and waved her business card. 'I'll ask, and I'll call if I have news.'

Bella smiled her thanks. Emotion had got to her; if she spoke, it might spill over.

She carried on with her mission after taking some deep breaths, repeating her spiel whenever anyone answered their door. Between calls, the memory of the motorbike which had followed Shane was high in her mind. It seemed increasingly likely that it had been Noah, and that they'd been travelling in convoy. She thought of Shane bad-mouthing him in the Hanged Man. He'd sounded vehement, which made sense if he'd wanted to put people off the scent.

Some of the residents on Heartsease Lane were friendly, some less so, but all unbent a little when she mentioned the hit-

and-run. It was natural to want to share. However, none of them had seen Olivia on her night-time walk.

Bella turned to dash across Castle Street, then cut through the castle grounds. She was determined to get back to Vintage Winter by afternoon opening time. Thoughts of buying a bike flitted briefly through her mind... As she strode on, her focus returned to Bea West. After getting no reply from her, John had sent her a text, asking how things were going. It was the most tactful way to proceed, but Bea hadn't replied by the time Bella had left. Bella hoped she was all right, but her gut instinct said she was. She still felt there was something slightly odd about Bea's tale. The way she'd left smashed crockery on the floor of the house she was trying to sell. Even though the row which had sparked the breakages hadn't triggered her departure. Apparently.

As she dashed up Castle Place and the high street, bits of information floated in her head. Bea's graffiti and the destruction of her plates, which she said she'd caused herself. The fact that she'd resigned from her job at the high school, but hadn't called the police. The way she'd gone AWOL, then contacted her dad but not her mum. Her mum's irritation with her. And the vandalism to her mum's car when her dad's hadn't been touched. And then there'd been Fiona, weary-looking, and Edwina's terrible singing voice.

Suddenly, Bella was convinced she knew the truth.

As she re-entered the shop, she turned to John, who'd naturally got back before her. 'Did you ever get a reply from Bea?'

He frowned. 'Yes, and it was odd. She said the trip to the police station went fine and that she was okay. Maybe it's just that Tony hasn't updated you yet.'

'I very much doubt it.' She told him what she thought.

30

BEA SPILLS THE BEANS

John was due to meet Gareth, so after they'd shut up shop Bella went alone to Upper Bewley to find Bea. She parked further away from the tiny, whitewashed house this time. She didn't want Bea to guess who was calling and hide. By rights, she ought to be wary, whoever knocked. Her life could be in danger. In reality, Bella didn't think Bea would be that frightened.

She hugged the edges of the fields as she walked, to keep her approach secret. After using the black iron knocker, she heard movement inside the cottage and rapped again gently. At last, the door opened a crack.

The moment Bea saw Bella, she started to close it again, but then paused. Bella guessed she didn't have the face to slam the door.

'Sorry to bother you again, and for everything that you're going through, but I think we need to talk.' She folded her arms. Bea needed to realise that she wasn't going anywhere.

Bea didn't meet her eyes. 'All right. You'd better come in.'

Bella closed the door after her and Bea ushered her through to the living room, offering her the sofa once again, but Bella took the chair.

When Bea had sat down too, Bella leaned forward. 'We need to know what really happened. It's important. As I said, I believe someone had a hand in Mary's death. They might not have killed her, but I think they would have if she hadn't died first. And now Olivia's dead too, of course.'

Bea flinched. 'You honestly think that someone set out to kill Mary, and the deaths are connected?'

'I'm convinced of it.'

Bea took an unsteady breath but didn't reply.

'You didn't see Adrian in a cloak near Mary's place, did you?'

She sighed. 'No.'

Bella should have seen the truth sooner. As she'd replayed their conversation in her head, she'd realised Bea hadn't mentioned a cloak until she had. 'Did you see *anyone* near Mary's cottage?'

She was blushing now, her hands over her face. 'No. It *is* in sight of my home, but only from an upper-floor window. I'd probably need binoculars.'

'I think I understand your graffiti now. *Leave her alone.* You were talking about your mum, weren't you, not Mary?' Bella might have guessed there'd been a powerful reason for Adrian to recruit Edwina as a backing singer. He cared about appearances, and she wouldn't boost the school's standing. She patted Bea quickly on the shoulder. 'I understand. I can see why you did it. Your mum and Adrian are having an affair, aren't they?'

A tear dripped from Bea's cheek onto her skirt. 'Yes. He's not Mum's first but he's the most cavalier. I'm terrified Dad will find out. It's been horrible, watching them walk hand-in-hand past my place when he's away. They take such risks. It would kill Dad. He still adores Mum, against the odds. Whereas I can't stand the sight of her these days. Or Adrian.'

'That's why you handed in your notice and you're moving away?'

She nodded. 'I just can't watch. I've tried to stop them, but it hasn't worked. I'm sorry I lied to you. It was very wrong. But when I realised you suspected Adrian of being involved in Mary's death, it was tempting to agree. I wanted to hurt him. To get him into trouble. But it was a spur-of-the-moment impulse. I knew the minute you left I couldn't lie to the police.'

It was as Bella had thought. 'Did you vandalise your mother's car as well?'

'I shouldn't have done that. I could be prosecuted. I bet she'd press charges.'

It had always seemed odd that the vandal had targeted just one expensive vehicle and not the other. Edwina's explanation, that they must have been disturbed, seemed unlikely. Who was there to disturb them in that remote area?

'And you smashed the crockery in a rage? After you saw them, on the same night that you did the graffiti?'

She nodded.

'Can you tell me what happened? The timing might be important.'

Bea frowned. 'It was latish. After twelve, I suppose. I saw Adrian appear in the lane. Dad was away and Mum came out to meet him. They stood there kissing in the moonlight, right outside my cottage. I was so angry. I felt as though they were taunting me. Mum knows how I feel about it. She thinks I'm a prude.' She drew in a deep breath. 'Then they went off towards Mum and Dad's house. To sleep in *their* bed. Well, not sleep...'

'So you grabbed the paint you'd been using to decorate, took your bike and made for Adrian's house.'

She nodded. 'I wasn't thinking straight. I suppose I wanted to make him worry about his precious reputation. Get his wife asking questions. But that was cruel. I was protecting my dad but throwing Fiona into the thick of it.'

Bella thought of her tired look. 'I have a feeling she might have known already. That he was out with *someone*, at least.'

Bea clutched at her hair. 'Why doesn't she put her foot down?'

'It's Adrian's fault. He's not a child.' He just acted like one. Her younger sisters flitted through her mind.

'No, no. You're right.'

'I see why you're asking, though. Maybe she still loves him, though why she should is a mystery. What did you do after you'd cycled home?'

Bea sighed again. 'I was still furious. I smashed the plates you saw, but it wasn't enough to get it out of my system. I could see a light in my parents' bedroom. It made me feel sick!'

Bella sympathised. Her mother had started to show a keen interest in other men before she and Douglas had divorced. Her dad had been well aware. She was sure they'd only stayed together for as long as they had because of her existence.

'I followed them,' Bea was saying, 'got some gravel and threw it at the window. I'm surprised it didn't break, I was so furious. Then Adrian pulled back the curtains to look. He had his shirt off already. It was disgusting. I suddenly felt I couldn't face him, so I ducked behind a tree and stood there, shaking. It was stupid to torture myself. They didn't turn the lights off. I could see them and hear them too.' She shuddered. 'Then at last, the window went dark. That's when I keyed Mum's car. I needed to do something to let my feelings out.'

'Do you know what time you arrived at the house, and how long you watched for?' Bella held her breath.

Bea frowned. 'I biked straight home from Adrian and Fiona's, dropped off the paint and broke the plates. I must have left Lilac Cottage again by quarter to two. I'd have been outside Mum and Dad's house within a couple of minutes.'

Before Mary had died. 'And do you remember when you got home?'

'About half past four. I checked the time because I saw

Adrian walk past just after I'd got in, as I was closing my bedroom curtains. Getting home before his neighbours could see he'd been out all night, I suppose.'

The rat. But rat though he was, he couldn't have been the one to scare Mary to death.

31

JEANNIE'S TAKE ON THE WHOLE AFFAIR

Bella dropped Thomasina home after visiting Bea West, then went straight to the Blue Boar. She should have trusted her instincts from the outset. At least she'd finally got the truth.

She knew John would be at the inn, and Gareth and Jeannie too, of course. She could update them and take stock. She'd forgotten she might also run into Boxer's ex (or possibly now current) girlfriend, Alison. She was sitting at the bar when Bella arrived.

It was the young barman, Bill, who served her, his eyes flicking to Alison for a moment. He blushed as he took her order for a glass of Gareth's summer cup. 'Er, just so you know, Boxer and Alison are back together. Isn't that great?'

Bella remembered to act her part just in time and replied with less enthusiasm than she felt. 'Ah... Oh, well, yes, of course.'

Bill gave her a sympathetic look. 'Want me to add something stronger to the summer cup?'

The very idea... 'Can you imagine what Gareth would say? No, I'll be fine, thanks very much.' Coming across as a tragic figure wasn't ideal, but perhaps a good deed didn't truly count unless you had to suffer for it. She didn't grudge Boxer. He'd been a hero when she'd needed a co-conspirator. Besides, she wanted him to be happy.

All the same, *bother*.

Jeannie appeared, her head on one side, and patted Bella's arm. Bella gritted her teeth. They'd all forget about it in a day or two.

'John's about,' she said. 'He hasn't eaten yet.' She glanced at Alison. 'Why don't you find a seat outside and I'll bring you some food? What'll you have?'

Bella chose, then Jeannie leaned forward and lowered her voice. 'Any news?'

She nodded. 'Plenty.' Jeannie wouldn't like it. She was longing for Adrian to be guilty, which Bella could well understand.

Jeannie nodded, her wild, flyaway hair escaping from under its scarf. 'I'll come out and consult.'

The beer garden at the Blue Boar was in the courtyard, between the inn and the old stables and coach house where Jeannie let Bella keep some of her stock. In winter and after dark, it sparkled with twinkling lights. On this sunny May evening, it was festooned with flowers in large pots and window boxes – from herbs for Gareth's dishes to tumbling purple aubretia and white-snow-in-summer, cascading over the sides of the planters.

The iron tables and chairs were painted cornflower blue and sat on the courtyard's ancient cobbles. It meant jiggling your table, so it wobbled less, but it was worth it. You could imagine yourself back in time, sitting out there. Besides, it was quite nice not to be under Alison's glare.

John appeared a moment later with a half of Hobsons Shropstar. 'How was Bea?'

Bella filled him in and he let out a long sigh. 'News indeed. So where are we?'

'Waiting for your mum. She said she'd come and consult too.'

John didn't commiserate with her over Boxer while they waited, which was a relief.

Jeannie bustled up minutes later with Bella's shallot and goats' cheese tarte tatin and John's crab risotto. A second later, she'd plonked herself onto a spare blue chair. 'Right. Let's have it then!'

Bella broke the news that Adrian had a cast-iron alibi for Mary's death.

Jeannie looked most put-out. 'You're absolutely sure?'

'Given the fact that Bea would be just as delighted as you if he were involved, I'd say so, yes.'

She groaned, then appeared to rally. 'The affair is bound to come out, though. Impossible for us to say anything, obviously. Poor Bob West. We can't be the ones to reveal the truth, but keeping a secret like that in a town this size never works.' Jeannie had her head on one side now. 'You're all right about Boxer and Alison, aren't you? I know you suspected they were still in love. I think my mediation must have finally paid off.'

John glanced at Bella for a fraction of a second, but didn't say anything.

'I'm pleased for them. Honestly.' *Enough, already.* 'But let's get back to the case.'

'You shouldn't push your feelings aside, you know.' Jeannie leaned forward. 'Very bad for you.' Then she frowned. 'I recommend you talk out your sorrow. You can come and see me about it, any time.

'The Fitzpatrick/West situation needs my attention too. They must put the spark back into their marriages. I might recommend one of our salsa nights, though of course people do swap partners during the sessions, so perhaps not. Leave it with me.'

John was clenching his teeth.

'So, what about our suspects?' Jeannie added at last.

'We're down to Fiona Fitzpatrick, Shane Sadler and Noah Elsworth. Though it's still possible Olivia was involved in some way.'

'She can't have been!' Jeannie's eyes were popping. Bella would have to defuse her before half the garden heard what she had to say.

'I agree it's very unlikely. We hardly need to discuss it.' The perfect precursor to doing just that. It always worked. 'But of course, she was under financial pressure with her business failing. And when you're in charge, that can consume you, especially if you have employees you mind about. And she was caring, wasn't she?'

'Oh, undoubtedly.'

'Quite. So I think she was under real strain before she died. She and Noah didn't get on, but what if they'd found some joint way of making money? Something that didn't seem to hurt anyone directly, and might save her business and her employees' livelihoods...'

'I suppose it's just possible.' Jeannie's brow looked like a three-dimensional map of the Lake District.

'And then, at a pinch, she could have known or guessed that Noah was involved in Mary's death.' Gently does it. 'Perhaps she saw him enter Springside Cottage and assumed at first that what happened was a prank, gone terribly wrong. I still haven't found anyone who can corroborate her claim that she walked near her house that night, and not in St Giles's Holt. She could have baulked at going to the police, either out of loyalty or if she was mixed up in Noah's dodgy dealings.'

Jeannie was about to rise again.

'It would be tiny, incremental steps into wrongdoing,' John said.

Bella shot him a grateful look. 'That's right. And once she went down that path, it would be hard to escape.' True or not,

Bella couldn't forget her look as she'd clung to her husband. As though the security meant everything to her, but it was under threat. Perhaps it was that feeling of fragility which had led to their relationship's renaissance. Olivia could have been shocked into realising the tremendous value of what she had. Her and Noah's arrest would smash it to pieces. 'In the last few days, Noah could have decided he didn't trust her not to talk. I'm convinced Olivia knew who Mary's blackmail note was meant for.' *I imagine you regret it now, but it's too late. It's time to pay your dues.* 'If it was for Noah, it might have convinced her he intended for Mary to die. Perhaps she tackled him about it or said enough to worry him. And we know he left the garage early for lunch the day she died. He could have done it if he'd hurried.'

'Noah would be the primary wrongdoer.' John's gaze was fixed on his mother.

Jeannie sighed. 'That I could see.'

'I think Noah is involved in some kind of clandestine activity,' Bella said, swallowing a mouthful of the goat's cheese tart. Gareth had done it again. It was the best she'd ever tasted. 'I saw him steal from a colleague, but it's more than that. He certainly wasn't using his compassionate leave to mourn poor Olivia. I overheard him agreeing to some kind of arrangement and he hared off on his motorbike at half past seven this morning. If only I'd been quicker, I might have found out where he went. Then a woman on Heartsease Lane said she saw him heading towards Shane Sadler's place. One of his colleagues had seen him in the vicinity too. I'm starting to suspect he was behind me the night I followed Shane.'

Jeannie shook her head. 'I blame myself. I saw this coming and didn't find a way to intervene. If he's not guilty, I must work out how to divert his attention to something more honest. That curfew! I ask you. How was that supposed to help? All that time in his bedroom, plotting and scheming. It must have been awful for Olivia too.'

Bella was keen to keep them on track. 'The upshot is, we think Noah's involved in something dodgy and that Mary had discovered it. Olivia might have been embroiled in it too, and possibly Shane Sadler. Noah could have been there the night Mary died and he had opportunity for Olivia's hit and run as well.'

Jeannie clasped her hands together. 'What have you discovered about Shane? He's long been a worry.'

'He loathed Mary after she made a fool of him, and if he's up to something criminal, maybe she found out. That could answer the "why now" question. It'll be hard to check his alibi – he does odd jobs according to Matt, so he's here, there and everywhere. But I've asked Matt to tell me next time he spots him in the Hanged Man, or heading out of town.'

'You'll follow him again?' As ever, Jeannie's disapproving shudder reminded Bella of a hen ruffling her feathers. 'You must take care, Bella. You're not to take the place of the police!'

Bella had already decided not to mention her plan to trespass on Shane's land. She could tell the suggestion was weighing on John's mind. He was jiggling his leg. She fought the urge to tap it. It was terribly irritating. 'Don't worry, I won't do anything you wouldn't.'

Jeannie looked at her narrowly. Bella was quite sure she'd do all sorts of things with gusto if she felt it was necessary, despite her words of caution.

'As for Fiona, she was home alone and miserable while Adrian made merry with Edwina West. She admits she'd noticed Mary's symptoms and for all we know she could have found out about the bequest. If her marriage is intolerable, she might be very glad of a lovely house of her own.'

'But she's a nurse, Bella! Or was.' Jeannie was back to being scandalised. 'It's her mission to preserve life, not take it away.'

'I know.' The number of times it had been mentioned... 'It's hard to believe, but she's clearly been having a difficult time and I also think she fell out with Mary.' Bella reminded Jeannie of Mary's letter which implied Fiona had been deceitful. 'Who knows what went on between them? Perhaps Mary planned to cut Fiona out of her will. She could have been blackmailing her, as well.'

'I hate to think of her as a suspect too, Mum,' John said quietly. 'But Bella's right; she has to stay on the list.'

Bella took a deep breath. 'The problem is checking Fiona's alibi. I can't ask outright. I'll try a dual approach: get enough evidence to force the police to link the cases and in the meantime, find out where she was via casual chit-chat.' Something as sad and horrific as Olivia's death was on everyone's lips. 'The astounding thing is that Adrian's called another fundraising meeting for tomorrow night.'

Jeannie sat up straighter. 'I can't believe the event will go ahead.'

'Perhaps he'll just pay tribute to Olivia and call it off. Either way, it means I can talk to Fiona. Carys will be there too, of course. She can have a go as well.'

Jeannie shifted in her seat. 'So, Noah Elsworth is our top suspect.'

Bella agreed. 'But Fiona's up there too, and Shane certainly has questions to answer.'

After Jeannie went back to her customers, John moved onto lemonade as they discussed the visit to Springside Cottage the following day.

Bella sipped the Crodino she'd ordered. 'We'll do the valuations, obviously.'

John raised his eyes to heaven. 'I thought that was a given.'

'But our primary objective will be to search Mary's belongings for anything that might relate to her death.'

The light was fading when a text alert sounded on her phone.

It was Matt. Shane Sadler was settling in for a drink at the Hanged Man, accompanied by a gaggle of friends.

I gather you won't have Boxer for company, Matt had written. *If you want a stand-in while you explore his place, I have a rare break in my busy womanising schedule. Also overheard Sadler take an interesting call this evening. I can fill you in.*

Great. He'd heard the Boxer gossip too. She turned the phone to show John, who gave her a sympathetic look.

'You could just not do it.'

'But we need the evidence, John.' She could feel her dad, powering her on, and she had the skills. Her job had taught her to take nothing at face value. If something was off at Shane's place, she was sure she'd pick up on it. 'Shane's up to something, and where does Noah fit in? If Mary was onto one of them, she was probably onto both. And Shane might have a key to Springside Cottage from when they were married.'

He nodded. 'All right, then. I was going to go home with Gareth as soon as he's finished, unless you want me to save you from Matt?'

It was no good; she couldn't do it to him. He deserved some time at home with his partner after a long day. Besides, she didn't need saving. If she couldn't cope with Matt for an evening, it would be pretty pathetic.

'It's okay, but thanks. Once more unto the breach...' She texted Matt back, telling him she'd meet him on the corner of Hope Clee Road and Meadow End as soon as she could get there.

'Do you want to borrow my bike?' John said. 'It's just outside and it's got a dynamo.'

She couldn't believe she was even considering using two wheels again. A few months ago, she'd have dismissed the idea out of hand. But she was wearing her 1950s capris, which would work, and Thomasina would stick out like a, well, a London taxi.

'Go on, then, if you're sure you don't mind. I can bring it back when I'm done.'

'Don't worry. Use it to get to Springside Cottage tomorrow and I'll borrow Gareth's.'

He was right. It would make the early morning trip to Mary's a lot quicker. Maybe she really should get her own.

As she went to unlock John's, her mind was on the cycle home. Matt would also be headed for Southwell Hall, unless he had some other late-night errand. He'd be on two wheels as well, no doubt.

It shouldn't be awkward. She wouldn't feel at all strange about it if she had to go with John or Leo.

Bother.

32

SHANE SADLER'S LAIR

Bella found Matt waiting for her on the corner: a shadowy figure standing against the thick trunk of an oak, almost invisible in the fading light. He was identifiable by his stance, relaxed against the tree in his scruffy black jeans and long-sleeved T-shirt, his dark hair wild in the evening breeze. She wondered if he ever combed it and decided probably not.

She locked up her bike and walked to join him. 'Thanks for offering up your rare free evening.'

She could just see his smile and his amused eyes. 'Think nothing of it. I wouldn't want to get bored.'

'Perish the thought.' She wanted to keep talking, so he didn't mention her reported rejection by Boxer. 'What's happened to Diana, or Delilah, or whatever her name is?'

They turned into Meadow End side by side and he laughed. 'Gone to see her brother.'

The fact that the model-like brunette had seen her in kimono-and-bedhead mode still rankled.

Matt gave her a sidelong glance and Bella tried to ignore the feelings it induced.

'So, what was this call you heard Shane take?'

She could just see him frown. 'It sounded like he was being called away again, but he refused. He said he thought he was followed last time.'

'Sweet Agnes, he must have spotted me. I love Thomasina, but she's not self-effacing. Still, it proves he's up to no good.'

Matt nodded. 'So, what are we looking for?' They were walking past an old red-brick house that sat beyond a hedge. Perhaps it belonged to the woman she'd talked to on Heartsease Lane.

'Anything that might prove criminal activity. Bernadette found a draft blackmail note of Mary's, but we don't know who she was targeting.' Her mind ran through the possibilities again: Shane, who drove off into the night on a regular basis; Noah, who'd been the topic of a heated discussion between Olivia and Mary; or Fiona, whose secret had shocked Mary when she'd discovered it. 'I also want to know if Shane could be working with Noah.'

Matt looked thoughtful. 'That wouldn't surprise me. Most of the types Shane mixes with are pretty shady.'

'The sort who hang out in the Hanged Man?'

He was smiling again. 'Exactly that sort. Myself excepted, obviously.'

Of all the Jenkses, discovering Matt dabbled in something nefarious would be the least surprising. He came and went at such odd times. He'd told her once that it was for work, but what kind of work took you out in the small hours in a place like Hope Eaton? It wasn't as though he was a vet or a doctor or something. 'How long d'you think we've got before Shane comes home?'

He flexed his shoulders. 'With any luck, hours. I heard the Hanged Man's having a lock-in tonight. I've never seen him leave before he's chucked out, barring the times he's gone off in his van.'

That must mean Matt stayed until the bitter end too, when

he was there. Not what you wanted in a guy. He was sounding more like her mother's boyfriends by the minute.

After the red-brick house, the dwellings were few and far between and then they reached fields, with just hedges and expanses of darkness either side of them. The road must peter out before they reached the river.

At last, they came to a stone cottage that had seen better days. She guessed it must date back to the early 1800s. It was low and squat, and the garden was overgrown with weeds, though there was a veg patch which was better kept.

Matt surveyed the area. 'I always did have Shane down as a minimal effort kind of a guy.'

As they took a step closer, a dog began to bark.

Bella met Matt's eye. 'Where is it?'

'Locked up somewhere, or we'd know it by now. I knew he had one, but it's normally in the house, from what he's said in the pub. Sounds like he dotes on it. He must have left it out here for a reason. To give any trespassers a fright, most likely, after he decided he'd been followed.'

Well, it had worked. The barking intensified, interspersed with snarling. Bella's heart was still in overdrive, but Matt was right. The dog wasn't loose. She could see its pen now, over by an outhouse. And looking around, the rest of the night seemed quiet.

'Think we're okay to carry on?'

Matt nodded. 'So long as we're ready to leg it if a neighbour comes.'

Unfortunately, the outhouse next to the dog's pen was a prime area to investigate. Bella peered through its window, the barking ringing in her ears. She was rewarded by the sight of tools, crates and a weird-looking implement with several spikes. 'You could do some damage with that.'

Matt peered over her shoulder. He was close enough for her to feel his warmth. *Distressingly distracting.* 'A broadfork. It's better than a spade. You can open the soil without disturbing it too much.'

He seemed to know a lot about it. 'Do you grow veg?' She hadn't seen any in his garden, which was next to hers. A benefit of a ground-floor flat.

'They take me on at Fox Hollow Farm sometimes. They're experimenting with traditional methods.'

That was all very well, but why didn't he do something regular? The commitment problem seemed to stretch to his work.

'Oh, his van's here.' Bella strode to the vehicle.

Matt nodded. 'I guess he knew he wouldn't need it, if he's put his dodgy trips on hold.'

She'd been banking on hearing it to warn her of Shane's return. It would be useful to examine it though; it seemed central to his operations. She glanced over her shoulder before peering into the cab, then swept her torch around the space. 'There's an enormous pair of gloves here. They've got a weird leather outer. In fact, they're not gloves. They're more like—'

'Gauntlets?'

Bella walked round to find him. 'How did you know?'

But at that moment, everything suddenly went onto high alert. The barking had changed. It was getting louder.

'Run!' Matt yelled, just as she grabbed his arm, ready to shout the same.

The next few seconds were a blur. The nearest fence, the quickest escape, no matter where it led. The dog – a big, dark, bounding shadow with bared teeth – snapping inches below them as they scrambled out of the way. As Bella lowered herself over the other side of the fence, she just had the presence of mind to look beyond the dog, towards its pen. A silhouette was disappearing into the undergrowth.

Matt raised an eyebrow. 'We had company after all, then.'

Bella nodded. 'Recognise them?' She thought she had.

'Not for certain, but it looked unpleasantly like Noah.'

'That's what I thought.' Bella was surveying their surroundings. A small area of grassland. Dog free and not obviously someone's garden. Good.

They walked in silence for a moment as Bella tried to get her breathing under control.

'How did you guess I'd seen a gauntlet?' she said, eventually.

'It went with the stuff I saw in the back. As well as a sleeping bag and a thermos flask, he had climbing gear. A hard hat, ropes, a harness and karabiners.' Matt looked at her from under his long lashes. 'Put that together with the heavy-duty gloves, the current season and Shane's late-night trips and I'd say he's been stealing eggs.'

'Eggs?'

He nodded. 'Birds of prey, usually. It's illegal but it still goes on. Makes the papers every so often. Maybe he's got someone who tips him off and gets a cut.'

Bella thought of the call she'd overheard in the Hanged Man. It fitted. Perhaps the numbers Shane had scrawled were coordinates.

'He might be driving as far as Cumbria or Scotland,' Matt went on. 'I hear some people do it for kicks, but knowing Shane, I'd imagine it's for money too. He'd get the thrill, and a pay-out into the bargain.'

Bella glanced back at his tumbledown house. 'He can't be doing that well out of it. But then I hear he gambles.'

'And then some.'

'So he's high-earn, high-burn.'

The dog was still barking its head off on the track adjacent to where they were walking. Hopefully it would have given up by the time they reached the main road.

'Think Mary found Shane out?' Matt asked.

'It's possible. This place and her house are at opposite ends of town but if Noah's involved, that might explain it. Ted Ashcroft from the auto repair shop says he saw Mary watching Noah. She could have seen him meet Shane.'

Matt nodded.

'I'll give my godfather a ring. See what he reckons.'

At last, the barks became scattered and quieter. They were off the dog's territory. And if it had been Noah who'd let it out, the dog hadn't gone for him. They must be well acquainted.

'Don't wait for me,' Bella said, when they arrived at their bikes.

'I'm not in *that* much of a hurry to get home. Debra's not there, don't forget.'

Funny boy. 'I'm not used to cycling. I'll be slow.'

'Not a problem.'

Bella unlocked John's bike. She would like to think Matt was being solicitous, what with there being a murderer on the loose, but she suspected he knew full well she could look after herself and simply found the sight of her on two wheels amusing. 'Go on then. You go first.'

But he nodded at the road ahead. 'No, after you. Then I'll keep pace. But I can't see you having any problems in those.' He nodded at her capris. 'They're practical.'

Ugh. 'Only coincidentally. I bought them entirely for their style.'

He laughed. Hopefully at her comment, not the sight of her wobbling as she set off. At least the journey was on the flat, across the river, then along Kite Walk. That made it quick.

Back at the hall she locked up as speedily as possible and bolted for her apartment. 'Thanks again for the backup.' She'd have been prepared to go alone, but she could see the arguments against it. If Shane had returned, she might have been killed twice over, once by him and a second time by Jeannie for disobeying orders.

'No sweat. By the way, I heard what happened with Boxer.'

Great to have it mentioned again. 'Ah. Yes.'

'I shouldn't know, but he told Gareth when I was standing behind them. I imagine Gareth's told John too.'

'What?' She was confused now.

'That you told Boxer to pretend he'd turned you down, to help win Alison back.'

'Oh.'

'Decent thing to do.'

She was unreasonably pleased that he knew the truth. 'You know what it's like,' she said lightly. 'I couldn't bear to see love frustrated.'

He opened his door as she fumbled with her keys and Cuthbert entered the hallway. He stroked the cat and grinned at Bella as she turned to say goodbye. 'I'd invite you in for a drink, but I know you'd say no, so see you around.'

She nodded and let herself into her flat. He was right. She would have done, so why did she feel so annoyed? Still, it was good to have avoided all that awkwardness...

33

SECRETS AT SPRINGSIDE COTTAGE

The following morning, Bella was due early at Springside Cottage to begin the valuation of Mary's belongings. She texted both Tony and Barry Dixon before she left. She gave Dixon the basic facts revealed by her and Matt's trip the night before. She couldn't admit to trespassing, so she left out the incident with the dog and Noah. She made Tony's message more personal.

> *Think Shane might have been stealing eggs. I'll explain when we speak. Reckon he'd kill to keep his secret?*

The reply came a few minutes later.

> *Done some digging. Looks possible if he's dealing in live eggs with the right distribution. They could fetch seventy grand overseas. Falconers think birds from wild eggs are genetically superior to ones from a breeder. Penalty would be loss of income, plus jail and a massive fine.*

Bella texted back about the person who'd let Shane's dog out, explaining she thought it was Noah.

Nasty. Think he got a look at you? Watch yourself, all right?

Tony at his most solicitous. On the upside, Noah didn't know her, and neither she nor Matt would have looked distinctive in deep shadow.

Bella googled egging after she got off the phone. It sounded as though making big money was rare, but there was still an active group of hobbyists who collected compulsively, no matter what it did to the species concerned. It looked as though some of them might pay smaller amounts to complete their collections. It was abhorrent. If that was really what Shane was up to, it had to come out. And if Mary had evidence of his and Noah's wrongdoing, it might be in her house. Bella showered, donned some fifties cigarette pants and a high-necked top, then downed a black coffee. Not bad for fifteen minutes' work.

She was just about to leave when Barry Dixon replied to her text.

Snowed under. Can't search Shane Sadler's van without a warrant. How did you get close enough to see what was inside?

Depressingly predictable. She'd answer him later. In a minute, she was away on John's bike, feeling a lot more relaxed than she had with Matt watching.

Twenty minutes after that, she approached her destination, having secured the bike in Holt Lane. John was waiting for her in the front garden with a stout, greying man who looked rather warm in a suit.

'My cousin, Tom Butler,' John said, indicating him. 'And Tom, this is my boss, Bella Winter.'

They shook hands and Tom shook his head. 'Sad business, this. I'd been Mary's solicitor for years. We'd got to know each other fairly well. I'm afraid you'll have quite a job, sorting through her belongings. She collected a lot of things.'

'She asked me to value some of them before she died,' Bella said. 'So we've got a head start with the larger items and a charming owl inkwell.'

Tom raised an eyebrow. 'I'd wondered if that might sell myself.'

'It's the sort of thing people fall for. So, she told you she was short of money?'

He blushed. That was a yes, then. 'Mary said she couldn't bear to let the inkwell go. A present from her boss, apparently, dating back years.'

Either her feelings for Adrian had changed or her financial situation had got more acute. That thought made Bella wonder about the blackmail again. Perhaps she *had* wanted the money for herself, and not to give to charity as Carys had suggested. She might have felt it was morally acceptable if her victim had behaved badly enough.

Or maybe, just maybe, she'd decided to sell the owl because she and Adrian had been lovers and they'd quarrelled. Or she could have found out about him and Edwina West.

Tom glanced around the room. 'I wonder about the statuette you mentioned, John. We looked, but it's possible we missed it. Perhaps you'll have more luck.'

'We already have.' Bella took it from her bag. 'It had been dropped by the spring. I'll put it on the dresser.'

At first, Bella had worried Tom might hang around, which would be very inconvenient, but eventually he left them to it, with a request to return the key before they went to open the shop.

'Right,' said Bella, as soon as he'd gone. 'You told Tom we'd need several sessions?'

He nodded.

'So we've got time. Before we start searching for evidence, I want to know where Mary kept her door key. I still think the one in her shoe belonged to the intruder. If I'm right, she must have a copy of her own somewhere – probably near the door.'

They skirted around the entrance. It didn't take Bella long to find one – it was on a hook just above the skirting board, between the wall and a bookcase. Unobtrusive but handy. Honestly, Dixon could at least have had a look.

She texted him, including an evasive reply to his previous message. He'd probably say the key was a spare.

'Let's have a careful scout round now, assess each room and work out where she kept anything private. We might find out what she had on Noah and if it relates to Shane's illegal hobby. It's crucial to know if she was a threat to him too. And I also want to search for anything that hints at Fiona's secret, or that she knew about the will.'

Downstairs, the room where they'd discovered Mary's body was large and open, with no hallway or porch to protect the contents from prying eyes. Yet there were still hiding places. 'We ought to check she hasn't tucked anything into the books, after what Bernadette found.' Bella pointed to a bookcase. 'I'm going to get an overview first.'

The other rooms on the ground floor were the kitchen, a dining room, a pantry and a study. The study looked promising. There were boxes of papers stacked up in there and an old metal filing cabinet too. It might be a long job.

Bella went upstairs next. There were four bedrooms in the eaves, atmospheric with huge oak beams and some lovely Regency chairs. She found the room she guessed had been Mary's, with a beautiful dressing table under a dormer window, a French swing mirror sitting on top.

'Searching up here will be quick,' she called down to John. 'I'll do a swift sweep and then come and help in the study.'

It was useful to get an overview for the valuation, too. The dressing table was pretty: French, like the mirror, in walnut with bronze decorations. There were bedside tables in a similar style. Bella opened the first dressing-table drawer carefully and found the usual sorts of things: cotton wool pads, a pot of powder, various make-up items and a bottle of scent.

She was investigating a drawer in one of the bedside tables when she discovered something interesting. Photos.

But they weren't of Noah or Shane. They were of the spring. She shuffled through the collection quickly. So peculiar. Each looked very similar to the last. The vegetation changed a little in bushiness, but other than that everything, even the lighting, remained the same, except for a couple of instances when there'd been rain. The photos had been taken at dusk. How many were there? Ten.

Ten nigh-on identical photos. What did it mean? She flipped them over. They each had a processing date on the back, and the dates were similar. The third week in May or thereabouts, one per year. And in each picture, you could see flowers laid in front of the stone carving of Sweet Agnes. They'd hardly wilted, as though it was soon after May Day.

Mary had taken them at this time of year. The last one had been developed twelve months earlier, and there wasn't one for this May. Because Mary had died before she could take one, in what was clearly an annual tradition? Or perhaps she'd bought a smartphone recently, and the latest shot was on that.

'John,' she called out as she dashed down the cottage stairs. 'I've found something odd up here.'

'Interesting.' John's voice was slightly muffled. 'I've found something peculiar down here too.'

34

NOAH AND THE MYSTERY WOMAN

When Bella arrived in Mary's study, she found John was also holding photographs – just two of them. He handed them to her. 'I found them under some run-of-the-mill paperwork in her desk drawer.'

They showed Noah Elsworth, talking to a woman wearing a wide-brimmed hat and a chiffon scarf with a black-and-white geometric print. The woman was turned away from the camera, obscuring her face, but you could see what was in her hand. A collection of bank notes. Bella had the impression she was handing them to Noah, though it was possible he'd just given them to her.

The second photo was even more tantalising. The woman had turned slightly so just a sliver of her cheek was visible, and they were both touching the money. If they could tell which was taken first, they'd know who was paying whom.

'You don't recognise her?' Bella said, indicating the woman.

He shook his head. 'She could be someone I know, but with the hat and her facing away...'

'I know. I wonder if Mary knew who she was.' It was quite possible, even if the mystery woman had never turned around.

Mary could have seen where she'd come from or recognised her voice or gait. 'She could have been blackmailing Noah, with these photos as evidence. But evidence of what?'

John looked up from the swivel chair he occupied. 'Maybe Noah was selling this woman something he'd stolen. It looks as though he's involved in Shane's egging, and we know he steals other things too.'

It was true. He'd taken something at the auto repair shop. 'At least your photos make some kind of sense. Have a look at mine.' She showed him the ones she'd found of the spring. 'They're very odd. Every one of them was processed in May, but I can't find one for this year. Perhaps Mary was killed before she took it. Or maybe it's still on the film in her camera. Unless she'd ditched it and started using her phone.' It would be a lot more usual, though Bella loved vintage cameras.

But John shook his head. 'I don't think she went digital unless it was very recently. I've just found an archive box full of negatives. The latest lot were taken at this year's Easter parade.'

'That will make it easier.' Trying to hack into a phone or laptop would have been impossible. 'We need to go through them to make sense of your photos. I'll look in the box you found. You carry on searching the desk drawers for any correspondence between Fiona and Mary.'

'Major!' He saluted as she turned to examine the boxes.

'Yes. Very funny. I'm doing you a favour. You've got the nicer job.' There were loads of photos. It could take hours. The ones of Noah must be recent at least. The weather had already looked spring-like.

Bella was thankful that Mary had been the organised sort, as went with her profession. The photos were in date order. But when she looked at the penultimate packet, some of the negatives were missing.

She should have realised Mary might take special precautions for any she'd gathered as evidence.

She cast her gaze over the room again. Mary would want somewhere secret and secure, yet easily accessible. She thought of the note Bernadette had found between the pages of a book.

Returning to the sitting room, she stared at the bookcase. Which one would Mary have chosen?

But then she saw one that harked back to the day Bernadette had found the blackmail note. It was a battered old volume on tort law, sitting on the top shelf. The book Carys had taken from Springside Cottage had been on tort too. The volume looked out of date, dry and dusty. Something no visitor was likely to pick up. It was interesting that the one with the draft note had been left on a side table. Perhaps Mary had referred to it shortly before she died.

Bella found a stool and reached for the book. A dead spider fell from the spine as she lifted it down and the smell of must hit her. But it was worth it. The pages weren't quite flat. There was something inside.

Negatives.

She went to show John. 'Mary was hiding her evidence inside books on law. I think she felt she was delivering justice.' She held the negatives up to the window. 'The photo of the woman clutching the banknotes comes first, then the one where they're both touching the money. She was paying Noah.'

John nodded. 'Nice work.'

'I wonder why Mary put the photos of the Sacred Spring in her bedroom. And why take the exact same shot, every year? Let's try to find her camera. I'd like to get her current photos developed if I can, to see if she took the same shot again.'

But though she and John searched high and low, they couldn't find a camera of any sort.

There was a prickling sensation on the back of Bella's neck. 'Either it's very cleverly hidden, or it's not here.'

John looked up from the bed he'd been searching under. 'I

think you're right.' He rubbed his chin. 'Do you suppose some-one's taken it?'

Bella nodded. 'The Sacred Spring clearly had huge signifi-cance for Mary. She went there every year and took a photo. I'm guessing it was on the same day each May and that she followed the usual pattern this year. But for some reason, the latest photo was far more significant than the others. It showed something that made the killer so frightened, they came to steal the camera and silence Mary.

'I didn't believe Mary would have taken her statuette and dropped it by the spring, but perhaps it was her after all. You can see it was handled regularly. Almost like a religious arte-fact.' It made her think of Carys saying Mary had been spiritual. And the way she'd seemed to hear voices in the trees. 'Maybe taking it was part of her annual ritual. It was a stylised depiction of the spring, after all. Then she saw something she shouldn't have as she took the final photo. Whatever it was, I think it frightened her so badly that she dropped the carving and ran.' It was as they'd thought before; there was no logical reason the would-be killer would want it, unless it could identify them.

'And then the killer came to get her soon after? That very night, in fact, because time was of the essence?'

Bella closed her eyes. 'Yes. Otherwise, she'd have gone back to fetch her beloved statuette.'

At that moment, a text came in from Dixon.

The key's probably a spare.

Honestly.

35

INTO THE DRAGON'S DEN

Bella and John made for Vintage Winter after returning the Springside Cottage key to Tom Butler. Bella texted Barry back and alerted him to Mary's missing camera, but with Olivia's death, she was sure the news would fall on deaf ears. They'd need to work out what had happened themselves. She switched to thinking about their lunchtime visit to the Hearst House Museum.

'I wonder if Danielle's found the records which show who donated the Sacred Spring carvings.'

'You still think it's relevant?'

She could see he was squirming at the risk of a run-in with Sienna. 'Vital. It sounds as though the same artist must have sculpted Mary's statuette. If that was Adrian, it points to a possible affair, which would give Fiona an extra motive. And if Mary took her statuette to the spring each year, I imagine it's linked to the reason she went there. If we can work that out, we might be a step closer to guessing what or who she saw. I think it's why she died.'

Vintage Winter was quiet for a Saturday. Once again, Bella propped their door open to try to encourage visitors. She was in a prime position, with a window directly onto St Giles's Close, but several people she recognised scuttled past her door, eyes down.

She'd been sufficiently caught up with the recent tragedies to put her worries about the shop on hold, but now a fresh tug of anxiety gripped her. What was going on? And what if it meant her business was doomed? She imagined having to let John go, just as Olivia had been about to lay off staff. It would be terrible. He'd given up his secure job at the museum to take a chance with her.

If Vintage Winter failed completely, she'd have to sell her father's old flat too. Move to wherever she could get work. What would her mother say? Bella was supposed to have all the answers. She usually claimed she had.

When they left for the Hearst House Museum at lunchtime she put the closed sign on the door, but would anyone even notice?

The museum occupied a large Regency townhouse on Uppergate, just around the corner from Vintage Winter. Old Mrs Hearst had lived in it and collected anything and everything throughout her long tenure, filling her rooms with objects, either personal or donated, that spoke of a changing way of life. There were old hats and clothes, vintage signs, paintings and furniture, toys, china and much more besides. When Bella had visited as a child, part of its charm was the eccentric stamp old Mrs Hearst had put on it. She'd got a pram in use as a drinks trolley and a vintage bicycle in the bathroom, its crossbar providing a towel rail. She'd heard that Sienna, who'd inherited the place, had 'rationalised it', selling some of the most charming pieces, though not to Bella of course. After her purge, she'd 'revamped' the rest, removing all traces of her aunt's creativity.

They found Danielle on the front desk as they entered. She

was taking ticket money from some out-of-towners who'd have no idea what they'd missed.

They stepped forward when it was their turn, and John introduced Bella.

'Thanks for helping us.' Bella shook hands. 'John mentioned the carvings you found, similar to Mary's statuette.'

'That's right, but we still can't find the records that go with them, I'm afraid. Old Mrs H was a gem, but you know what she was like on the admin side, John. The carvings are still in the basement. Follow me and I'll show you.'

They trailed after her down a corridor, past the odd visitor peering at the displays.

'She's put *all* the smaller items in glass cases?' They looked awful. Just like any other mediocre collection.

John looked upset and Bella resisted the urge to hug him.

'I know.' Danielle looked miserable too. 'We said we thought it would look sterile, not like a lived-in home where you could imagine being the owner. She said if she'd wanted our opinion, she'd have asked for it. Bea and I are thinking of resigning. She hasn't replaced you, John. She thinks she can carry on, using extra volunteers.'

She was just the sort to exploit people. It was such a shame. In a book, Sienna would get her just deserts, but real life wasn't so obliging. Bella had to make do with revenge fantasies.

Danielle opened a panelled door and they creaked down a flight of poorly lit stairs. At the bottom, two carvings sat on top of a box marked 'not for display until 2050'. That was some forward planning.

They were clearly worked by the same hand as Mary's; the style was distinctive. The museum pieces were less successful than Mary's version though. As though the artist had made three attempts and the practise efforts had been donated to Mrs Hearst.

John approached them. 'May I pick them up?' Sienna had put 'do not touch' notices everywhere upstairs.

'Of course. You're practically staff.'

'Sienna would self-combust if she heard you say that.' Bella watched as John lifted one of the carvings.

He showed her the bottom. *For darling M, from Fitz.*

Oh, my word. They checked the second statuette, and the inscription was just the same. Bella looked at John. This was something to discuss outside. 'If you ever find the records, we'd love to know.' Perhaps Adrian had given them to her one by one, each more accomplished than the last. In which case, it was probably she who'd donated the earlier versions to the museum, to commemorate a love affair she felt bound to keep private until no one cared any more. But she couldn't bear to part with the last, Bella imagined. She'd scratched out the giveaway inscription instead. 'It's definitely the same artist.'

They thanked Danielle and were about to leave when Bea sidled up to them.

'I'm sorry again about lying to you.' She blushed.

'We understand,' John said.

Bella nodded. 'And I'm sorry about your mum and dad's troubles. I hope things work out.' Though she was sure Bob West would be better off without the thoroughly disloyal and tuneless Edwina.

Bea nodded. 'Thanks. As a matter of fact, Mum says she's not seeing Adrian any more. She thinks his wife found out. Not that I'd take her word as gospel, obviously. Look, I just wanted to say, I heard Sienna mention you the other day. It was odd.'

Bella stepped forward. 'How do you mean?'

Bea's blush intensified. 'To be honest, I couldn't think how to bring it up with you. But you've been so kind, and you ought to know. She was telling someone in the bakers that you'd stolen a very valuable vase.' The words came in a rush. 'Or well, not stolen it exactly, but conned a vulnerable woman out of it. She said it wasn't surprising you had enough money to set up here. Then she told the woman to boycott your shop.'

Bella's eyes met John's. *Sweet Agnes, how many people had she told?* No wonder Vintage Winter was losing customers.

At that moment there was a noise and they realised Sienna Hearst had returned. She strode into the reception area, her cold blue eyes on Bella's. Her sharp face was caked in expensive make-up and she laughed. 'Oh, Bea, I can't believe you're telling tales. I do expect some loyalty from my volunteers, you know.'

Please resign, before she sacks you. Bella knew how satisfying that was.

'I don't think you need come back after your session today.'

Too late. What a missed opportunity.

But Danielle had folded her arms. 'In that case, I'm out of here too.' Her expression was grim. 'Good luck with finding a replacement. Your reputation's known far and wide.'

Sienna waved her comment away. 'People still listen to me, that's the point. You'd do well to remember that, Danielle.' That sounded like a threat. She turned to Bella. 'There are blog posts that say how duplicitous you were, currying favour with a vulnerable elderly lady.'

It hadn't been a bit like that, but Bella had no intention of engaging with Sienna. Never feed the trolls. She turned to Danielle and Bea instead, and promised to explain it all to them later. She just wished she'd already told John the story. What must he be thinking?

'Of course, I wouldn't have wasted my time looking into you,' Sienna went on, her eyes still on Bella. 'You're nothing to me. But I got an anonymous tip-off, telling me there was dirt to find.' She smiled now. 'I shouldn't think you've got long in this town, and I shall be delighted to see you go.' She turned to John. 'I'm afraid I won't be offering you your old job back. As you can see, I've turned this place around. I'll be looking for someone who's more in keeping with the new ambience.'

36

THE SCANDAL

As Bella crashed out of the Hearst House Museum, she almost ran into Fiona Fitzpatrick. Thoughts collided in her mind, topmost being Fiona's whereabouts when Olivia was killed. She stopped herself probing just in time. She was too full of adrenaline and she'd mess it up. Fiona would be at the fundraiser meeting that night. She'd talk to her then.

'Are you all right?' Fiona looked slightly anxious.

Bella had been staring at her for too long. Bother Sienna Hearst. She'd made her lose her poise. 'I've just remembered why I don't visit the museum these days.'

Fiona lowered her voice. 'I feel the same way. The new manager reminds me of Adrian's sister-in-law, all polished veneer hiding a heart of pure venom.'

'She reminds me of Cruella de Vil.'

Fiona laughed suddenly. 'I call Adrian's sister-in-law Rebecca behind her back, à la Daphne Du Maurier.'

They said their goodbyes and Bella watched Fiona disappear around the corner.

'Sorry, John,' she said, as they crossed St Giles's Close towards the antiques centre. 'It's time for you to hear about the scandal. It catapulted my move here, but I don't often talk about it. It sends my blood pressure through the roof.' They entered the shop but she didn't turn the sign to open.

'Long story short, it happened when I was still managing the antiques shop in London. I discovered a valuable client of ours was doing a private deal with a woman called Julietta Montgomery, who had a beautiful, rare vase to sell. He'd got a friend of his to undervalue it. I just happened to be visiting his hotel, dropping off some goods, when I overheard him discussing it and got suspicious. I warned Ms Montgomery and – again, long story short – she hung on to the vase and the hotelier and his friend were tried for fraud. They got off on a technicality. They and their pals have been out to get me ever since. I've seen the anonymous blog posts about me. Vague and just this side of libellous. Even the owner of the shop I managed didn't like me taking a stand. He said I'd make their clients jumpy.' It still made her furious. 'Other knock-on effects included the break-up with my idiot boyfriend, who apparently "saw my boss's point of view". And then poor Ms Montgomery died.' She'd been in her nineties. 'It was a huge shock to find she'd left me the vase. There was a letter in her will, telling me how grateful she was not to have lost it to a greedy fraudster. She said she wanted me to have it, either to keep or to sell for its true worth and fulfil my dreams. She had no family. The rest of her estate went to charity.'

John faced her. 'You sold the vase and put the money into the business?'

She nodded. 'The proceeds from my London flat helped too. I'm sorry, John. I've dragged you away from the museum and now I'll probably go bust.'

'I hope you don't imagine I'd have carried on working for Sienna if you hadn't come along.'

She met his eye. 'No. But you might not have chosen Vintage Winter as an alternative.'

'When people know the truth, they'll soon come round.'

'It won't be that straightforward with Sienna on the case. It's so easy to twist things and if she contacts the hotelier or his pal, they'll gang up on me. It would be different if the prosecution had been successful. As it is, Sienna's clearly portraying me as a malicious troublemaker who managed to get my hands on the blessed vase myself.'

She tried to steady her breathing, but the situation felt out of control. It must have been going on for days. Most of the town had probably heard the rumours by now.

'The situation plays to my strengths,' John said lightly. 'I like problem-solving. Give me the details of the people involved and I'll have a think.'

She wrote the names down for him. No wonder John was good at selling stuff. He left you feeling in safe hands. Bella tried not to think about winding up her business. She needed to focus on Mary and Olivia. Some brutal, self-centred monster had robbed them of their futures in a beautiful town – hers and her father's – where they should have been safe.

But John drew her mind back to the scandal. 'I wonder who sent Sienna the anonymous tip-off about you.'

'Me too.' If she could get her hands on them...

'You have to wonder if it's to do with the deaths.' John moved towards the coffee machine.

'What?'

'Well, why would someone look for dirt on you now? And feeding the information to Sienna can't have been chance. They picked the one person who's only too glad to help spread gossip. They did their research.'

'Of course. John, you're brilliant, and I'm not thinking straight.' She sat down at the refectory table, her mind poring over the facts. 'Someone's trying to muddy my name and ensure no one listens to a word I say.'

John handed her an espresso. 'It seems quite likely.'

'They must think it's less risky than trying to kill me.' But that might change if she got too close to the truth. She thought of Noah, releasing Shane Sadler's dog. She had no idea if he'd recognised her or Matt.

Bella felt like hiding in the office that afternoon. People might come in if they thought it was just John on duty. The whole town loved him. But it wasn't a sustainable solution. She kept thinking of all her hard work – the number of customers she'd spoken to individually. People she'd started to think of as friends.

She needed to work on the case. Find their villain and she might find her detractor.

'At least the lack of customers gives us time.' Bella couldn't believe how calm John sounded. 'Where are we at? What about the inscription on the base of the museum's statuettes? Is "Fitz" Adrian?'

She'd been all set to discuss their latest findings the moment they left the museum. She couldn't believe the upset had distracted her so badly. 'Yes, that was a bombshell. I heard Mary call Adrian "Fitz" on May Day. I thought how informal it sounded at the time, but they'd known each other for years, so I put it down to that. But it's like Carys said, Adrian's a bit of a stuffed shirt. I doubt many people address him that way. And we'd already wondered if he and Mary could have had an affair. I just couldn't believe it, somehow. Aside from it being out of character, I wouldn't have thought he'd be her type. Then again, the same applies to Shane.'

'So you think Adrian carved the statuette, and gave it to Mary, and she scored out the dedication to avoid discovery?'

'That's what it looks like. She took care to keep the museum ones secret too if she was the donor – asking that they be kept sealed for fifty years. And your cousin Tom told us Adrian bought her that owl inkwell. She didn't want to get rid of it, originally. Maybe she changed her mind if she realised he was sleeping with Edwina.'

'And it's as we thought before: an affair would compound Fiona's motive for attacking Mary if she found out. But you're frowning.'

'Why would Mary admit to her solicitor that Adrian bought her the inkwell, yet go to such lengths to hide the origins of the statuette? If she was being that cautious, you'd think she'd avoid highlighting anything that might link them.'

'Maybe she slipped up.' John turned the shop sign to open.

'Maybe.' Bella needed to let her thoughts settle. Her mind was all over the place. 'I need to find out more. I'll have to drop it into conversation with Adrian. I can't see another way. If the annual visit to the spring relates to their relationship then he probably knows the truth about that, too. We need to know what Mary saw there, and why her camera was stolen.'

John looked drawn. 'For pity's sake, don't see him alone. He's got an alibi for Mary, but what if he and Fiona are in it together?'

'Your concern is very touching, but I'm not a complete fool. The combined schools' fundraiser meeting is tonight. I can talk to him then, surrounded by people. Fiona's sure to be there too. I'll be watching her. But the crucial thing is to find out what Mary saw at the spring. I only hope it relates to her annual tradition. If it doesn't, then it could be anything. Perhaps she witnessed stolen goods changing hands, or a couple cheating on their other halves.

'Let's go back there after we close, before I head to the Fitzpatricks'. We never had a proper search after we found the carving. If Mary saw something shocking, we might find evidence of it.'

37

BLOOD

The Sacred Spring was deserted when Bella and John reached it after work. The remnants of the May Day flowers still sat to either side of the stone carving. There was nothing untoward. The water trickled into the pool and the pondweed at its edges sat undisturbed. But to either side, there was bracken and undergrowth.

Bella glanced over her shoulder at John. 'Anything could be hidden in there. Want to take the right-hand side if I take the left?'

She turned and parted the bracken, checking to see if there was anything on the ground at its base. No joy.

She moved beyond it, peering into the heather. What was that? But it was nothing. Or nothing much. Just some lamb's wool amongst the plants. But then she saw the rock behind the heather.

What on earth? It had a huge bloodstain on it. She pushed aside the vegetation. More blood. It hadn't rained since Mary had been killed. It could have been here the whole time.

'John, come and have a look at this.'

Bella took photos. She'd tell Dixon of course, but she could guess what he'd say: that it was probably the result of one animal killing another. But if a lamb had been killed by a fox, say, surely you'd see signs of it, even if it was only a trail of blood where its carcass had been dragged away. Instead, there was just the wool and the blood was all in one place.

Bella called Dixon the moment she got home. She was in luck – he was still at the station. She told him what they'd found, from the photos of the spring to the blood.

'Mary must have seen something that frightened her, and that's what made her drop the statuette. Couldn't you at least get someone to take a sample of the blood?'

'Ms Winter—'

'Bella.' They'd shared childcare advice. That had to equal first-name terms.

'*Bella, I'm going through a hundred and one reports, trying to work out who might have stolen the car that killed Olivia Elsworth, and who she had dealings with in the run-up to her death, in case it was deliberate. I had no sleep last night because the four-year-old had a nightmare about giant dog biscuits and I happen to know we have no food at home apart from one can of tuna and a packet of sponge fingers.*'

'But the place I think Mary visited the night she died looks like a bloodbath.'

'*I presume you've remembered that her death was natural causes?*'

'But under suspicious circumstances. You must admit it's odd that a door key was found dropped in her shoe, when her own was hanging on a hook by the skirting board.'

'*We've been through all this. The one on the hook was probably a spare. As for the blood, I expect it came from an animal.*'

'There's no sign that's the case.' She decided not to mention the lamb's wool.

He heaved out a sigh. '*You haven't got any tips on children who keep having bizarre nightmares, have you?*'

'I used to talk through the day with my younger sisters. Let them get everything out before they went to sleep.' Bella had wanted to know what they were thinking anyway. She always knew if they were bottling something up and it had kept her one step ahead. Exactly where she liked to be.

'*Thanks. I'd kill for a decent night's sleep.*' She heard him slurp something that was probably coffee. '*I didn't mean that literally.*'

'Could someone at least have a quick look at the blood?'

He grunted. '*That's a physical impossibility; even getting to the spring isn't quick.*' There was a long pause. '*But I'll see what I can do.*'

Bella was short of time before the fundraiser, so she went to grab supper at the Blue Boar, though she couldn't really afford it. On the upside, Vintage Winter's lack of customers was making her stomach turn, so she only felt like something light.

She found Jeannie serving. The landlady demanded updates.

'Bravo!' she said, when Bella explained her small victory with Barry Dixon.

'I think it was just less effort to give in. It doesn't mean he'll actually *do* anything.' But maybe he would. She felt she and Barry were inching towards some kind of understanding.

Bella sat over her food, her mind on Adrian Fitzpatrick. Fitz. She'd want to tackle him about the statuette that evening, but something about it was making her twitchy. Now she stopped long enough to analyse it, she realised it was the thought she'd had about Adrian's character. On paper, he and Mary could have had an affair. They'd been closeted together, all day, every day, for years. And Mary hiding the origins of the statuette fitted the theory.

But the details brought Bella up short. Carving multiple copies of Sweet Agnes for Mary, gradually perfecting the process, spoke of heartfelt dedication. And him, or more likely Mary, donating the early versions to the museum suggested a deep love too. It was as though they represented something so important that the donor didn't want them hidden forever. Bella guessed it had hurt them not to shout their love from the rooftops. Donating the carvings meant the declaration would be public one day. It was intense and romantic. None of that worked with a relationship involving Adrian. He seemed physical, practical and cynical. Yet Bella had heard Mary call him 'Fitz'. They'd been at the spring, which was clearly a special place for Mary. Somewhere she didn't want to leave, which brought out the spiritual in her. Where she made a pilgrimage each year and talked to herself. Or to someone who wasn't there...

And then, suddenly, a memory struck her. In seconds, she was googling. Testing an idea. Speculating about Adrian's snobbish parents and his sister-in-law like Daphne du Maurier's Rebecca. She found the woman online and details of her two children. She was a banker's daughter, currently running a political think-tank. After that, Bella's mind turned to poetry, a memorial and the nickname Fitz. As she walked to the Fitzpatricks' house, her plans to talk to Adrian took an entirely new direction.

Bella arrived two minutes late for the fundraiser meeting, wishing she didn't have to listen to Adrian blathering on before she could act. She stood next to Carys in the Fitzpatricks' elegantly proportioned sitting room with its floor-length silk curtains, feeling cross. How could she have thought for a moment that Adrian would have carved the statuettes for Mary?

He stood there, the welcoming host in his well-cut grey suit, but all she could think of was him in the arms of Edwina, wearing a cat-like smile and nothing else. *Ugh.* It would be hard to unsee that image.

She couldn't spot Edwina herself. Perhaps she'd pulled out, after what Bea said about her and Adrian breaking it off.

Fiona Fitzpatrick looked tense, her jaw tight. She was wearing a neat shift dress and a pale pink silk scarf which contrasted with her almost-black hair.

'Ladies and gentlemen, dear friends.' *Yuk.* Adrian waited for quiet. 'Thank you for coming. I wanted us to meet to share our grief over the loss of Olivia. It's unspeakable. I'm still in a state of shock and I'm sure you are too. And so soon after Mary's death. I immediately thought we should cancel or at the very least postpone the combined schools' fundraiser.'

There was a murmur of agreement. Carys's assent was especially audible. Still no progress on the second-hand clothes, presumably. But Adrian held up a hand.

'However, I'm not the one who's most closely affected by these tragedies. I spoke to Harry Elsworth to offer my condolences and he's asked us to go ahead.'

There was a collective intake of breath.

'Harry wants us to do the fundraiser as a tribute to Olivia. And to Mary of course, as we originally planned. He's going to invite some of Olivia's celebrity friends down from London and make it the most marvellous send-off for her that we can manage. Between ourselves, I think he's desperate to keep busy and focus on something while the police investigation goes on.'

Bella had felt the same after her dad died. For a day she'd been knocked completely flat. Unable to function. Then she'd gone into organisational overdrive. Blotted everything out and not let herself feel. Of course, when the funeral was over, his flat sold and possessions distributed, she'd had nothing left to focus on. It had been like a dam coming down, the tide of grief. Poor Harry Elsworth.

Adrian cleared his throat. 'For his sake, I think we have to carry on. I hope you're all willing.'

There were lots of murmurs of agreement, combined with Carys's almost inaudible groan.

'Thank you. We'll meet again on Tuesday evening for a full practice, with all stall holders and acts ready to discuss logistics or perform a run-through as appropriate. For this evening, please help yourselves to food and drink. And we need ideas. The Year Twelves' play requires vintage farm equipment as props. Any thoughts on where we might get some?'

A hand went up at the back. 'Fox Hollow Farm has some. Sorry, I thought I'd mentioned it. The family are exploring traditional farming methods and opening a museum as a side-line. I was talking to Fred about it. I can ring and ask if they'd loan us some bits.'

Adrian smiled. 'Thank you.'

The woman who'd raised her hand nodded. As the Fitz-patricks' guests began to talk and the hubbub increased, Bella saw her take a mobile from her pocket and disappear into the hall.

She turned to Carys. 'I've got news, but I might have more soon. I need to talk to Adrian Fitzpatrick.'

Carys's eyes sparkled. 'Go to it! Want me to do anything?'

'Chat with Fiona, please. My goal is to find out where she was when Olivia was killed, though that'll be tricky.'

'Got it.'

Bella spotted Adrian across the room, standing next to a baby grand piano. She wove her way through the crowds, carrying her wine carefully.

During a gap in conversation, she inserted herself.

'Ah, Bella.' Adrian looked suitably sombre. 'This is a strange situation, isn't it? But I'm glad we'll hear you sing. I expect you've heard that Edwina has had to drop out. We'll be relying on you and our accomplished music tutor.'

'What a shame about Edwina.' *You sleazy old slimeball.* She smiled innocently at him. 'Yes, it is odd, isn't it, having to carry on like this?

'By the way, John Jenks and I found Mary's missing statuette in the grass by the Sacred Spring. You remember I asked you about it?'

A flicker of anxiety twitched Adrian's features. He nodded.

'We think Mary took it there, just before she died, and dropped it.'

Adrian shifted his weight from one foot to the other. 'Why would she take it to the spring?'

'I think you know. And why she scratched the dedication off its base.'

Adrian flushed and drew Bella further from the throng. 'What do you mean?'

'The carving was a present from your brother William, wasn't it?'

He paled. 'I can't imagine what you're talking about.'

'His nickname was Fitz and he and Mary adored each other, but I imagine your parents weren't keen. The woman your brother married in the end was a banker's daughter, and a high-flyer to boot, whereas Mary's dad was a rag-and-bone man and she was a secretary.'

Adrian opened his mouth, then closed it again. That answered that one. She'd guessed correctly. The other possibility was that Mary hadn't met Fitz until after he was married, but that seemed less likely, given Mary's sense of propriety.

'I don't know how your parents managed to keep them

apart. Maybe they used emotional blackmail. I can imagine
Mary not wanting to come between them and Fitz. She had a
strong sense of duty.' She thought of Mary's father and the
threats he'd made if she wasn't 'good'. 'But in time, they started
seeing each other, as friends at least. I'm not sure Mary would
have gone further, though Fitz's wife was hateful and unfaith-
ful.' Just like Daphne du Maurier's Rebecca. Bella had found
enough online gossip to make the nickname Fiona had given her
seem justified. 'Fitz must have been deeply unhappy. Perhaps
he didn't leave his wife for the sake of their children, but I'm
quite sure it was Mary who he loved.'

Adrian was looking over his shoulder. He wouldn't want
anyone to hear this. Fitz's wife was hugely influential these
days. As well as running the think-tank, she'd remarried
someone in government. If she turned on the Fitzpatricks,
Adrian probably imagined it would affect the publicly funded
research project he'd been asked to lead. 'This is all rubbish,' he
said at last.

'I don't think so.' Bella explained about the statuettes at the
museum. 'I heard Mary say "Fitz" on May Day. I thought she
was addressing you, but she was talking to you about William,
wasn't she? I hear she did all the work to get his memorial
erected on Kite Hill. He wrote poetry about the spring and
loved it as much as she did.' Bella should have remembered
what Carys had said sooner. She'd portrayed Adrian's brother as
a romantic. Carving three statuettes to get one which was
perfect made total sense now.

'Suddenly, it all added up. The way Mary would talk softly
to someone who wasn't there, her determination not to leave the
spring and her annual pilgrimage. Did you know about that?'

There was a very long pause. Adrian looked as though he
was weighing up options. Eventually, he sighed. 'Yes, all right.
She went every year on the anniversary of William's death. It
was especially agonising for her because she blamed herself: he

was on his way to meet her when he was killed in a car accident. I didn't know she took the statuette with her.'

'Mary scratched off the dedication in case Fiona saw it and word got out?'

He nodded reluctantly. 'It was rash of William to carve it in the first place. Protecting his kids was paramount. His wife was barely there and they needed him.'

It must have hurt Mary to obliterate a message that had meant so much. Bella thought of the guilt and torment she must have gone through after losing Fitz. And then of what she'd said to Carys and Leo's daughter. *Doing wrong only leads to misery.* There were the people she'd reported to the police too; Mary had been determined to set them on the straight and narrow. Bella was starting to think that her zeal had been driven by what she saw as the consequences of her own wrongdoing. She focused on Adrian again. 'The annual pilgrimage explains the photos we found.'

He raised an eyebrow and she filled him in.

'I didn't know she took photos, but I can imagine it.'

'Does anyone else know all this?'

Adrian frowned. 'Not as far as I know. I'd appreciate it if you kept it quiet. Going public would only hurt my niece and nephew.'

And Adrian, who'd make a powerful enemy by revealing his sister-in-law's sham first marriage. 'I won't say anything.'

She let him go. So Mary had lost the love of her life: a poet and sculptor. A man who'd shared her love of the Sacred Spring. Someone who'd married unwisely to keep the peace, then regretted it bitterly. She couldn't get over Mary scratching off his dedication. It must have made her heart bleed. No wonder she'd picked the statuette up often and clung to it. It brought Olivia to mind, clinging to Harry.

Bella was starting to see how Mary had come to throw herself into the relationship with Shane Sadler too. She'd taken photos of the spring on ten anniversaries of Fitz's death, eleven if you counted this year's, and she'd been divorced from Shane for ten years. She must have married him in the aftermath of Fitz's death. After such a crushing blow, she'd gone for someone totally different, to blot out the pain, probably. But it had been a mistake. She'd realised it the moment he'd moved into Spring-side Cottage. In her heart of hearts, she'd wanted to be alone with Fitz's memory. Shane had known something was up – the affair he suspected had been over, yet ongoing.

Bella doubted Mary had been jealous when Shane started sleeping with Olivia's employee. It was more likely that she'd simply reverted to her father's strict, black-and-white morality. She knew Shane was making the same mistakes she had, and her childhood values had come back into play. Carys had reported Mary's views: that humiliation was the only way to get Shane to mend his ways. A proper deterrent. Not that it had worked, obviously.

Bella caught up with Carys and filled her in.

'No wonder the poor woman was scared of the hooded figure. She must have thought it was the demon from the legend, come to get her for her sins, just like her father warned her.' Carys shook her head. 'It must have been hard to throw off a tale he'd drummed into her from childhood. So where d'you think it leaves us?'

Bella gathered her thoughts. 'Anyone who knew Mary visited the spring on the anniversary of Fitz's death wouldn't do anything criminal there on that date. But that doesn't help. Adrian's the only person who definitely knew about her ritual, and he's already out of it. I suppose it hints that he and Fiona weren't working together. He'd have warned her that Mary would be there if they had been.'

'Shane might have noticed the pattern of her visits too.'

'True, but I don't think we can rule him out on the strength of it. And Fiona could have known independently, as her best friend, but the same applies. Did you get to talk to her?'

Carys nodded. 'But it was inconclusive, I'm afraid. I told her where I was when the news about Olivia broke, and she responded in kind.'

'Well done!' Fiona's readiness might imply she was innocent, and just as horrified as Carys. But of course, if she was guilty, it would be sensible to have a story lined up.

'It came quite naturally in the end,' Carys went on. 'You know what it's like after something shocking happens. Everyone wants to share and relive it to try to rationalise it all.'

She picked up a vol au vent from a nearby tray. 'According to Fiona she'd nipped out from the charity where she works for some office supplies and got the news from the woman at the stationers. I managed to get it out of her that she had no one to confide in at her office, so there was probably no one to check up on her either.

'After that, I got her on to Mary – it wasn't hard when we'd already been talking about a recent death. Fiona sounded fond of her. The nearest I got to touching a nerve was when she admitted she could be overbearing when it came to her opinions on right and wrong.'

That fitted. Perhaps Fiona was thinking of the secret Mary had brought up in the letter. She'd be sensitive about that.

Bella's mind went back to the earlier part of the evening. 'It's interesting that Harry Elsworth is happy to support the fundraiser in Mary's memory, as well as Olivia's, given Mary was instrumental in Noah's arrest.'

'Ah,' Carys picked up a glass of white wine from a tray and handed it to Bella, 'not if you know Harry. He's all about lofty ideals, fairness, peace and reconciliation. Not that I'm getting at him; it's admirable. But not everyone finds it that easy. I don't suppose Noah approves.'

Bella could imagine. He probably got more resentful each time his dad's principles blinded him to problems at home.

Carys sighed. 'I'll have to look lively with the second-hand clothes stall.'

'You could get Jeannie to ask the customers at the inn. Maybe they could drop their donations off at the bar.' Jeannie would go at the problem like a dog with a bone.

Carys brightened. 'Now there's a thought.'

'You could call her now. It'll be busy on a Saturday. Plenty of sitting ducks to accost.'

Carys grinned. 'I'll do it.'

Adrian called order before they left. 'We've had word back from Fred at Fox Hollow Farm. They'll lend us their vintage equipment. We can use the school van to collect it on Monday lunchtime. Fiona and I will come, of course. Please could I have some additional volunteers? Some of the items will be heavy.'

Bella raised her hand. Extra time with Fiona would be a bonus.

Bella was back at her flat, nursing a cup of raspberry tea and enjoying Beverley Knight on vinyl when her mobile rang. Tony.

'Interesting little development for you.'

Bella put her tea down. 'Go on.'

'Shane Sadler's been arrested. And you're right – he has been stealing eggs.'

'Wow! But Barry didn't seem interested when I told him what I'd seen in his van. And it feels too quick for them to get enough evidence to act on the back of that, anyway.'

'Hmm. I have to say, my contact at the nick was a bit cagey about how they got a warrant. Your tip-off could have played a part though. I'll be asking more questions, naturally.'

And for once they'd be legitimate. Tony might be retired, but he still worked for the police part-time, watching out for anything that didn't meet standards. The thought always made Bella laugh. Tony wasn't one for rules.

'Thanks, Tony. Has Shane mentioned working with Noah?'

'No. *The team suspect he has an accomplice or two, but so far he's tight-lipped.*'

38

WRESTLING WITH THE FACTS

Sunday came round again – John's day off. Bella couldn't afford a stand-in, and that wouldn't change if Sienna kept up her hate campaign.

She opened Vintage Winter alone and wondered what John was up to. He hadn't mentioned the scandal since they'd visited the Hearst House Museum the previous day.

She tried to banish it from her mind as a lone customer left the shop without buying anything. Filling her head with the case was the answer. Whatever happened she had a contribution to make. She made a list of everything she knew. The result was a horrendous jumble of facts and ideas, but help would be at hand at lunchtime. She and John had arranged to meet the rest of the gang at the Steps.

At one o'clock, she sat opposite him, with Carys and Tony also in attendance and Leo darting between their table and the customers.

'I'm on WhatsApp duty,' Carys said. 'Jeannie wants to know what we discuss.'

'Sounds good.' Bella gave them an update, then turned to

Tony. 'What news from you?' She opened her prized notebook and turned to a fresh page for psychological advantage.

'Shane Sadler's been bailed. I told our boy Barry to ask about Noah before they released him. Sadler insists they didn't work together, but he flinched when his name was mentioned. Make of that what you will.'

Bella had been thinking it through all over again. 'In favour of them collaborating, I'm all but certain it was Noah who let Shane's dog out. The dog treated him as a friend. And as far back as May Day I thought the pair of them had a connection. They managed to communicate with a raised eyebrow and a nod. When I asked Shane about Noah he was rude about him, but I thought at the time he might be trying to put me off the scent.'

Tony swallowed a sizeable mouthful of bacon bap. 'Noah's definitely been moonlighting, which would also fit. And he was away from the garage when Olivia was killed too, for part of the window. Time enough.'

'And we know Noah hated Mary,' Carys said. 'He's a promising suspect, especially if Mary was blackmailing him.'

'I agree, but when it comes to him and Shane working together, some things don't make sense.' Bella's doubts had been nagging at her. 'Noah sneaking across town when he was meant to be at the dentist, for instance. I can imagine Shane hiring him to smuggle the eggs to a port or airport, I suppose, given what you said about the overseas market for live eggs, Tony. The motorbike would come in handy for that. But the short, oddly timed absences from the garage don't fit, unless he's found several locals willing to pay through the nose for eggs. That doesn't sound likely, and even if he has, why fix the appointments in the middle of the working day? Trumping up excuses at the repair shop just makes him look shifty.' It was as she'd thought before – whatever Noah was up to, the time and place were important, and outside his control. 'I wonder if he's got a second string to his bow, though that probably involves theft too. We saw him stealing at the garage and Mary had a photo of him taking money from a mystery woman, as though he was selling goods on.'

'Mystery woman?' Leo came briefly to rest at their table.

Bella showed him the picture she'd taken of Mary's photo on her phone. 'Here.'

'Distinctive hat and scarf,' Carys said, leaning over.

Bella closed her screen again. 'Whatever Noah's up to, maybe he works for himself as well as Shane.'

Carys was busy tapping updates into WhatsApp. As she paused, her expression was sour. 'I could believe it.'

'What does Jeannie say?'

She referred to her phone. 'That whatever Noah's up to it has to be something more exciting than working at the garage. She thinks he enjoys an adrenaline rush.'

'She's probably right. Perhaps being Shane's wingman isn't sufficiently thrilling, so he's thieving too. But why steal from a colleague?' Bella's head was starting to ache. 'That was high risk. They'd know someone they worked with was guilty.'

'Except the theft was never reported. Isn't that right?' Tony raised an eyebrow.

'Yes.' It made no sense whatsoever and was trying her patience. Bella thought of her surveillance on Friday morning. 'Noah shot off on his motorbike the day after Olivia was killed, following a phone call the evening before. He could have been transporting Shane's eggs further afield, I suppose.

'Anyway, too much speculation. To sum up, Noah's definitely up to something, possibly in addition to Shane's operation. And Mary was investigating Noah and had taken photos. She could have been blackmailing him. He hated both Mary and his stepmum. He's my top candidate for killer.'

A WhatsApp ping emanated from Carys's phone.

'What is it?' Bella craned forward.

She peered at the screen. 'Jeannie says someone's donated a scarf with a geometric design for my stall. She's sent a photo.'

Bella almost knocked heads with Leo as she craned to see it. It was an exact match for the one in Mary's photo. 'Who donated it?'

A moment later Carys grimaced. 'She's not sure. She's going to ask the bar staff.'

Bella took a deep breath. There was no point in stressing. Jeannie was probably bellowing demands for information as they spoke. 'All right. So, onto Shane himself. I think it's entirely possible Mary knew what he was up to.'

Carys nodded. 'But he's less likely because Mary was following Noah, not him, and it's Noah's photo we found in her house?'

'Sounds about right,' Bella said.

'And what about Sadler's motive for Olivia, now we know what we know?' It was Tony who'd butted in. He turned to her and raised an eyebrow.

Back to being a performing seal. 'Originally, I didn't think he fitted. I didn't see how Olivia might have guessed he was Mary's blackmail target, if he was, and I'm sure something clicked when she saw that note. But if he and Noah were working together, that gave her a far better chance of working it out.'

'What about Fiona Fitzpatrick?' Carys said.

'We know she got that letter from Mary.' Bella looked at the photo she'd taken of it. '"I'm horrified at what you've been keeping from me. Why didn't you come clean? I thought we were friends. We should talk now. This changes things."

'And there's Adrian's affair. It could have made her desperate to get out of their house. If she knew about the bequest, then blackmail coupled with the threat of Mary changing her will might have pushed her to act.'

'And we know she was home alone the night Mary died,'

Carys said. 'Maybe she went out after you spoke to her without Adrian realising.'

'But in her case, why the hit-and-run?' Tony put in.

Bella rallied her thoughts. 'Fiona could have decided Olivia was a threat if she spotted her digging for evidence. As before, it's possible Olivia saw Fiona enter Mary's cottage if she lied about where she walked that night. She could have lacked the confidence to go to the police given the death was natural causes. Or perhaps Olivia witnessed something that made her think Fiona was Mary's blackmail victim.'

Tony nodded. 'Not impossible.'

'There's one more thing to bear in mind: I believe something made Mary drop her carving near the spring the night she died.' It was so sad that she and Fitz now shared a date of death. 'I think she saw a crime and captured it on camera. Adrian knew she made the pilgrimage, but it wasn't common knowledge. Other people might not realise they'd run into her. I don't know what took place or how it might relate to the other clues. But there's a fair amount of blood in the undergrowth. Maybe someone was attacked. I've been trying to get Barry to take an interest.'

'Could be animal blood,' Tony said.

'Gee, I never thought of that.' Bella gave him a fixed smile. 'It's what Barry said too. There was a wisp of lamb's wool nearby, but no sign of a carcass.' For a moment, Bella wondered about agricultural crimes, but the only thing she could think of was the farm Barry had been investigating for the way it disposed of dead animals – Stockett's, was it? She mentioned it to Tony. 'I suppose that must be a crime of sorts, but I can't imagine anyone killing over it. And even if a farmer had dumped a dead lamb at the spring, it wouldn't explain the blood. Whatever the case, I'm convinced the scene holds the key to why Mary died.'

Tony grunted. 'All right. I'll mention the blood again in case it's slipped Barry's mind.'

Leo had reappeared. 'So where are we? I demand to do the summing up.'

Carys raised an eyebrow. 'You haven't even heard everything. I'll do it. Noah's most likely but there are questions to answer about what he's been up to. Shane and Fiona are both possibles and they're definitely up to something. Adrian's out of it, much to Jeannie's disappoint—'

Her phone pinged. 'Oh.' They all sat forward. 'The geometric scarf came from Fiona Fitzpatrick.'

39

FIONA FITZPATRICK AND THE LETTER

Back at Vintage Winter, Bella made herself a coffee and set about rearranging the shop window. It was essential to keep the display looking fresh, as though stock was selling. It was an old trick, but it wouldn't save her. Out-of-towners were still coming in, but there weren't enough to keep her afloat.

As she worked, her mind picked over the details she'd amassed about the case. What had Mary seen at the spring? If Noah was guilty, how on earth had the photo she'd taken there threatened him?

And what had Fiona been paying him for? Perhaps she'd buy stolen eggs. Not live ones, just shells to secretly hoard as a collector. They almost felt more likely than a standard trinket. Something usually unattainable, with rarity value, might appeal. Bella thought of the lost birds and the endangered species. Fiona would have to be self-centred with no conscience. Either that, or totally lacking in imagination. She hadn't struck her as either, though some people had blind spots.

But as Bella put a beautiful Japanese Imari bowl in the centre of the window her mind turned to the value. You could see the money in the photo. A few notes, certainly, but not a huge amount. Bella doubted Shane would have got his petrol money back from the cash Fiona had handed over. So maybe Noah hadn't sold her an egg. Did that mean she'd bought something he'd stolen himself, and the link between him and Shane was irrelevant?

Whatever the truth, Mary had seen the pair of them and taken the photos. She'd probably confronted at least one of them. And written to Fiona about a secret.

Bella sighed and switched to dusting. It was more mechanical and better for thinking.

Once again, she wondered how the police had come to arrest Shane. She'd love it if it were down to her tip-off, but it seemed unlikely.

Then her mind returned to the auto repair shop and Thomasina's service. It was weird that none of Noah's colleagues had reported a theft. He'd taken something from a coat pocket before her very eyes and he'd clearly been operating in secret.

She thought of the gossip she'd overheard when she'd called to book her car in. One mechanic was off work because of a domestic emergency, Ted Ashcroft had said tactfully. In the background, someone had sniggered and given the game away. *The lecherous old goat. Bet his wife's giving him hell.* It sounded as though he'd been having a fling and she'd found out. All sorts of things were coming home to roost at the moment. Fiona had discovered Adrian's infidelity, of course, according to Bea. And Shane was about to pay for what he'd done.

Perhaps Noah would be next. Bella needed to make sure of it, if he was guilty. She wouldn't let him ruin her beautiful hometown. She'd have to be clever though; he had a habit of wriggling out of things. Even when he'd got caught stealing the quad bike, he'd kept parts of his wrongdoing secret: the source of the unexplained cash he'd had on him when he was arrested. Perhaps he'd been working with Shane back then, too.

Then thoughts mingled: secrets coming to light, clandestine meetings, money changing hands and Noah going AWOL. A tiny thread-like link formed in her mind. As she followed it, a whole web took shape and light dawned. The illumination showed just how things might make sense.

The moment it was time to close the shop, Bella called Fiona Fitzpatrick and asked to meet her at the Blue Boar.

She wasn't keen. '*I'm sorry. I'm feeling low.*'

'Would you like me to come to you instead? Only what I've got to say is private and the garden at the inn might give us some space if Adrian's at home.' She waited, then pushed again. 'I'm afraid it is important.'

At last, Fiona sighed. '*All right. I'll come. I can be there in half an hour.*'

Bella walked into the Blue Boar to see Boxer and Alison in a clinch. Jeannie shot her a look of sympathy. At least Matt, John and Gareth knew the truth. She went to find Fiona, then ordered them each a gin and tonic.

Jeannie leaned over the bar. 'She looks utterly washed-out. I wonder if it's a vitamin deficiency. I'll put an extra slice of lemon in her drink. I must see if I can tempt her to Gareth's superfood salad shortly.'

Bella had better get to the crux of the matter before Jeannie arrived to monopolise the conversation. She went outside to their chosen table and put the drink down in front of Fiona.

'Thanks.'

Bella sat down too. It was time to show a bit more of her hand. Always a gamble, but if her guesswork was correct, it wouldn't do any harm. 'I'm sorry to drag you out. You probably guessed from the start that I was worried about Mary's death. I know it was natural causes, but there were so many oddities around it and she looked terrified. I couldn't just leave it.' Her dad wouldn't have; it was in her blood. 'It's Adrian I need to talk to you about. I wanted to let you know that I understand the graffiti now.' Talk about delicate, but there was no way to have the conversation without mentioning it.

Fiona's face creased, the controlled, brave front falling away. 'Oh.' She stared down into her drink. 'But that's got nothing to do with Mary.'

'I know that now. But from the beginning I thought someone was frightening her and she probably died at the sight of them. That theory made me worry over every unexplained event around her death, including your intruder. It became even more urgent when Olivia was killed too. I realised I needed to understand each oddity, to work out which I could ignore, and which were crucial.'

At last, Fiona put her head in her hands and tears fell. 'I was so worried when you found Mary's body. Noah was hateful towards her, and her ex-husband was horrible too. There'd been the dead rats and all the rest of it. It was a relief when I heard the death was natural, though I wish to goodness she'd seen a doctor. She could have been saved.'

'It sounds as though she was a tough woman with some major regrets. If you couldn't persuade her, I doubt anyone could.' She was sure it was true, but now, she needed to steer Fiona back to her husband. 'So you knew what Adrian was up to?'

After a long time, Fiona spoke, still not looking up. 'I always do. There have been many women. But I've never known who or had proof until now.'

Bella was sure she knew why it was different this time. She thought of Noah stealing something from a colleague's pocket but never being challenged. Why wouldn't someone accuse him, unless what he'd taken wasn't money at all, but something secret and incriminating? A love letter, perhaps, or a photo? And then there was Noah watching Shane Sadler leave the valley, then tailing him on his motorbike. And hanging around at his house, just like her and Matt. Not what she'd thought. At. All. She reckoned she knew now why Fiona had secretly handed him money. And why an extramarital affair at the garage, Shane's egging, and the identity of Adrian's lover had come to light.

No wonder the police were being cagey if they'd got their evidence on Shane from Noah. They'd hardly want to admit they'd relied on him after all that had happened. She'd get the truth about that next. For now, she needed to focus on Fiona.

'You hired Noah as a PI, didn't you? Got him to tail Adrian to see where he went?' It would explain him accepting a telling-off from her on May Day. She was a client. Someone who might recommend him to others.

Eventually, Fiona nodded. 'I got the idea from Jeannie, funnily enough. I overheard her say Noah needed something exciting to keep him occupied. Everyone said he was bright, after cash, and a risk-taker, so I thought, why not?'

'He did a good job?'

She nodded. 'He saw where Adrian went weeks ago now. Got the photos. He certainly earned his fee. But when I confronted Adrian, I found it was all for nothing. He just laughed.' She sounded desperately weary.

Bella sipped her drink. 'But he's so careful about his reputation. And isn't he in line for a top government-funded role?'

Her look was bleak. 'Have you ever heard of someone being turned down for one because of an affair?'

She had a point.

'He told me to go right ahead and tell everyone. He didn't mind. He said it would probably add to his kudos in certain circles. It might cause a bit of a stir in the town, but Adrian said people would soon forget. It was something and nothing. But not to me it wasn't.'

'It wouldn't be to Edwina's husband either.'

Fiona's chest rose and fell. 'I know. He was one of the reasons I decided to keep quiet in the end. Edwina's not taking part in the fundraiser any more and Adrian seems to have got bored with her, but she won't be the last.'

Bella still needed to ask about the letter she'd found in Fiona's room but there was no way she could admit she'd gone through her wardrobe. Thank heavens her business and upbringing had taught her to think on her feet. The draft black-mail note was inspiration. 'Fiona, there's something else I need to ask you. Mary was in the habit of roughing out letters before she sent them. John and I visited Springside Cottage to value the contents for her executor and I found a draft letter to you. I'm sorry. Mary sounded hurt and talked about something you'd been keeping from her. Did she see you with Noah and misunderstand the situation?'

Fiona pushed her hair out of her eyes. 'Yes, and that triggered the letter, though not directly.' She sighed. 'She wanted to know what on earth we were up to. We'd been meeting in secret, for obvious reasons, so it must have looked iffy. She left a message on my voicemail, demanding an explanation. I was so humiliated that I waited until I knew she'd be out before I called her back. I left her a message too, telling her the truth about why I'd hired Noah, and admitting to Adrian's affairs. After that, I switched off my mobile and hid for three days. I just couldn't face talking to her about it. That was when she wrote me the note. She was terribly hurt that I hadn't confided in her.'

Dear Fiona, I'm horrified at what you've been keeping from me. Why didn't you come clean? I thought we were friends. We should talk now. This changes things.

Sweet Agnes, and she and Leo had both thought the note

implied Fiona knew about the will and whatever she'd done had changed Mary's mind. Why hadn't she listened to Tony's irritatingly sage advice? *Imply is the operative word. You can't tell Mary's tone from the letter.*

It probably *was* at that point that Mary had changed her will, but to write Fiona into it, not out. She'd have known she might need a bolthole.

'Mary and I had it out,' Fiona went on. 'She felt I hadn't trusted her. I explained how embarrassed I was and how worthless I felt and she forgave me. She wanted me to tell everyone what Adrian was up to. She thought it would stop him doing it again, but I knew it wouldn't. And by that stage I'd taken a deep breath and realised the effect it would have on Edwina's husband. And her daughter too. She's very protective of her father, from what I hear. Mary pushed and pushed. She said Bob West would be better off knowing and Bea would get over it.'

There was a lot in that. Jeannie would certainly agree. Still, it was Fiona's choice. Her comment about Mary being overbearing when it came to her opinions on right and wrong made total sense.

Fiona sighed. 'In the end I put my foot down, and then of course poor Mary died. I assume it was Adrian's infidelity that gave her the idea to leave me her house, as an escape route.' She was crying again. 'I was devastated to lose her. The options she gave me show you just the sort of friend she was.'

Bella finally felt sure that Fiona hadn't known Mary's plan. It probably explained Mary's decision to get rid of the owl inkwell too. She'd gone off Adrian, a man she'd once associated with his brother, but who was now revealed as a serial adulterer, with no concept of true love.

Bella sipped her drink. 'So, Mary had decided Noah wasn't breaking the law by the time she died?'

Fiona nodded. 'That's right.'

Noah had just moved down the list of suspects. He'd left the auto repair shop early the day his stepmum was killed, but that could have been to cover a job for another client. If he was spying on people, he'd need to follow their schedules. In the back of her mind, she'd been wondering who'd hired him to follow Shane. She'd discounted Mary herself. She'd never use him, Bella was sure, and Noah wouldn't have carried on after she'd died if no money was coming in. But now, she thought she had the answer, though it turned her thoughts on their head. She'd need to check it with Noah himself.

Meanwhile, Shane had shot up the suspect list. With Fiona and Noah's demotion, he automatically became more likely, but it was also entirely possible Mary had been blackmailing him. She'd been following Noah, and Noah had followed Shane. She could have seen Shane handling stolen eggs, or loading equipment into his van. Maybe she'd got sufficient evidence to make herself a threat, but not enough to interest the police.

After they'd finished talking, Bella reported back to Jeannie.

'I should think private detective work will suit Noah very well,' Jeannie said, 'but I must warn the townsfolk not to expect any loyalty. I'm afraid he's entirely unprincipled. He needs guiding. I must think of how to arrange it. You don't suppose Tony—'

'I really think not. But for now, the key point is that Mary knew what Noah was up to. She had no reason to blackmail him. Even if she'd written the letter before she found out the truth, it doesn't fit. You remember the wording? "I imagine you regret it now, but it's too late. It's time to pay your dues." That implies she knew for sure that the addressee was guilty, and that she understood the specifics. I think she must have been targeting someone else.'

'So other than old scores, Noah had no reason to try to kill her?' Jeannie looked thoughtful.

'Exactly. I don't think it was him.'

'You're *sure* it couldn't be Adrian?'

'Cast-iron alibi.'

Jeannie sighed heavily.

'But Shane's another matter.' Bella explained her thinking.

Jeannie gave her a firm pat on the shoulder. 'Keep at it. But don't let that godfather of yours make you do anything dangerous. I won't have it. Ah, excuse me. I must talk to Fiona about nutrients before she leaves.'

40

NOAH AT NARIN'S

Bella went back to the flat to plot her next moves. The progress she'd made had given her a huge buzz. She didn't want to stop now.

She needed to speak to Noah. The thought of going to his house didn't appeal. It would be unthinkable to go barging in when the rest of the family were grieving. She searched for him online instead. If he was making a serious go of the detective business, he must be publicising it somehow.

When she searched for Elsworth and private investigations she got a result.

She was just about to call the mobile number listed when her phone rang. Number unknown.

'Is that Bella? Bella Winter?'

'Yes.'

'Ah, good. My name's Marion. I live on Meadow End, but we met on Heartsease Lane. You called when I was babysitting for my daughter. They're back from their long weekend now, and I remembered to ask if she'd seen Olivia Elsworth walking along her road the night Mary Roberts died.'

'I'm afraid it was a long shot.'

'*I thought so too, but their little one still sleeps badly and she was up. She did see her, so there you are. It was worth asking. I hope it helps. I'm so glad to know you're Douglas's daughter. He was very good for this town.*'

Bella was instantly choked up. She swallowed hard, thanked her, hung up and took a deep breath. So Olivia *was* on Heartsease Lane at some point the night Mary died. It didn't prove she hadn't walked to St Giles's Holt, but it made it a lot less probable. It sounded as though she'd gone exactly where she'd told the police.

She called Tony and passed it on.

'*Interesting. Not likely she saw a hooded figure with a medieval weapon heading into Springside Cottage then.*' Tony made a ruminating sound. Either that or he'd just put a toffee in his mouth. '*So what made her a target? Unless the two deaths are unrelated after all.*'

'Yes, thanks, Tony. Not helpful.' She paused for thought. 'It's like we said before, Olivia could have discovered the identity of Mary's would-be killer another way, by guessing they were her blackmail victim, perhaps. Or maybe the killer wanted her and Mary out of the way for another interconnected reason.'

'*You want to be looking at where Olivia and Mary's worlds intersected.*'

'Noah is the obvious answer.' Back to him again. She filled Tony in on her discoveries, theories and plan to talk to him. 'But there's the estate agents too. Olivia was selling Mary's cottage. Or trying to.'

'*Maybe Olivia knew about Mary's bequest. Mary could have told her in case she shuffled off before the sale went through.*'

'I don't see why. If she really thought she might die, I hope she'd have taken Fiona's advice and seen a doctor.' Though Bella half wondered if Mary had wanted to be with Fitz. 'Even if she did tell, why would that knowledge get Olivia killed?'

'*All right. Just chucking out ideas. Any other connections?*'

'None come to mind.'

'*But they'll be there. Keep thinking and I'll give it my attention. I reminded Barry about the blood at the Sacred Spring by the way. Pointed out there's rain forecast for Tuesday.*'

'Thank you.' She'd go round to his house and start telling his children ghost stories if he didn't pull his finger out.

After they'd rung off, she called Noah. She told him she'd heard he was taking on private detective work and asked to meet him at Narin's on the high street. Perhaps she'd get herself a kebab instead of cooking.

Half an hour later, Bella and Noah were sitting opposite each other in a window seat at the café. Bella had a halloumi and cherry tomato kebab. Delicious. Noah clearly thought she was a new client. Might as well enjoy the food before the tensions set in.

'So what's the job you want to discuss?' Noah said.

'The information you gave the police on Shane Sadler.'

His look turned cool. 'I can't talk about work for another client.' Then he glanced speculatively at Bella's handbag. 'Unless there's a very good reason.'

Bella ignored him. She'd pay him at the end of the conversation, if she felt like it. 'I don't think there's a confidentiality problem.' Their eyes locked. 'There was no client, was there?'

It had gradually come to her. If Noah had been following Shane to collect evidence, then he wasn't his current accomplice. Yet at Shane's house, Shane's dog had treated Noah like a friend. At some stage, his master must have presented Noah as such.

And then Bella had thought of the money Noah had on him when he was arrested. He'd been involved in *something* organised, back when he'd stolen the quad bike. It seemed likely that he'd worked with Shane then. After which, Noah had been prosecuted. He'd had to lie low for a while, and presumably, the partnership had been on hold.

'You had it in for Shane and you went after him of your own accord.'

Noah's eyes narrowed. 'And why would I do that?'

'I saw the pair of you exchange a glance on May Day. As though you were asking something of him, and he was acknowledging it. I'm guessing you wanted to work with him again, but he'd been fobbing you off. Between May Day and last Monday, I think you'd finally pinned him down and he didn't want you any more.' By the time Bella had talked to Shane at the Hanged Man, he'd been bad-mouthing Noah. Bella had leaped to the conclusion that he'd been disguising their friendship. Now, she was sure she'd been wrong.

Noah's fist was clenched. 'I kept him out of it completely when I got nicked. And that's how he repays me. Decides he can operate alone and keep more of his cash.'

'That figures.' Bella thought back to the phone call she'd heard Shane take in the Hanged Man. 'He said his overheads had gone down.'

The fist clenched tighter. 'It was satisfying to pay him back.'

'Won't he drag you down with him?'

Noah smiled. 'Not if he's got any sense. I haven't told the police everything...'

The look in his eyes made Bella want to get up and walk out.

Noah was running his finger idly along the table. 'I wouldn't bother telling anyone about all this. I'll just deny it, and so will Shane.'

No doubt, but she'd still tell. Noah was dangerous. She could sense it, sitting opposite him.

He put down his kebab. 'How come you know so much?'

'Just stuff I picked up on the grapevine. As a private detective, have you worked out who killed your stepmother?' He must have wondered.

'I haven't had time and I don't care. I never liked her. When

I was arrested she "worked with the school" to try and fix things. She never saw it from my point of view. She's always preferred my sister.'

'Why did you leave the garage early, the day she was killed?'

He smiled again and it was chilling. 'You think I might have done it? I can see that. But the idea never crossed my mind.' He sounded surprised about it. 'I was working on another job. A wife cheating while her husband's at work.'

Bella was inclined to believe him, though it didn't make her any more comfortable in his company.

Noah leaned forward. 'Time for me to do some deduction. I think it was you I saw round at Shane's place. I enjoyed setting his dog on you. No way was I going to let you dig the dirt I wanted. So,' Noah's eyes met hers, 'you don't want to hire me?'

'I did, but only for the half hour we've just spent talking. Here's the fee for it.' She handed him a twenty-pound note.

'I charge more than that.'

'Not this time you don't.' She got up to leave. He was making her feel clammy.

Back at home, Bella had a therapeutic shower and changed. She couldn't stop shivering. After that, she put a Caro Emerald LP on the record player, put her feet up on her velvet sofa and thought.

In the wake of Olivia's death, she'd almost lost sight of the questions she'd had about Mary. It wasn't just who'd dressed up and entered her house to kill her and why. It was also who'd planted the rats and meat. That could have been Shane and Noah before they'd argued; it would fit with a low-level desire to get even. For Shane, the vengeful feelings could have gone into overdrive if Mary had started blackmailing him. She might have seen it as an effective way to get him to change. He got through a lot of cash, so it would hurt.

But how would any of that fit with Mary's stolen camera and her intruder, who'd no doubt come for her shortly after she'd used it at the spring? And what was the blood doing there? Bella still couldn't believe it was the result of animals fighting. There'd been too much, and *something* had made Mary drop her carving.

If only Barry would send someone to look at the scene. She sent him another text with updates on Noah and a reminder.

41

PROPS AND PLOTS

It was Monday, and Vintage Winter was closed, but Bella went in to worry over the books, and John dropped by for an update. Bella got up to make them coffees. As she worked, she explained about Noah's hints. 'The egging is appalling, but it sounds as though Shane's guilty of something that would carry a longer sentence too. Noah's holding it back to retain some control.' She tried not to think of the most gruesome possibilities. 'I've passed it all on to Barry but I'm not sure it'll make a difference.'

'I told you it was dangerous, going to search Shane's place.'

'I won't go back. And I find Noah just as frightening. I think he's entirely amoral and he was full of hatred for Mary and Olivia. But I doubt that's enough motive on its own, and Mary didn't have anything on him, in the end.'

'But she must have thought she had, when she spoke to Olivia about it at Springside Cottage. That had to be before she found out that Noah was working as a PI.'

'Sweet Agnes, that's a good point.' She put a black coffee in front of John, sat down and took a sip of hers. 'I need to check when Fiona admitted to Mary that she'd hired Noah. She's probably in her office by now. Let me give her a call.'

When Bella asked her question, she could hear the frown in Fiona's voice. 'I can't quite remember, but a while back now. Well before May Day.'

Hell's teeth. So, when Olivia had told Mary to leave her family alone, she'd been talking about something else.

Bella was distracted when she went to help the fundraising team pick up the vintage agricultural machinery from Fox Hollow Farm. Harry Elsworth was there, mucking in. She watched as he lifted one end of a set of potato drill rollers. She wouldn't have known what they were if it hadn't been for Fred the farmer's explanation. She'd never been into industrial antiques.

There was an intensity about Harry that was heartbreaking. As though he was putting every fibre of his being into doing this job, and then the next. Not pausing for breath lest reality catch him up. Her eyes met Carys's for a moment. She was wheeling a turnip cart while Bella took care of a whey strainer.

'We're so close to where Olivia was killed.' Bella couldn't imagine how Harry could bear it. Her body had been found on that very road. She remembered Olivia hugging Harry within an inch of his life and Carys talking about the renaissance in their relationship. They'd had troubles and conquered them, only for her to be killed. Life could be so unfair.

Adrian strode up to them. 'Do you always dress as if you're going to a party when you're handling farm equipment?' There was a twinkle in his eye.

Carys glanced at Bella and winced.

'Yes.' That wasn't strictly true. John had hinted that her kitten heels might be impractical, which had influenced her to keep them on. The ground was dry and hard and there was no point in owning nice things if you didn't use them.

For a second, Tony's words came back to her. *You are the product of two parents.* But she was nothing like her mother.

Adrian's smile faded when he realised she wasn't treating his quip as a merry topic of conversation. He went off to help another fundraiser lift a churn.

She and Carys were far enough away from the others to talk.

'Any progress?' Carys asked.

'Not to the extent that I can identify the killer.'

'What are the main sticking points?'

'I don't know who planted the Ginny Greenteeth paraphernalia at Mary's place. I suspect it's the same person who planned to attack her, though. I've a hunch that the rats and rancid meat are a separate issue.'

'So if you're right, and the Ginny Greenteeth tormentor is also our killer, you think they began by trying to scare Mary, then upped the ante?'

Bella nodded. 'The timing suggests Mary saw something crucial at the spring the evening she died. An attack on someone maybe, because of the blood. But there's no news of anyone going missing or anything like that.

'Either way, I'm pretty sure Mary's would-be killer took her camera because there was an incriminating photo on it. And they probably intended to kill her because she was a witness.'

'Yet she didn't call the police straight away. You'd think she would if she'd seen a crime being committed.'

'Yes, you would. And why was this person trying to frighten her before all that? Nothing makes sense.'

They'd put their kit in the school van and turned back to fetch more, which took them closer to the others again. It meant they had to finish their chat, but Bella carried on thinking.

In the end, someone had wanted Mary dead, but that might not have been the case when they staged the Ginny Greenteeth

references and stood around chanting in the wood. Things had
changed when Mary went to the spring.

But how did Olivia fit into the mystery? It didn't look as
though she'd been anywhere near Mary's house the night of the
would-be attack. There had to be another reason the killer
wanted her dead and it must relate to the blackmail note. Bella
was still convinced she'd known what it had referred to.

What had Olivia meant when she'd warned Mary off? *How
many times do I have to tell you, Mary? He's done nothing
wrong! Haven't you done enough to my family?* Was there any
chance she'd been talking about Harry, not Noah? Or had Noah
done something fresh, after Mary had realised there was an
innocent explanation for the photo she'd taken? It wasn't impossible. In reality, there was nothing innocent about Noah.

She didn't even know who Mary had been blackmailing.

Crammed into the back of the school van with the ancient
farm machinery, Bella willed a breakthrough to come. She
focused on Olivia. The draft blackmail note could have
confirmed a suspicion she'd had about someone. Then maybe,
for whatever reason, she'd decided to confront them rather than
go to the police. That could fit for Noah or Harry. Or if she'd
had something to hide herself. She'd have been desperate to
protect her marriage.

They arrived back at the high school and offloaded the
machinery, putting it at the back of the hall.

Adrian had a hand on Harry Elsworth's upper arm. He was
commiserating, coming out with all the right words. After they'd
finished talking, Adrian turned to the rest of them. 'Thank you,
everyone. Rehearsal tomorrow night.'

Carys and Bella parted outside the school. 'I'd better get
back to my little darlings,' Carys said. 'It's painting this afternoon. Oh joy. I will cover myself from head to toe in overalls.'

'Good luck.'

Bella's mobile rang before she'd gone any further. Tony. She tapped to answer.

'News?'

'*Hello to you too, Bella.*'

'Hello. But have you got news? It's not the blood, is it?'

He chuckled. '*Got it in one. Our boy Barry's got the analysis back. Turns out he did pay attention to what you said after all.*'

Wonders never ceased. 'Thank you for letting me know. He hasn't called me about it. And?'

'*It was theatrical.*'

'Theatrical?'

'*Yup. The sort actors use on stage. The report mentions the lamb's wool you noticed too. It made me think of a sacrifice.*' Tony's voice held a bloodthirsty note of interest. '*But it's not that, because the blood wasn't real.*'

42

A LITTLE KNOWLEDGE IS A DANGEROUS THING

Bella ended her call with Tony and carried on her way. Ordinarily, she'd head back to Vintage Winter and work on the stock, but it was shifting so slowly that there wasn't much point. She wanted to go back to the spring instead. Walk through what Mary did the night she died to see if she had a brainwave.

She cut through to St Giles's Holt via Holt Lane – the quickest route from the school – then used the right of way through the grounds of Springside Cottage. As she passed, she could just see the upper floor of Lilac Cottage in the distance. Someone was home. There was movement at a window. Perhaps Adrian wasn't forcing Bea to work out her notice. What he'd said to Fiona was true: his political contacts wouldn't worry about a run-of-the-mill scandal, but he could probably do without Bea bad-mouthing him in the staffroom.

Minutes later, Bella stood looking at the spring, imagining the scene there. A sacrifice, Tony had said. Except the blood was theatrical. Just like this whole affair. The chanting figure dressed in a cloak, the clever tricks to make it look as though Mary was cursed. The medieval weapon. It had all been so stagey.

Bella's skin pricked. So, had the scene here at the spring been mocked up to look like a sacrifice? She shivered, though the air was warm. Could someone have taken a dead lamb from the farm Barry had been investigating? Perhaps they'd brought it up the hillside and pretended to kill it, using large quantities of theatrical blood.

It could have been someone continuing the same campaign against Mary. Terrorising her.

Goosebumps crept up Bella's arms. If so, instead of it being someone who'd had no idea she'd be there, it was probably someone who knew she would be. Her mind fixed on Adrian. He knew she went there every year on the anniversary of his brother's death. But he'd been with Edwina West when Mary died. He couldn't have entered her house and triggered her heart attack.

Who else was there? It was possible Fiona knew about the pilgrimage, and Shane could have. And then there was Opal, who kept watch. She'd told Bella and John about seeing the hooded figure. She could have talked to someone about Mary's ritual. Bella bet she'd noticed it.

Her thoughts ran on. If someone had staged a sacrifice to scare Mary, they'd have worn a disguise. The hooded robe, most likely. They'd have hidden their face. Any photo Mary took shouldn't have identified them.

Something must have gone wrong. Perhaps the hood had snagged on the trees by the spring. If Mary's photo revealed the tormentor's face, things would change. But even so, it didn't seem like something to kill over.

But then Bella realised: to Mary and anyone viewing the photo, it would look as though the person concerned really was sacrificing a lamb. No one would like the town seeing them as a weird cultish fanatic who was cruel to animals, but who would kill for that? Shane? Fiona? Someone who Opal had told? And why had they wanted to scare Mary so badly? Was it all a game, or revenge, or—

A text arrived on her phone. John.

Making progress over the Sienna business. Didn't like to say earlier in case it didn't come off. Will tell you more tomorrow.

She messaged back:

Intriguing. You are my top employee; did I ever tell you?

He really was the best, but despite her light tone, thoughts of Sienna set her heart thudding. How dare she try to ruin Bella's name? Make it so none of the locals trusted her? Though of course it hadn't been Sienna's idea. Someone had sent her that anonymous note. Maybe the killer, wanting to discredit Bella.

And then it came to her.

Perhaps *that's* what the killer had been doing to Mary. She was known for her conversations with trees and her spiritual nature, triggered by losing Fitz. Had the killer been capitalising on that? They could have hoped she'd talk about the hooded figure, the chanting in the wood and things moving in her home without her touching them. People might decide she'd lost her grip on reality. Carys had started to worry about her, and Adrian had mentioned it too.

If so, Noah – and possibly Shane – had made it harder: tormenting Mary in a similar way, with items that were just as sinister but clearly real, like the effigy and the dead rats.

Perhaps that had made the killer up their game. Go one step further to put on a show which would sound totally unbelievable if Mary described it. Something to convince all and sundry that she'd lost control. But they hadn't banked on accidentally revealing their identity in the process. Nor on Mary taking a photograph. Could that possibly be the answer?

If so, if so... then they must have been trying to discredit Mary because she might spread something damaging about them. She couldn't have had definite proof; Bella imagined the killer would have attacked her immediately if she had. Or that she'd have gone to the police. Instead, the killer must have thought they could handle the situation without violence. It was only when they'd been photographed in such a compromising situation that they'd panicked and taken that terrible next step.

What had Mary known?

Bella perched on a rock near the spring.

The oddity she kept coming back to was the draft blackmail note. Olivia had been killed shortly after she'd seen it. That surely must be significant. And Bella had never discovered who it was intended for. Shane was still a possibility, but he didn't fit with Olivia warning Mary off. His downfall wouldn't affect Olivia's family.

Maybe it was the note that was the problem. Tony's words about Mary's letter to Fiona came back to her. Leo had said it *implied* Fiona had known about the bequest, but when she'd told Tony that, he'd said 'implied' was the operative word. And he'd been right. They'd misread the meaning completely.

What if it was the same with the blackmail note, and it wasn't what they'd thought at all? Why else would you write something down like that?

A wave of realisation flooded over her. Because you wanted to remember it. They'd always acknowledged the note had been partial, as though Mary had begun a threatening letter but not finished it. What if it was something she'd overheard instead? Part of a telephone call perhaps?

If so, who had been on the other end of the line? Olivia, who'd died soon after she'd seen what Mary had written? Had she recognised the threatening words because she was the one being blackmailed?

After that, it wouldn't take much to put two and two together and assume the blackmailer was Mary's tormentor. Olivia had been on to them; she'd needed managing.

No wonder she'd looked so upset.

It would explain why she hadn't gone to the police too. Whatever her secret had been, it must have been very important to her. Bella thought again of the way she'd clung to her husband, and Carys's talk of the rocky patch in her marriage, around the time of Noah's arrest. An affair. Bella bet that was it. Infidelity had felt like a theme in the last few days, yet she hadn't thought of it in Olivia's case.

It all made sense. Olivia had been through a very difficult time with Noah and though Harry was supposed to be wonderful in many ways, he was often absent. Bella could imagine her making a mistake, falling into the arms of someone sympathetic. Taking comfort then bitterly regretting it. She'd have realised afterwards how much Harry meant to her, but it was too late. Someone – possibly her lover – had decided to capitalise on her lapse in judgement. It was unspeakably cruel.

Bella should get back to town and chew it all over with John. She set off towards Springside Cottage again. Walking helped her think. She'd cut through to Holt Lane and see if John fancied a lemonade at the Blue Boar.

The more she thought about it, the more convinced she was she'd got it right. So who was guilty? She'd walked ten more paces when icy waves rushed over her.

Surely she couldn't be right? The question was how, and why the blackmail? And what to make of the argument she'd overheard between Mary and Olivia?

She turned towards the trees, and suddenly, the facts she'd amassed rearranged themselves and fell into place, one after another. The 'how' was the last bit to make sense, aided by a distant memory of something Carys had said, before any of this terrible business had started.

At that moment her mobile rang. John.

She picked up, feeling a surge of adrenaline. 'I was just about to call you. I know who did it!'

As she spoke, she was flung forward, pushed violently from behind, her phone snatched from the ground next to her, the wind knocked from her lungs.

Adrian Fitzpatrick lunged down at her and Bella felt a thrill of pure panic.

'I knew you'd work it out. Right from the beginning when Fiona mentioned you suspected foul play.' His hands were round her neck. 'Then someone told me who your dad was. How you had something to prove. I heard you take that call outside the school. Knowing the blood was theatrical must have helped. I tried to remove it but the stain wouldn't budge.'

His hands were pressing tighter. Bella could see the blue sky behind his head but there were stars in it. She fought terror and the urge to use both hands to prise his fingers open. She'd never manage it.

She wriggled, bending one leg up to one side. Closer and closer, straining for her foot. She was gasping as she got a finger inside one of her kitten heels. Adrian's brown eyes stared into hers.

In one move, with all the force she could muster, she swung the shoe up and whacked it into his head. He yelled in pain as the sharp heel hit him. His grip loosened but he'd got her shoe.

She twisted away from him, her other leg bent. A moment later, she had the second kitten heel. But she was coughing and spluttering and he was rounding on her again.

If she let him get close enough to attack him, he could use the other shoe to fight back. But if she threw the shoe at his face, he'd end up with two implements sharp enough to do damage.

He was coming for her. She scrambled to her feet and edged back. He'd be on her in a second.

But at that moment, she realised her surroundings were familiar.

In a fit of desperation and hope, she flung the second shoe, putting every ounce of strength she had into it. It glanced off him, barely causing him to break his stride, but his momentary flinch had given her enough time to reach under the nearest tree. It was where Adrian had hidden the homemade weapon. If only the cudgel-like stick was still there. It would have far more reach than her kitten heels.

She felt, grabbed and swung it all in one movement. It took Adrian by surprise. She knocked the shoe he still held from his hand and he yelled again. With any luck she'd broken something.

Then, at that moment, something amazing happened. A figure came bounding through the trees, long-skirted, hair flying.

Adrian was totally disorientated as Opal flew at him, something green in her hands. She pushed it into his face and he howled again, grabbing the leaves and flinging them aside as Bella threw Opal her phone and swung for Adrian with the stick once more.

'Please, Opal – call the police. Then call Boxer at the Blue Boar. He owes me a favour and he'll get here quicker than they will.'

But before Opal had dialled, they heard voices through the trees and thudding feet. A moment later, quite inexplicably, John and Barry Dixon appeared. The pair of them fell on Adrian, ably helped by Bella and Opal. In fact, Barry had to tell Opal to get off.

43

EVERYONE WANTS AN EXPLANATION

When uniformed officers arrived to ease the situation, Barry glanced at the kitten heels Bella had retrieved.

'You do realise it's illegal to carry something you intend to use as a weapon?'

Seriously? 'I always wear party shoes to walk through the woods.' She met his gaze head-on. 'Ask any of my friends.'

Barry sighed. 'Perhaps I won't bother.'

After she'd given a statement and Adrian had been removed, her presence was demanded at the Steps. It was after hours, but she and John sat in the garden with its trailing climbers, trees and dappled sunshine. Most of the gang were present and demanding the lowdown. Jeannie had left her bar staff and Peter in charge at the inn. Gareth, Tony, Captain, Leo and Carys completed the party. They'd invited Opal, but she'd dashed back to her house as soon as Barry had let her. She'd got away with carrying a handful of stinging nettles with intent to harm.

Tony pulled Bella into his usual half embrace. 'Don't reckon your dad ever sailed *that* close to the wind. I did, though. But in the spirit of do as I say, not as I do, next time, tell me where you're going.'

'Always? Whenever I go anywhere?'

Tony raised an eyebrow and Captain gave her a stern look.

'Definitely! Tell all of us!' Jeannie said as Leo patted Bella on the shoulder.

John was quiet and pale. 'I'm so glad you're all right.' Gareth patted *him* on the shoulder.

Bella bit into her scone with Shropshire farm butter. She was finding it restorative though her throat was sore. Some medics had checked her over before she'd left the holt. They said the bruising and pain would ease over the next couple of days. 'Since I didn't tell anyone, how did you find me, John?'

'The moment you got cut off, I called Carys,' he said. 'I knew you'd been together. But she didn't know where you'd gone, so then I rang Tony.'

Tony nodded and smiled. 'I told John I'd called you about the blood. We guessed you might have headed to the spring to have another look.'

'Honestly, you could have been anywhere,' Jeannie said heatedly. 'It's just as well they were right.'

'Sounds like you were winning by the time John got there.' Tony sounded gratifyingly proud. 'What would you have done next?'

'I'd have had to ask Opal to tie Adrian up with twine or something while I threatened him with a bumpy stick.' She turned to John. 'On the whole, I'm glad you turned up when you did.'

'So you understand how Adrian managed it?' Gareth put down the flapjack he'd been nibbling. 'I thought he had an alibi.'

'That's right,' Carys said. 'He was out of the running.'

'It suddenly came to me, but that was my undoing. Adrian had been following me. I guess he wanted to check how much I knew. He'd heard me take the call from Tony and mention the theatrical blood. He knew I was getting close. Then you rang, John, and I told you I knew who'd done it. That was when he attacked me.'

'Honestly, John!' Jeannie turned to him. 'You might have thought!'

Leo laughed and John didn't waste his breath replying.

Bella did it for him. 'It was me who brought it up.'

'All the same!' Jeannie said. 'Of course, I always said it must be Adrian. But what made you decide it was him, Bella?'

'A number of things.' Bella explained how she'd started to question the blackmail note and the alternative explanation that had come to her. 'If it was a record of a conversation, it seemed highly likely Mary had heard it at the school. Her life was divided between there and Springside Cottage.'

Carys nodded. 'And her desk was right next to Adrian's office. So it made you question his alibi in a way you hadn't before?'

Bella nodded as Gareth took another mouthful of flapjack. 'This is remarkably good, Leo.'

Leo beamed. Gareth was notoriously hard to please. 'I'll give you the recipe. But only for a straight swap.'

Gareth eyed him narrowly, then turned to Bella. 'So how *did* Adrian do it? And how did you work it out?'

'It was something Carys said that came back to me. When I very first asked what she thought of Adrian, she said he was well off: "All heated gilets, horses, jeeps and sherry parties." For some reason, as I walked along that came back to me. Irritating really, because it was clearly there in my memory all along. It was the heated gilet that was significant.'

Carys, who'd been leaning forward expectantly, gasped. 'You think he put it on Mary's body to make it look as though she'd died later than she really had?'

'That's what I'm betting. I suggested it to Barry Dixon, so I guess he'll ask about it. If we take it that Adrian planned to kill

Mary, I think he must have charged up the gilet and worn it under his cloak. In the end, Mary died before he struck a blow, but I assume he was still worried the police might suspect foul play. He'd had to steal her camera, apart from anything else. Someone could have spotted that. And it was what Mary saw that evening at the spring that triggered his actions. It was always possible she'd told someone about it. He needed to make sure that he could prove he wasn't involved if anyone investigated.'

'Wow, he was bold!' Carys looked stunned. 'He put the heated gilet round her body, then went off to Edwina's?'

Bella nodded. 'Then returned after some hours of passion to remove it again, if my hunch is right, giving himself an alibi. He must have decided it would cool sufficiently while he was gone to make it look as though Mary had died in the intervening hours. I imagine he searched for the key he'd dropped too, but he didn't find it. It wasn't obvious, tucked inside poor Mary's shoe, and I doubt he wanted to hang around. He probably left her door open to give the impression she'd opened it, and seen something which scared her to death.'

'It's monstrous,' said Jeannie.

'So Mary was a threat to him because she knew he was blackmailing someone.' Carys sipped her drink. 'But who?'

'That was where the two sides of the case came together. We'd already concluded that Olivia knew what Mary's blackmail note was about. We saw the fear in her eyes when she saw it. Once I'd decided that it was a snippet of something Adrian had said, I realised the only way she'd recognise it was if it was said to her.'

'Nice thinking.' Tony stroked Captain's head and gave her an approving smile. 'So what had he got on her?'

Bella explained her theory about an affair. 'I think it was with Adrian himself.'

'Oh no!' The distaste in Jeannie's voice echoed Bella's feelings. 'What on earth possessed her?'

'I can only imagine, but Noah said Olivia worked with the school after he was arrested. And then, Carys, you said the rocky patch in Olivia's marriage was around then. Adrian probably presented himself as a shoulder to cry on. When I thought back, I realised Olivia seemed to be under his thumb. Look at the way she agreed to do that talk about the old days, even though she hated harking back to her former life. You could see how unkeen she was.'

Carys nodded. 'True.'

'As to why, not for money, I'd say, since he's got plenty of that. I thought about what he values most instead: position and power.'

'Absolutely.' Jeannie gave an emphatic nod.

'The thought reminded me of another thing Carys said.'

Leo snorted. 'Someone's getting all the credit today.'

Carys gave a dignified smile.

'You told me Olivia was related to the royal family and a couple of senior Members of Parliament. And then I thought of Adrian's appointment to lead this government-funded schools project. It sounds very prestigious.'

Jeannie looked scandalised. 'You mean he asked Olivia to push for him to get it?'

Bella nodded. 'That's what I suspect. What happens to people who get that sort of role, do you think, long-term?'

Carys shrugged. 'A CBE for services to education? Posh receptions and dinners?'

'Quite possibly.' Thoughts of Adrian climbing the greasy pole sickened Bella. 'Knowing his character, I wouldn't be surprised if he wooed Olivia deliberately, knowing what good use he could make of her. He seemed to know all about her smart London contacts.'

'I always said he was a megalomaniac!' Jeannie swept her gaze over them all. 'Didn't I say so?'

'But why did Adrian frighten Mary so cruelly before he went to kill her?' Carys sounded like Bella felt, furious and desperately sad.

Bella dug her nails into her palms to combat her emotion and explained her theory about Adrian discrediting Mary. 'At first, I think he thought it would be enough. Mary had heard him blackmailing *someone* and she'd guessed it was Olivia, but she couldn't prove either thing. Under the circumstances, I think Adrian decided not to risk killing Mary; he went for a safer option instead. The fear he induced was a by-product of that. If he'd heard about the way her dad treated her, he'd have known she'd be susceptible to the legends he was referencing. I overheard him expressing worries about her state of mind on May Day. It came across as concern, but really, I think he was reinforcing the impression he wanted to give: that Mary had lost her grip on reality.'

'What a despicable brute,' Carys said. 'How did he find out Mary was on to him?'

'I'd wondered that.' Bella gathered her thoughts. 'I don't think Mary had confronted him. She was outwardly polite to him on May Day and I imagine she didn't quite know what she was dealing with. She might not even have known Olivia's secret. Perhaps she simply overheard the call, then saw them acting oddly together. I guess she didn't have enough to go to the police, so she went to Olivia to try to get the information that way. It would have felt a lot less dangerous than tackling Adrian.'

'Olivia was talking about Adrian, not Noah, when they argued and she said he'd done nothing wrong?' Carys looked aghast.

Bella nodded. 'I think so.'

Jeannie shook her head. 'If only Mary had gone to the

police and told them he was blackmailing *someone*. She should have let them investigate.'

Bella glanced at Tony, remembering what he'd told her. 'Unfortunately, she had a history of reporting people. The police finally convinced her she shouldn't do it unless she had evidence and I suspect that's what stopped her. It would have been her word against Adrian's. I think she went looking for proof instead.

'So as a result, there she was, trying to pump Olivia for details. But of course, Olivia wasn't going to tell. She was desperate to shut the topic down to save her marriage. My theory is that Mary had aired her suspicions with Olivia well before I heard them arguing. Olivia said, "How many times do I have to tell you, Mary?" They were going over old ground. And what would your reaction be, if you were Olivia and you realised Adrian had been careless enough to let Mary overhear him?'

'Oh my word.' Carys was ashen now. 'I suppose I'd have gone to Adrian and begged him to be more careful.'

Bella nodded. 'I think that's what she did.'

'You mean it was Olivia who put Adrian on to Mary?' Jeannie's eyes were wide.

It was a miserable thought. 'I'm sure she didn't mean to, but she probably panicked because she was desperate to keep her secret. You could see how much she minded about Harry by the way she clung to him. She might not have told Adrian who'd overheard him, but it wouldn't be hard for him to guess.'

'So he started his campaign after that,' Carys said. 'But how did a plan to discredit Mary turn into a decision to kill her?'

Bella sighed. 'He must have been rattled already, and then came another bit of bad luck.' She explained how someone, probably Shane or Noah, planting nasty things in Mary's garden had weakened Adrian's plan.

Carys nodded. 'I see what you mean. Suddenly, if Mary

talked about seeing a hooded figure in the woods, people might believe her, because the dead rats and the rotting meat were real.'

Bella sat back in her seat. 'Exactly. I think that's when Adrian decided to up his game.' She told them about the dramatic animal sacrifice he'd staged for Mary to witness at the spring. 'It would have sounded unbelievable if she'd talked about it, and it was clever because this time it would look as though it was something she'd witnessed by accident, not a personal attack on her. It made it less likely that people would associate it with the rotting meat and so on. But something went wrong. I think he revealed his identity by accident and Mary got a photo. It must have made him look like some kind of devil worshipper and that's probably what she thought too. I imagine it was shock, fear and her own incredulity that stopped her going straight to the police at that point. He was an old, old friend of hers. The brother of the man she loved. She knew he was an adulterer, and probably a blackmailer, but this was something else. It was late evening and I guess she dashed home, locked the door, and wondered what on earth to do. She'd probably have told someone the following day, if she'd lived.'

'Poor, poor Mary,' Carys said.

'I know. I think her fate was sealed at that point. If word got out that Adrian had been seen, wearing a hooded cloak, seemingly sacrificing a live lamb, it would be the end. The contacts he'd made in government wouldn't want him running their project, and people in Hope Eaton would either mock him or be horrified. He could never have carried on as headteacher. He'd be an outcast.'

'And there'd be nothing he could say to defend himself,' Carys said. 'Not without admitting his whole scheme.'

They were silent for a moment, the only sound a blackbird singing in a tree under the blue sky.

'Mary would never have opened the door to him that night,

of course,' Bella said, 'but he could easily have pinched her keys at school and copied them. I think he did that much earlier, as part of his campaign. I assume he let himself into Springside Cottage to move things around. It came in handy in the end.' It was horrific.

'And what about Olivia?' Jeannie asked.

'I think the day she visited Vintage Winter triggered a catastrophic chain of events. I thought at first that it was her seeing Mary's note that was crucial, but in fact that was nothing new. She was probably horrified that we'd found it, but Mary had already talked to her about what she'd overheard. It was the information we let slip that mattered.' It was an awful thought. 'Although Mary's death was natural causes, we'd worked out that someone had been tormenting her and she heard us say so. She knew Mary had been on to Adrian, so she saw his motive immediately.'

Carys closed her eyes. 'If only we'd realised she was behind us when we were talking.' She looked at Bella again. 'And because of her secret, she wouldn't go to the police?'

'That's right. My guess is she blamed herself for telling Adrian he'd been overheard, and probed for information out of guilt. I doubt she'd have risked it if she'd realised he'd entered Mary's house intending to kill her, but everyone knew the death was natural.' Bella imagined Olivia, desperately hoping she hadn't triggered Adrian's cruel campaign. 'I expect she tried to be subtle, but by that stage Adrian was panicked enough to kill her. She was found very close to Fox Hollow Farm, where we collected the vintage machinery. Maybe he asked her to meet him there to pick up some stuff. The person who suggested borrowing their kit at our fundraiser meeting said they thought they'd mentioned it before. Adrian could have told Olivia he'd asked several people to help when in fact, it was only her. If he made the request at the last minute, it would reduce the risk of her telling anyone what she was up to.'

'And of course, he had a hold over her, so she had to jump to it.' Jeannie's knuckles were white on the cup she held, her look fierce.

'It's all very sad, and ironically, I think Mary only wanted to help. She went through agonies of guilt and sorrow when she broke her own rules and had an affair with Fitz, only to lose him. I think she'd made up her mind that lies only lead to trouble, so she wouldn't leave things be.'

She glanced around the group. 'In trying to stop Adrian, who deserved it, Mary was threatening Olivia's marriage. As far as Olivia was concerned, she'd done what Adrian asked and life was about to come right again. So long as Mary stopped asking questions.'

'Poor, poor Olivia,' Carys said.

'And poor Mary.' Jeannie set her teacup down on the table.

It was a funny thought that Mary, Noah and Bella had all been sleuthing. Mary, because she'd seen the light after what she'd felt was a fall from grace, Noah for financial gain and kicks, and Bella to keep her father's memory alive and Hope Eaton safe and happy. Solving clues gave Bella a buzz too, of course, just as it did when she struck a deal for Vintage Winter. Using her skills for the common good was the icing on the cake.

44

SOME SILVER LININGS

The following day, Bella arrived at Vintage Winter for work as usual, though normality felt weird and there didn't seem much point. She'd fathomed out who'd tormented Mary, but not in time to save her or Olivia, and she hadn't got a solution to Sienna Hearst's malicious rumours either. She could barely sustain another month like this. John must realise; he did the books. She was glad he'd come up with an idea to help but she couldn't imagine it working. Once word had got around, it was already too late.

'It's so quiet,' she said to him.

'It's early. Besides, I have a plan, remember? I've been doing some additional sleuthing of my own.'

Bella frowned. 'Really? What sort?'

'I've managed to track down a friend of the late Julietta Montgomery.'

The woman who'd bequeathed her the vase. 'How on earth?'

'I found an obituary which mentioned a charity board she sat on. I went to the other board members and Bob's your uncle.'

'Amazing.'

'The friend knows exactly what went on. She heard it all first-hand – and how grateful Julietta was for your help. She was horrified when I explained the trouble Sienna's causing. She's agreed to come and give a talk with you, advising the locals what to look out for when selling antiques and bigging you up as someone they can trust.'

'She hasn't!'

'Your surprise at my success is a little hurtful.'

'No, but it's just... well, it's wonderful.'

'Mum says she'll hold the event if you're up for it.'

'Just try and stop me.'

The ghost of a smile crossed his face. 'The town's bound to believe in you after that. This woman couldn't be more upstanding. She's a dame for services to young people and philanthropy.'

'John, you're a lifesaver. I owe you Champagne.'

'Thank you. Though perhaps not at ten o'clock in the morning.'

Over the coming days, Tony kept her up to date. Even Barry Dixon got in touch, but it was partly to ask for advice about headlice.

From the pair of them, she gathered that her conclusions about Adrian had been correct. Barry had gradually wormed it out of him with dogged questioning. He'd taken Bella's advice and poked Adrian where it hurt most – in his ego – and got him to talk that way, though finding the car he'd used to kill Olivia with traces of his DNA inside it had been crucial too. He'd been responsible for all the more subtle moves to frighten Mary, from the Ginny Greenteeth references and chanting to moving things around in Springside Cottage. And he had indeed gone into her house the night she'd seen him at the spring, intending to kill her.

The tech team had not only found searches on his computer featuring Olivia's cousin, who worked for the Department for Education, they'd also proved he'd read the blog posts casting doubt on Bella's honesty after the vase debacle. She was now sure it had been he who'd set Sienna off. It could only help when it came to convincing people she was blameless.

Fiona had been into the shop. She'd cried a lot, but by the time she left, she'd dried her eyes and looked resolute. A long overdue divorce was on the cards. She was planning to sell Springside Cottage and buy somewhere central in town.

'I won't leave Hope Eaton,' she said. 'Why should I? The talk will die down eventually and I'll want my friends around me.' She, Carys and Bella had arranged to go for a meal together.

As for Noah, he'd misread Shane. The older man's anger was so great, he'd finally decided to shop his old partner, and to hell with the consequences. The police were furious with Noah for only giving them partial information. What he'd kept back meant he and Shane would both serve time. Tony had muttered something about aggravated burglary. Shane had also admitted encouraging Noah to plant the rotting meat and rats in the grounds of Springside Cottage before the pair of them had argued. He hadn't liked Mary booting him out all those years ago. Scuppering the sale had amused him.

Harry Elsworth and his daughter were hunkering down together. The fundraiser had been cancelled, but they were organising a concert in Olivia's memory. It didn't look as though Olivia's affair had lessened Harry's feelings for her. Or his grief. The entire town was rallying round.

And Boxer and Alison's relationship was just as lovey-dovey as it had been before their split.

Lovely.

. . .

It wasn't long after that that Bella and John were given the go-ahead to remove and sell Mary's furniture. Even the spacious Thomasina couldn't accommodate items like the dresser, so Bella hired a truck and she and John went together, with Boxer, Gareth, Leo and Carys as extra muscle.

'Right,' said Bella, when they'd loaded up, 'let's get this lot back to the Blue Boar and then I'll buy you all a drink.' Free storage at the old coach house was invaluable.

After they'd got everything unloaded, Bella noticed a small gap in the coach-house wall. She'd never spotted it before. It allowed her to peek through to the former stables. She loved thinking back to the days when stagecoaches had stopped at the inn. As the others stretched their tired muscles and chatted, she put her phone torch to the gap.

The old stables weren't empty, as she'd thought they'd be. She could see furniture, and it looked incredible. There was the most intricately carved table. It was flat on top, but the base was a diorama, with trees, and a fox weaving through the undergrowth. It was St Giles's Holt! She could make out Springside Cottage. There was another table in sight too, with a beautiful inlay on its surface. The artist had used a variety of woods to depict the Town Steps.

'What's up?' Leo's voice made her jump.

She pointed.

Leo peered through. 'Oh! I hadn't realised you could see Matt's workshop from here.'

'Matt's?'

Leo looked at her strangely. 'Yes. You don't mean he's never mentioned it? But you're neighbours.'

Carys had joined them now. 'He tends to be rather secretive about it, to be fair. He never lets me watch him work.'

Leo snorted. 'I wouldn't want to. He does most of it after midnight.'

'Midnight?'

'He spends his days doing other work to pay the bills.'

Bella was practically dumbstruck. She indicated the old stables. 'That ought to pay the bills.'

Carys sighed. 'There are so many things in this world that aren't quite as they ought to be.'

She was right there. And there was Bella, thinking Matt was directionless with no overriding passion. 'Why didn't any of you tell me?'

John looked surprised. 'I didn't know you didn't know. And although his work is beautiful, I hadn't realised you'd expect me to announce it.'

Carys was looking at Bella speculatively. If she was getting ideas, they needed to be quashed.

They exited the coach house and Bella locked up. After that, she took them to the bar, where posters advertising her event with the dame John had found were everywhere. Jeannie had already told people the true story and the locals were smiling at Bella. She was increasingly confident she'd be able to sell every bit of stock she had and have people coming back for more.

Pleasingly, everyone was saying how grumpy Sienna had looked in the last couple of days.

When they sat down with their drinks at last, Bella snatched a surreptitious look at Carys. *Bother.* She was staring straight back at her, a knowing spark in her eyes.

'Whatever you're thinking, you're wrong,' Bella said.

Leo looked confused. 'I don't know what you're talking about, but Carys is always right. She tells me every day.'

A LETTER FROM CLARE

Thank you so much for reading *The Antique Store Detective and the May Day Murder*. I do hope you had fun solving the clues! If you'd like to keep up to date with all my latest releases, you can sign up at the following link. Your email address will never be shared, and you can unsubscribe at any time. You'll also receive an exclusive short story, 'Mystery at Monty's Teashop'. I hope you enjoy it!

www.bookouture.com/clare-chase

The idea for *The Antique Store Detective and the May Day Murder* came to me after I realised I'd misread a social interaction, despite having witnessed it first-hand. It made me appreciate how much our expectations skew the conclusions we draw and how important it is to keep an open mind!

If you have time, I'd love it if you were able to write a review of *The Antique Store Detective and the May Day Murder*. Feedback is really valuable, and it also makes a huge difference in helping new readers discover my books. Alternatively, if you'd like to connect with me direct, you can find me on Facebook, X, Instagram or via my website. It's always great to hear from readers.

Again, thank you so much for spending some time reading *The Antique Store Detective and the May Day Murder*. I'm looking forward to sharing my next book with you very soon.

With all best wishes,

Clare x

www.clarechase.com

 facebook.com/ClareChaseAuthor
x.com/ClareChase_
instagram.com/clarechaseauthor

ACKNOWLEDGMENTS

Much love and thanks to Charlie, George and Ros for the feedback and cheerleading!

And as always, I'm more grateful than I can say to my wonderful editor Ruth Tross for her inspiring input, constant encouragement and patience.

I'm also indebted to the entire Bookouture team who work on my novels. You can see what a fantastic group effort it is by looking at the following page, where everyone involved is mentioned by name. They are the most wonderful, skilled and friendly group of professionals and it's an honour to work with both them and Ruth.

Love and thanks also to Mum and Dad, Phil and Jenny, David and Pat, Warty, Andrea, Jen, the Westfield gang, Margaret, Shelly, Mark, my Andrewes relations and a whole bunch of family and friends.

Thanks also to the lovely Bookouture authors and other writers for their friendship and support. And a truly heartfelt thank you to the generous book bloggers and reviewers who pass on their thoughts about my work, including some who have been with me right from the start. Their support is wonderful and it's also a joy when newcomers join in.

And finally, but crucially, thanks to you, the reader, for buying or borrowing this book!

PUBLISHING TEAM

Turning a manuscript into a book requires the efforts of many people. The publishing team at Bookouture would like to acknowledge everyone who contributed to this publication.

Audio
Alba Proko
Melissa Tran
Sinead O'Connor

Commercial
Lauren Morrissette
Hannah Richmond
Imogen Allport

Cover design
Debbie Clement

Data and analysis
Mark Alder
Mohamed Bussuri

Editorial
Ruth Tross
Melissa Tran

Printed in Great Britain
by Amazon

56922548R00172